ALSO BY GWENDOLYN KISTE

Boneset & Feathers

The Invention of Ghosts

The Rust Maidens

Pretty Marys All in a Row

And Her Smile Will Untether the Universe

GWENDOLYN KISTE

SAGA PRESS

LONDON SYDNEY **NEW YORK** TORONTO NEW DELHI

SAGA PRESS
AN IMPRINT OF SIMON & SCHUSTER, INC.

1230 AVENUE OF THE AMERICAS, NEW YORK, NEW YORK 10020

First Saga Press trade paperback edition August 2022

SAGA PRESS and colophon are trademarks
of Simon & Schuster, Inc.

For information about special discounts for bulk purchases, please contact Simon & Schuster Special Sales at 1-866-506-1949 or business@simonandschuster.com.

The Simon & Schuster Speakers Bureau can bring authors to your live event. For more information or to book an event, contact the Simon & Schuster Speakers Bureau at 1-866-248-3049 or visit our website at www.simonspeakers.com.

Manufactured in the United States of America

1   3   5   7   9   10   8   6   4   2

Library of Congress Cataloging-in-Publication Data is available.

ISBN 978-1-9821-7235-0
ISBN 978-1-9821-7236-7 (ebook)

To Charlotte and Bram
Thank you

one

It's almost sundown in Los Angeles, and Dracula's ashes won't shut up.

He's been at it since yesterday, calling out for me, calling out for anyone, his voice strained and distant, so soft I can never quite make out the words, so unforgiving I can never escape him. I cover my ears and recite a prayer I no longer believe, but it's not enough to blot out the sound of him.

I have to try something else. I have to bury him. Again.

So now here I am, standing in the shadow of the Hollywood sign, a shovel in one hand, an urn of his ashes in the other. Up here on Mount Lee is as good a place as any to lay him to rest. It's remote and hard to get to, and at the very least, I won't forget where I put him.

The last bits of daylight have dissolved across the horizon, and I move through the overgrown weeds, picking a spot between the letters *Y* and *W* where the earth is soft and malleable.

Then I start digging.

Below me, the city buzzes pleasantly like a swarm of locusts. It's the middle of June, the heat creeping in, and this isn't how I wanted to spend my evening. Of course, I never want to spend my nights with him, but what I want doesn't count for much.

As I work, the urn quivers on the earth next to me. The color of midnight, it's not much bigger than a man's fist. This isn't the only urn of Dracula's ashes, but right now, it's the only one that matters. It's the loudest of the bunch, that's for sure. The others back at the house are usually content to keep quiet, murmuring no louder than common sleepwalkers, but not this one. It's made up its mind to make my life hell. And I've made up my mind to do the same to him.

Another whisper from the urn, and I nudge it with my heel.

"Stop," I say, my feet sinking in the mud. I hiked all the way here in my pilgrim pumps and satin dress, up the Santa Monica Mountains, even snagging my hem on a low-lying shrub. Dracula doesn't care. He just keeps at it. He's never been very good at keeping his mouth shut. Not that he's really got a mouth, not now, not after I buried that stake in his cold, dead heart.

Anybody who knows the story—and let's face it: these days, who doesn't know the story?—will always wonder the same thing. He's dead, right? Turned to dust decades ago? Shouldn't everyone be safe now?

Please. As if men like him are ever that easy to vanquish. They always figure out the best way around the rules, bending the world in their favor. For most of us, death is the undeniable end. For him, it's only a minor inconvenience.

A sharp breeze cuts through the dusk, rattling the letters in the sign like restless bones. The air harsh and sweet, I close my eyes, the buzz of the city fading away. That's when I hear them. All the sweet heartbeats in Los Angeles, thrumming inside me at once. They waft up from the valley like steam, and my skin hums, my teeth sharpening, reminding me of what I am, what he's done to me.

The sound of Dracula rises again, almost singing now, and even though I still can't hear him clearly, I can guess what he's saying.

"Take what belongs to you, Lucy," he used to tell me. "Take anything you want."

I do my best not to listen. My hands blistered, I keep digging, promising myself the same thing as always: that I won't end up like him. I won't become a monster. I'd rather waste away, which is exactly what I'm doing, hunger gnawing at me night after night, my stomach aching and cavernous and raw. It turns out a vampire can live a very long time without taking a drink. It just hurts like hell to do it.

I grimace, eager to get this over with, as a shadow passes over my face.

"Are you all right?" A voice materializing, thin as mist, next to me. I turn and see her, moving like a phantom in the twilight, so quiet I never heard her coming.

I smile. "Hello, Bee."

She grins back. "Hello yourself."

The melody of the city fades to static, and it's just me and her and these ashes that won't ever rest. Her head down, Bee huddles close to me, and the hollowness, the silence within her, reminds me of how we're connected. There's no heartbeat inside either of us. We're at once alive and dead, even though we aren't the same. Bee's no vampire like me. She died and came back a different way, a way she doesn't like talking about.

That means Dracula's not her problem, he's mine, so I try to keep her out of this. When I left, she was waiting in the car, back where I parked it on the street, in a quaint little neighborhood where the only boogeyman they know is rising inflation.

"You didn't have to come all the way up here," I say, digging a little faster now.

"Figured you could use the company." Bee fidgets in the dirt next to me. "Besides, I'd rather not be alone."

An uneasy silence twists between us. I'm not the only one with secrets.

The Hollywood sign looms over us, the rusted sheet metal trembling in the breeze. For a lonesome town, this might be its most lonesome landmark. At the far end, the *H* rocks back and forth, the same letter actress Peg Entwistle chose when she took a swan dive off the sign back in '32. That was thirty-five years ago, ancient history in this town, and by now, everyone's mostly forgotten her. That's how it goes here. This is a glittering city haunted by the ghosts of dead girls and dead dreams. In that way, Bee and I fit right in.

The shovel hits sandstone, and this is it, the best I can do. My hands shaking, I deposit the urn of Dracula into the dark. There are no words of prayer and no curses, either. Just a flick of the wrist, and he's nestled in the ground. I fill the hole back in, almost frenzied, my fingernails limned with darkness, my pumps pounding on the earth, packing down the soil.

Bee helps too, kicking some dirt into the grave. "How long do you think he'll stay put?"

I shake my head. "Not long."

Beneath our feet, I already feel him, restless as always. He'll work his way back up, bit by bit, crawling like an earwig, the urn writhing in the earth on his command.

I grind my heel into the ground one last time. "Goodbye," I say, but he and I both know it's a lie. I'll come back at the end of the week. It isn't safe to leave him alone for long. At least this way, though, I get a few days' reprieve from his complaining.

It's darker now, and Bee and I trek back to the car. Halfway down the hill, she takes off her shoes, lemon-yellow Mary Janes we picked up last year at the Salvation Army.

"Easier than hiking in heels," she says, and I laugh and do the same, the two of us barefoot in the trail dust, sneaking through the Santa Monica Mountains, dragging the shovel behind us. There are snakes in these parts, but they slither beneath the sagebrush when they see us coming.

We emerge at last under a streetlight, and parked on Mulholland is our Buick LeSabre, rust on the bumper, one taillight cracked.

Bee tosses me the keys, and we both slide in, the torn leather seats spewing yellow foam. It takes two stalled starts before the engine roars to life. The car's already seven years past its prime, but who's counting? Not us, not when we have less than a hundred dollars in cash to our names and can't afford a new ride. This is the only thing we've got, so we make the best of it. With the canvas top pulled down, we rocket toward the state highway, the California evening settling around us like a false promise.

As the oleander trees rush past, Bee twists the chrome dial on the radio, and we sit back, listening in. It's the same news as always. The death toll in Vietnam. The people in power pretending to care. Nothing good ever happens here. Cape Canaveral launched *Mariner 5* at Venus this morning, which makes sense, because the only way things might ever improve is to give up on this planet altogether.

"Do you think we could survive on Venus?" Bee asks.

I shrug. "I hear it's made of fire."

She exhales a laugh. "Aren't we?"

Bee tips her head back, the wind rustling through her long, dark hair. The night's cooling off already, and the canopy of trees draws us closer into its embrace. I wish we were safe here, but we're not alone. We're never alone, not really. Something's always whispering after us, lingering on the breeze, hiding in the static of the radio. I press the gas pedal harder, ready to rev it so fast nothing could ever catch us, but that's when I see it. The marquee emerging around the bend, the cornflower-blue neon flashing like a beacon.

Munroe's Drive-In. Double screens, open seven days a week. Chockful of loud music, louder explosions, and images so bright they nearly blind us. This is exactly what Bee and I need. It's the only way we've found to escape ourselves, to escape the past, if only for a few hours.

The engine turns over as we idle up to the ticket booth, its faded paint flecking off like chunks of dirty snow. Inside, hunched over in a folded chair is Walter, the purveyor of the place, his hair fright white, thick whiskers coming out both his ears. He squints into the convertible and brightens when he sees it's us.

"Hello, girls," he says, flashing us a toothy grin, oblivious as always. Bee and I have been coming here for ten years, neither one of us ever aging a day, but he doesn't seem to notice. He's just happy to have the patrons.

We pay our five dollars and rumble slowly into the lot over chunky gravel, pulling into the last spot in the front row. This speaker's the best one in the place. Never been broken, not that we know of, and you can crank the volume high enough to drown out almost anything.

The first movie starts a minute later, barely long enough for us to turn off the engine. Walter must have been waiting for us. He knows we're here every night, rain or shine.

Our eyes fixed on the screen, the trailers flash by, as Bee sits cross-legged in the passenger seat, her dusty pumps on the floor, her feet bare again. All around us, the scent of Pic permeates the air, everybody with a mosquito coil lit on their dashboards except for us. Bee and I don't have to worry. We're in the only car the bugs never bother. They know there are no signs of life here.

But there are signs of life elsewhere. Windows fogged up, heavy panting, the whole nine yards. Young couples necking in the back seats of their parents' borrowed cars, their guards down, their pulses thrumming faster. My fingers clench tight on the steering wheel, the soundtrack of the movie fading out, everything fading, until all I hear are those rhapsodic heartbeats.

These eager lovers are easy pickings. Too easy. They'd never expect me, what I'd do to them. I could stroll right up to their cars and climb on in, and they wouldn't even have time to open their mouths and scream before I'd open my mouth and make sure they never screamed again. Sometimes, I think I like coming here just to test myself, to prove I'm not a monster. I can sit right in the middle of a smorgasbord, and I won't do a single thing about it.

I look across the mountains in the dark, and there it is, hanging over me in the distance like the blade of a guillotine. The Hollywood sign. You can see it from all over town, peeking between buildings, shining through the smog. That means I can see him, too, the place where I've hidden him.

Seventy years, and what he did to me still feels as fresh as yesterday, every detail branded into my mind. The scent of roses, the scent of him, sweet and inviting, like a home I'd never known. The night it happened, there was no black cape or black bat or blood clotting Technicolor red across a crisp white blouse. It was far duller than that. Just me and him on an iron park bench at midnight. My broken curfew, his broken promise. A man who takes what he wants, and a girl who has to pay the price. That's the way these stories always go.

The first movie ends, and the floodlights come up for intermission. The couples in the other cars climb out and stretch their legs, their bodies glistening with sweat, fresh hickeys on their necks. I watch them, thinking how quick it would be, how simple. One pointed glance from me, and they'd be under my sway, mine for the taking. Dracula's voice ripples through me again.

Take what belongs to you, Lucy.

As though on his command, I fling open the car door, my whole body quivering.

Bee's head snaps toward me, her dark eyes wide. "What's wrong?" she asks, and under the weight of her stare, shame washes over me.

"Nothing," I say. "I'm going to the concession stand. You want anything?"

"The usual," she says, and hesitates. "You sure you're okay?"

"I'm fine," I say, and stumble out of the car and across the lot, past the flushed couples, past everything, not looking back, not even when I'm sure I hear something in the hills laughing at me.

When I get inside, the lobby's empty: no heartbeats, no danger. Narrow and cramped, it's not much more than a shack, fingerprints smearing the walls, half the overhead light fixtures burned out. A red velvet rope, matted and stained, snakes around from door to counter, even though there probably hasn't been a line long enough to fill the place since Clark Gable was a matinee idol.

I follow the rope around and lean up against the counter, waiting until the side door creaks open and Walter hustles in, his breath rasping. He does it all around here—takes the admission, roasts the hot dogs, runs the projector. That's because there's nobody left to help him. He's a widower from way back, his life a domino game of losses. His youth, his wife, his peace of mind. By the look of this place, it might be the next to go.

Still, he never stops grinning. "What can I do for you, Lucy?"

What I want isn't on the menu, so I settle for ordering two medium Cokes and a popcorn, extra butter. Bee and I don't need to eat—we don't need much of anything—but going to the movies is all about make-believe, right?

His gnarled hands trembling, Walter fills two waxed cups with ice. "Glad you could make it out tonight," he says. "Wednesdays are always slow around here. You know, just last week—"

And with that, he starts into his latest yarn about the patron who bought three boxes of Milk Duds and paid in pennies. I quiet my face, trying my best not to roll my eyes. Small talk. Why do people always make small talk? Sometimes it's about the weather, sometimes a singer or television actor I've never heard of. Not that that means much. Perry Como is still modern to me.

As Walter chatters on, scooping yellow leavings from the bottom of the popcorn machine, I turn away, gazing out the smudged window in the lobby. Across the lot, Bee's watching me from the Buick. She waves when she sees me looking, and I wave back, smiling.

Bee won't come in here. She doesn't like confined spaces, doesn't like feeling trapped.

"Oh, did I tell you?" Walter nearly bursts toward me with excitement, his pulse surging. "My grandson Michael's coming to visit. You remember, the one that just finished his tour overseas."

I hesitate, something settling deep in my guts. "Of course," I say. How could I not remember? Walter hasn't stopped talking about his grandson ever since the draft notice landed in the mailbox like a grenade, shattering their lives into bits. This is the one bit of small talk I'd never deny him.

"He'll be here tomorrow," Walter continues, as I fork over a dollar, and he makes change, one careful nickel at a time. "I'll be sure to introduce you to him."

"If that's what you want," I say, even though I should tell him no. His grandson's been at war, an ugly war, even uglier than most. He's seen more death in two years than I've seen in two lifetimes. He doesn't need to meet me, too.

Walter doesn't understand that. When he looks at me, he sees what everyone else does: a perfectly fine young lady, red curls in her hair, red rouge on her cheeks. Never mind the dirt beneath her fingernails and the teeth that sharpen if you catch her on a bad night. He never seems to notice those things. Nobody does. That's why I can hide in plain sight. Everything about me is a disguise.

The drinks and popcorn gathered up in my arms, I get back to the car just in time for the next film to start. A beach movie I never heard of called *Don't Make Waves*. Bee and I clutch our drinks, downing them in a minute, barely tasting anything.

The movie drags on, Tony Curtis's character pestering a pretty blonde who isn't given much to do besides bounce around in a bikini. Sighing, I glance in the rearview mirror. Behind us on the other screen, it's the latest James Bond film. *You Only Live Twice*. We'll probably see that one tomorrow night. We see every movie that plays here. Anything to escape what's waiting at home.

Or what's waiting for us here. A change in the wind, and we're suddenly not alone.

Bertha, a man's voice calls out, sharp and cold as a fistful of straight pins.

It isn't Dracula this time, and it isn't for me. It's for Bee. She seizes up in the passenger seat. No matter how many times this happens, she's always caught off guard.

He comes at her again, louder and more determined. *Where have you gone, Bertha?*

She won't look at me. She won't look at anyone. Bee with her own secrets and a name she never uses anymore.

Bertha Antoinetta Mason. The so-called madwoman in the attic. The first wife of one Edward Fairfax Rochester. A man with a sprawling estate and a sprawling ego and a temper that could set the whole world on fire. She married him young, married foolishly, and when she wouldn't bend to his will, pliable as clay in his calloused hands, he locked her away in an upstairs room before he went searching for someone else, a woman to replace her.

That was over a century ago, thousands of days separating her from him. He shouldn't even remember her now. But men like him are never eager to lose what they consider theirs.

His cruel laughter lilts on the wind, and I fumble with the speaker, cranking up the volume, desperate to drown him out. This is one of his favorite tricks: calling her from afar, throwing his voice across the miles like a wicked ventriloquist. We have no idea where he is, but he can somehow always find us.

Bertha, he whispers again, and Bee grabs my hand, the two of us holding tight to each other. I look to the other cars, the couples in back seats blissfully unaware. Like always, nobody can hear him but us.

"Do you want to leave?" I ask, but Bee shakes her head.

"It won't do any good," she says, and she's right. Nowhere is safe for us.

Bee and I wait, barely moving, until what's left of his voice dissolves into the night. This is how it always goes—he never sticks around—but the damage is already done. For the rest of the film, she and I stare blankly at the screen, seeing nothing, hearing nothing, thinking only of the two men who won't ever let us escape.

There are tales about Rochester and Dracula, books and movies, ones where Bee and I have been mostly written out, deleted from our own story, our own lives. Every time I turn around, it seems there's another version of Dracula, another casting call for nubile young women, corseted and blushing and breathless for him. He's become an unlikely hero, a bloodsucking James Bond, and I've become less than a footnote. The disposable victim who should have known better.

Bee's fared even worse. In all the movies about her life, she's no more than an extra locked away in a flimsy attic. She gets a few meager frames of screen time before a fire gobbles her up in the third act. She's ash; she's nothing; she's an obstacle to overcome. She has to die so Rochester and his new wife can live. Bee and I are the same in this regard: the only way that others can have their happy ending is if we don't get ours.

The end credits roll on the second film, all beachy sunsets and lovers united, and the floodlights come up again, for good this time, garish and accusing and spiriting us on our way. Walter waves goodbye from the ticket booth, and Bee and I drive home, midnight brimming all around us. The sky crackles, the heavy clouds threatening rain, but we don't bother to put up the top for the convertible. Too claustrophobic for Bee. Besides, we both like the fresh air. We might not need to breathe anymore, but on cool summer nights like this, it's nice to pretend.

We turn down Wilshire Boulevard, storybook houses whizzing past us in the dark. My entire body tenses. We're almost there now, the one place I've been dreading all night.

Bee gazes at me, the glow of the passing streetlights flickering on her face. "We don't have to go back yet," she says. "Norm's might still be open. We could hang out and drink coffee until tomorrow."

She's trying to buy us time. Buy *me* time. She knows what's waiting for me.

"It's okay," I whisper.

Bee didn't hide from her nightmare tonight. I shouldn't hide from mine.

The car slows, and we reach a stone house veiled thick in shadows, dead ivy clinging to the facade. I pull into the long driveway, desiccated weeds sprouting up through the cracks in the cement, the empty swimming pool silent and gaping as an open grave.

Welcome home.

The engine cuts out, and Bee and I climb out of the car. On the cracked cobblestone path, we walk together, past the former garden, gray and thorny and crying out silently for help, everything fading here.

When we get to the front step, the air turns heavy and fetid, and once again, I want to run. I want to be anywhere but here.

Bee studies my face, her eyes shining and calm. "Are you sure?" she asks.

"Yes," I say, and with a steady hand, I turn the key in the lock.

We open the door, and the rest of Dracula is waiting to greet us.

two

As we step into the house, the pieces of him murmur all around us, permeating every room like a sickly sweet cologne. Even locked inside his urns, he's louder than he has any right to be.

If he's still locked inside the other urns. I need to check on him. I need to make sure he hasn't tried another escape.

Bee and I drift through the vestibule, past a decapitated statue of the *Birth of Venus*. (We didn't do the beheading, by the way; it came like that with the house.) In the living room, the curtains flutter in the night breeze, and Bee crosses to an open window, gazing out at the skyline, glinting like faded diamonds in the distance.

It's dark in here, so I strike a match and light a pair of taper candles. This is all we have. There's no electricity running to the house. No heat or water, either. We can't afford utilities, but then why would we need them? Being dead means being frugal.

Bee watches me with the match, her lips pursed. She doesn't mind candles, but she never lights them. That's because she won't touch fire. Not anymore, not after what happened the last time she struck flint against steel.

"Sometimes," she once told me, "it still feels like my skin is burning."

Then she said no more about it, and I didn't ask.

My hands steady, I leave one candle on the antique desk and take the other to guide my way. "I'll be back in a moment."

Bee looks at me, her brow furrowed. "Do you need help?"

"I'm fine," I say, and even though it's a lie, she pretends to believe me.

"Good luck," she says, and I'm off on my nightly errand. Checking on these murmuring remains. Guarding the urns of Dracula.

For seventy years, I've separated him from himself, his ashes never kept in one place, never even kept in the same room. He's too powerful that way. If I put him in a single vessel, he'd break free and cobble himself together in an instant. Instead, the urns are scattered throughout the house like silly knickknacks.

The first urn's in the parlor, locked inside a small glass cabinet, the kind that used to display odd Victorian artifacts like narwhal horns or monarch butterflies. It's the quietest urn in the house, and when I run my fingers along the outside of the clay, looking for cracks, for any sign of weakness, it barely quivers in reply.

When I get to the next one in the kitchen, I'm not so lucky. This urn's in the wall behind the decommissioned icebox, nestled in the horsehair plaster, and as I yank it free, it shivers in my hands, practically sighing in ecstasy, the brush of my fingertips giving it a cheap little thrill. I hold back a gag, scanning it quickly for flaws. A chip on the rim perhaps or a half-unscrewed lid or a thin fracture in the clay like the fault line beneath Los Angeles. Fortunately, there isn't anything to worry about tonight. No cracks, no movement, nothing alarming at all. I place the urn back where it belongs, inside the wall.

That leaves the last one. The worst one. It's always waiting for me, pushed to the back of the cellar. Because I've got no excuses left, I go to it now, through the door at the end of the hall and down the stairs, dread clenching in my throat.

In Los Angeles, basements are rare as coelacanths. It's something about the waterline along the coast, the way the sea pushes in toward the land, stealing into places where it doesn't belong. Bee and I got lucky with this house—or unlucky, depending on how you look at it. It's not a very pretty cellar. The stone walls are slime and grit, and the splintered wooden stairs have no risers, the backs open to the darkness, to anything that wants to reach out and take hold of you.

I descend deeper into the bowels of the house, the gloom creeping closer. This single candle isn't nearly enough to light my way, but it will have to do. Especially since I'm almost there.

The final urn is on the floor, trapped beneath an upside-down milk crate, the rusted wire like prison bars. I edge forward, but I don't touch this one. I don't even get too close. It isn't safe, the outside of it hotter than the others, like a gas lantern left to burn all night. It never tries to speak. It only seethes, the rage in it so potent it chokes the air out of the room.

My head spins, and I steady myself against the oily stone wall. The weight of his wrath always makes me seasick standing still, everything in me heavy and dizzy and outsized.

This isn't what I want, to be tethered to Dracula for eternity. I wish I could cast his remains out into the Pacific or seal him in concrete, leaving him behind, leaving him in the past, but that wouldn't be enough to hold him. He'd escape in a day if I did.

It has to be these urns. They're the only thing stopping him.

When we first moved in, Bee asked me if I wanted to leave the urns outside. Buried in the garden, maybe, or left in the bottom of the empty pool.

"We don't have to invite him in," she said, and even though I knew she was right, I brought him inside anyway. I might exile an urn for a little while, but it isn't safe for all of him to be too far away for too long. Day or night, I need to keep him close. I need to watch him. That way, I can always be sure at least a part of him isn't free. Some days, that's the only comfort I have, knowing that I've prevented a monster from being unleashed on the world.

I retreat upstairs, back to the living room, and Bee looks up at me from the sofa.

"How was it?"

"The same," I say, which is the best we can hope for.

A heavy breeze cuts through the air, and Bee's face twists, as if in pain.

"Could you?" she asks, and motions to the other side of the room.

One of the windows has blown shut.

I hurry to it and fling it open again, moonlight pouring in. This is another of our rituals. We leave all the windows open, even in the dead of winter, even during the worst thunderstorms. Rainwater leaks down the sills, seeping into the plaster, the yellowed paint cracking and bubbling, but that doesn't matter. Bee doesn't like to feel closed in. A decade locked in an attic will do that to you.

"Thanks," she says, calm settling over her as she leans back on the withering Queen Anne sofa.

"No problem," I say. I'll do anything I can for her. She'll do the same for me. Bee, my best friend, my only friend, the two of us sisters not by blood but by circumstance. We've been unlikely roommates for decades, ever since we stumbled upon each other outside London, no money in our pockets and no pulse in our veins.

"Are we the same?" she asked as we sat together at the St Katharine Docks, watching the ships come and go in the dark. I wanted to tell her yes, but it wasn't true. Bee's never been like me. There's no bloodlust in her heart, no faint scar on her throat. Like Dracula, Rochester did something to her, something violent, something arcane, but those men had different methods. Dracula stole me from my bed at midnight, but Rochester was always more elaborate than that, having a flair for the dramatic. He lured Bee all the way from her home in Spanish Town, Jamaica, carrying her across the Atlantic, just to lock her in that attic. Then when she finally escaped, when she burned her prison to ashes, he started calling out to her, searching the world for her. And he hasn't stopped since.

His voice from earlier tonight still burns in my bones. "Where do you think he is?"

Bee hesitates, her hands clenched in her lap. "Too close."

"In L.A.?"

"No," she says, her mouth a harsh line. "But somewhere else in California."

I nod, not asking any more. I've probably asked too much of her already.

The candles burn down to nothing, the breeze carrying the darkness into the room, and we know what that means: it's time to call it a night. Another day of eternity crossed off the list.

Upstairs in the hall, Bee glances back from her bedroom doorway.

"Good night, Lucy," she says.

"Good night, Bee."

She leaves her door open, anything to keep the claustrophobia from seeping in, but when I get to my room, I lock myself in tight. Anything to keep Dracula out.

In the dark, I kick off my shoes and curl up on my dusty four-poster bed. I don't own a coffin, never have. I also don't sleep during the day. I don't need to sleep much at all, so long as I'm not like him, wasting all my precious energy stalking unsuspecting victims. It's remarkable how much spare time you have when you don't fritter it away on being a monster.

But that's all he is, all he knows. His whispers linger on my skin, and even though the pieces of him are downstairs, a whole floor and a locked door separating us, it still feels like he's right here, in the same bed with me, his breath hot on the back of my neck, his fingertips tracing a path up my thigh. I can't escape him. He's everywhere at once.

Defiant to the last, I close my eyes and drift out of myself, out of my body, back to the places I came from. Across a continent, across an ocean, back to England. Past Carfax Abbey, long since abandoned, and over the house where I grew up, where I died, curled in a bed not so different from this one.

I drift on, through the streets of London, down back alleys and into the gloom where nobody goes. At least almost nobody. There's someone else with me now, someone I haven't heard from in a very long time.

Miss Lucy, the voice singsongs, slicing through the dark like a dull knife. *Where are you, lovely?*

Renfield. He materializes like fog in my mind. His clothes are tattered, his face obscured, his appetite for strange creatures unabated. If I look closely, I can see a cockroach leg, thinner than a toothpick, stuck between his molars. I do my best not to look closely.

He's calling me from afar, lingering like a specter in the margins of the city. He shouldn't still be alive, but then again, neither should I.

Even after all these years, Renfield and I have never met, but we know of each other anyhow. Through whispers and rumors and visions we can't escape. When we close our eyes, we can both see it. The past, as though it's still happening. I'm the one Dracula chooses first, plucked from my bedchamber like a daisy in May, and Renfield is the one he casts aside, a useless weed, a vestigial limb.

You never realized how lucky you were, Renfield says, gnashing his teeth in envy, and I wonder what he knows of luck or love or anything else.

He's not a vampire, never has been. He's a drudge, a thrall, mesmerized against his will, powerless and lost. So long as I don't call back to him, he can't see me the way I see him. That doesn't stop him from trying, his graying eyes staring into the gloom, searching for me. Or rather, searching for what I have.

Master, he whispers, but before the urns can try to answer, I open my eyes and let him slip away.

Shivering, I bolt up in bed. I'm alone now. Dracula's receded from the room, and there's a yawning emptiness in his wake. An emptiness inside me, too. I hate the way he comes and goes, the way he still claims me for his own, how I can't stop him even when I've got him captured.

Rage rises in the back of my throat, acrid and stifling, and I can't sit still. My blanket gathered up around me, I wander to the window. It's quiet outside. Hollywood is settling down for the night. Only the glitzy denizens of Chateau Marmont are still up at this hour.

And maybe something else too. A shadow's moving at the edge of the yard, the figure lithe and close to the ground. A coyote maybe, come up from the canyon, prowling for squirrels or stray cats.

I grit my teeth. "Go away," I whisper, as it rustles past the weeds, still hidden from view. I've never liked coyotes. Too much like wolves, and wolves were always Dracula's favorite. His "children of the night," he called them. What a weirdo.

I wait at the window, listening for a howl, listening for hours, but whatever the animal is, it doesn't return.

I WAKE UP HUNGRY.

It's Thursday. Another day, another tally mark. I slink out of my tangled bedsheets. My shoes are somewhere on the floor where I left them, dirt from the Hollywood sign still caked around the heels. But as I lean down to search, bits of daylight creep across the room, and my chest constricts. I forgot to close the curtains last night.

My eyes bleary, I tiptoe to the window, as though I can sneak up on the day. With a careful hand, I reach toward the curtain, but a sliver of morning hits my face anyhow, and I flinch, nearly crying out, my mind whirling, my flesh tightening on my bones. There's pain, but not the kind you might expect.

Sunlight doesn't kill us. It never has. That wasn't one of the original rules, but these stories become twisted, don't they? They take on a mind of their own, and suddenly, you're living in someone else's invention of what you should be.

But here's the thing: the sun does something else, something almost worse. It takes me away from here, pulling me into the past, putting images in my mind I'd rather forget. I see Dracula, the way he looked the night we met. So prim, so proper, so appallingly handsome. His scent like ash and roses, like a fistful of coffin dirt.

"Good evening, Miss Lucy," he'd said, and I hate this part. I hate remembering how I swooned for him. How I believed him. The worst mistake I've ever made was trusting someone who only saw me as temporary.

And he's not the only one awakening inside me. Mina's with me too, back when we were only foolish girls, too young to know we should be afraid. Her fresh face is so gauzy in my memory that it's almost lost to time. The face of my first friend, my only friend other than Bee. I see the garden maze where Mina and I used to giggle and run and share our secrets, the two of us weaving blooms of wisteria through our long hair.

"Let's never grow old," she would whisper, and I'd squeeze her hand and promise, never realizing the price I'd pay for keeping up my end of the bargain.

These memories burn in me, brighter than a hundred suns, and I don't want this. I don't want to remember. At last, I take hold of the curtains, and with my fingers clenched, knuckles white, I yank them closed. Then I collapse to the floor, my head in my hands.

I want to crawl back into bed and not leave this room at all today, but that won't happen. Through the closed door, I hear her. Bee, battling her own past. Down the hall, she's having another nightmare.

When I get to her, she's thrashing in her bed, her limbs gone wild, her face twisted.

"It's all right, it's all right," I keep saying, perched on the rim of the mattress. I put one hand on her arm, and instantly, I feel it there.

The thing crawling beneath her skin, thin as worms, tough as iron.

This is what Rochester did to Bee. What that attic in Thornfield Hall did.

"I barely remember it," she always tells me. But sometimes, when she's having a nightmare, she'll say things that don't make sense.

"Don't let it get me, Edward," she wheezes. "Please don't do this to me."

It was hiding in that attic where he imprisoned her. Something that got into him and got into Bee, too. That's why neither one of them have died. The secrets of that burned-down house are keeping them alive.

There are so many things she still won't tell me. There are things I haven't told her, too. It's a promise we made to each other the night we met: to not ask questions we aren't eager to answer.

"Wake up, Bee," I whisper, and with a final thrash, her body goes still, and she opens her eyes.

"Did it happen again?" she asks, and I nod.

She sits up, wiping salt tears from her cheeks. The skin on her arms is quiet now, no more crawling, no more movement. The thing inside her has settled down, retreating deeper into her body.

"I shouldn't have slept in so late," she says, as if that's to blame.

I start to say something, to tell her it's okay, but Bee's too quick for me. She's up and out of bed, rushing downstairs, determined to make up for lost time. I linger in the doorway, listening to her dashing back and forth through all the rooms, into the parlor and the hallway and settling finally in the kitchen. By the time I come down, the house is quiet and dark. She's already tugged all the curtains closed, sealing out the worst of the sunlight. This is our compromise. The windows stay open for her, the curtains stay closed for me. We help each other. We're only safe if we're in this together.

And we're only safe if we keep to our routine. It's been a few hours, so I check on the urns again.

"He hasn't made a peep," Bee says brightly when I inspect the one behind the icebox in the kitchen.

I watch her at the counter, polishing silver and porcelain and brass for the imaginary guests we'll never have.

"You don't have to keep an eye on him," I say. "He's not your responsibility, Bee."

She shrugs. "It's fine," she says, as if it's a perfectly normal request, asking your roommate to babysit the ashes of your ex.

The day already heavy in my bones, I go to the other urns, first in the parlor and then the cellar. At the bottom of the rickety steps, I hesitate, staring at it. At him.

"Why won't you stay dead?" I whisper, and it's the same question Dracula could ask me. I try not to speak too loudly. I don't want Bee to hear. I don't want her to know I still talk to him, still have these useless conversations with the man who murdered me.

Back upstairs, Bee's finished with the silver and she's waiting for me in the parlor, two brooms propped up next to her.

"Ready?" she asks, her eyes flashing gold as I pick one broom, and, smiling, she grabs the other. Then we take off running, her down the hall, me up the stairs, our laughter ricocheting off the crumbling plaster, loud enough to drown out everything else, even Dracula.

This is another of our routines, and the only one I don't mind: tidying up the house together. Each day we make a game of this. Bee gets the cobwebs, sweeping them out of the doorways and the archways and all the corners, and I get the dust, the veils of it draped over the house like lace, and when we're finished, we sit back in the parlor and see how fast the decay returns. Usually before nightfall. That's how quickly our lives rot out around us.

This property wasn't so bad when Bee and I purchased it. Sure, it had been abandoned for years, set for demolition, which is how we got it so cheap. But back then, it still felt alive. The ivy, thick and verdant, crept over the outside like it owned the place. The weeds in the garden grew neck-high, and there were strange wildflowers nobody could even name. The furniture hadn't moldered yet, and the ceilings hadn't sagged.

I changed all of that. A single touch from me, and everything started withering to gray. Vampires don't just settle down in decrepit castles. We make them that way, the death within us seeping out into everything we're near. I could take one step into glittering Versailles, and by nightfall, it would look like a tomb.

Today's decay comes even quicker than we expect, and we watch it sneak closer to us, Bee sprawled out on the fainting couch, me in a winged-back chair.

"Look at the ceiling," Bee marvels, the shapes on the plaster dancing and whirling.

"How about the wallpaper?" I say, as it curls away in the corners like stiff flesh.

As the afternoon light wanes, the decay settling around us, we laugh together and play the old Victrola. It's the wind-up kind, and after every song, we take turns crossing the room and making it start again. *Tea for Two. Thanks for the Memory. Smoke Gets in Your Eyes.* We've heard these tunes a thousand times, and we'll hear them a thousand more. This is all the entertainment we've got in the house.

Bee sings along, her voice an uncanny aria, and I tip back my head, listening. She's like a thousand cathedral bells in Paris, ringing all at the same moment. Nobody in the world sounds like her.

The Victrola lazes down, desperate for another windup, but Bee doesn't notice. She just keeps on singing, adrift in a melody only she can hear. There are times like this when I catch her gazing off into nothing, her eyes unfocused, her heart on her sleeve. She's thinking of something lost. Or someone.

"If you could have one wish," she asks, staring across at the rolltop desk, splintered and faded with age, "what would it be?"

I hesitate. Bee's never asked me something like this before. Nobody has.

"To be free," I say at last, though I don't even know what that means. "What about you?"

"To never be alone," she says, and my heart twists in my chest. Bee was lonely enough in that attic to last ten lifetimes. If it weren't for me, she'd fill this house to the gills with guests. Streamers in the rafters, champagne in a dozen punch bowls. But so long as I'm here, it isn't safe to have people in the house. They could find out about him. They could find out about me.

It's dusk now, almost time to head to the drive-in. Bee's already up and across the parlor, closing the Victrola, when there's a knock on the front door. She and I freeze, her hand suspended in midair above the turntable, my body stiff in the winged-back chair, both of us waiting, hoping it will go away.

Another knock, and it's clear we won't get what we want.

I clamber to my feet. "I'll answer it."

I can already guess who it is, his heartbeat through the door giving him away every time. Tyrone, our sour-grape neighbor. I see him in my mind, scowling on our front step. His face perennially pinched, his hair sullenly white, he's got the look of someone who would gladly pass an ordinance against joy if he could muster up the votes.

I cross into the vestibule as he knocks again, and I throw open the door, fast as I can. It gives him a start, his whole body flinching.

I grin. "How can I help you today?"

He glares back at me. "You know why I'm here."

That's true. It's the same reason he's been bothering us for the last year, ever since he moved into a bungalow across the street. According to him, we're a scourge on everything: the neighborhood, the property values, basic decency. All of that, and he doesn't even know we're dead.

"There are regulations," he says, and snuffs, his gaze roaming over the dried ivy dangling from the roof. "And this place has got to be a fire hazard."

I snap my tongue. "I don't come to your house and criticize your decorating skills."

His eyes turn sharply toward me. "Addams Family is not an aesthetic." He snuffs again. "Clean it up, Miss Westenra, or I'll be forced to take my complaint to city council."

His hands balled into fists, he marches back toward the gate, only to stop suddenly on the path.

"Oh, wonderful." He glowers at our graveyard of a garden. "You have a dog now?"

My brow twisted, I step off the front step to see what he sees. Up and down the yard, there are paw prints, the claws sharp enough to dig thick divots into the ground.

"It's not mine," I say, and that's not even a lie. That coyote last night was busier than I realized.

"Like I said," Tyrone says with a sneer, "fix up this place. Then maybe stray dogs won't terrorize the neighborhood."

And with that, he's off. I watch him go, thinking how there could be something far worse terrorizing the neighborhood, something that could make sure he'd never get all the way to city council, maybe not even across the street.

Back in the parlor, Bee barely glances up. "Another threat from Tyrone?"

"Always." I glare out the window, clenching my teeth. "I could devour him whole."

"True," Bee says, "but I can't imagine he'd taste very good."

I exhale a piercing laugh, one that reverberates off the ceiling, practically shaking the whole house. For a moment, I'm sure I hear Dracula join in.

With the sun vanished in the sky, Bee and I drive across town. On the Sunset Strip, there's already a line around the block at the Whisky a Go Go. Tall boots, taller egos. I envy those kids. Years ago, I was just like them. I used to dance at every party, in every parlor. Sometimes I danced alone, and sometimes I danced with Mina, the two of us turning in circles until we were giddy.

Then I met him. On a lonely street in England, he asked me to dance, and all these years later, I'm still dizzy from it, the ghost of his hand on my back still enough to make my skin crawl. Enough to make me never want to dance again.

We pull up to the drive-in just as the first film's about to begin. "Good to see you two again," Walter says from the crumbling ticket booth.

Of course he's glad we're here. Other than a couple in a Studebaker toward the back and the two in the silver Pontiac Banshee in the front row, the lot's mostly empty. These days, Bee and I are about the only regular customers left. Everyone else has drifted away to the Cinerama Dome on Sunset or the Golden Gate Theatre on Whittier. Drive-ins are quaint now, relics of the past. Maybe that's why Bee and I like it so much here.

We opt for James Bond tonight, and it's all squibs and swelling music and well-coiffed women whose names 007 forgets long before the end credits roll. I try to focus on the film, but everything aches inside me. My hunger's sharper than before, coming over me in waves.

At intermission, I stumble out of the car. "You want anything?"

"The usual," Bee murmurs, and I know what that means. Two drinks, one popcorn, extra butter. This is it, all there is. An eternity of reruns.

My head down, I push through the door into the lobby, but I'm not alone this time. There's a young man behind the counter, his back to me, moving like a ghost past the popcorn machine. This must be Michael, Walter's grandson. He turns a little, still not seeing me, his face in profile. My gaze slides slowly over him. Sharp jaw, sandy hair, steel-blue eyes. He could be a young William Holden, a golden boy, a promise the world won't keep.

A strange sensation flickers in me, and I'm leaning against the counter now. I should say something—get his attention, get my popcorn, get back to Bee—but I keep watching him. And listening.

That heartbeat, a relentless melody in his chest, strong and rich and unapologetic. He's alive, and he's acutely aware of it. Most people don't think much about whether they're breathing or not. It just becomes so automatic, so banal. But not for him, not with where he's been, what he's seen at war. He knows death more intimately than a lover. We're the same in that way.

A flush of heat surges through me, and I suddenly can't help myself. I think of all the lovely, terrible things I could do to him. How sweet he'd taste. The way he'd moan my name. The way he'd scream my name, too. I wonder which I'd like better.

My head goes gauzy, and I won't do this. That's the one thing I've promised myself: that I won't become like

Dracula. I start to inch backward, to do the right thing, but outside in the lot, an old clunker backfires, the noise sharp as shattering glass. Michael startles, his whole body going rigid, his head twisting toward the sound. That's when he sees me standing here. His eyes lock on me, and I should turn away, I should run, but I don't. I gaze back at him, just for a moment, just long enough for it to happen.

I don't move any closer. I never even lay a finger on him. That doesn't matter. Something in his face shifts. Something in me shifts too.

"Hello," he whispers, and a heavy veil of shame settles over me.

"I'm so sorry," I say, but it's too late. I can already see what I've done to him floating behind his eyes.

When it first happens, it's intoxicating. Like a spoonful of laudanum, like being lifted through the sky and then plummeting just as quickly, clouds pulsing past you, the whole world drifting away.

This is what Dracula did to Renfield. It's the same thing Dracula did to me. A bewitching, a thrall, a single look that turns you pliant. Something like love. Something like death, too.

"Are you Lucy?" Michael asks, his face so sweet and eager.

"I am," I say, and wish I wasn't.

"My grandfather's told me about you." He busies himself behind the counter, still looking at me, his eyes glazing a little from what I've done. "You and your friend Bee come here every night, don't you?"

"We do," I murmur as I watch him. He's pouring me two Cokes. I haven't ordered anything yet, but he already knows what I want. I'm doing this to him, putting thoughts in his head without even meaning to.

He sets the drinks and a box of popcorn on the counter. We're close now, the scent of his skin like pine, everything about him earthy and grounded and real. He extends one hand to me, maybe for my money, maybe for something else, but I won't reach out for him. I'm afraid if I put my hands on him, I might never let go.

"What else would you like?" he asks.

"I don't need anything," I whisper, even though it isn't true. My stomach raw, I need the very thing he could offer.

His eyes are still on me, but I can't stay here. The door swings open, and I'm outside, rushing back to the Buick empty-handed, back to Bee.

When I get to the car, the second film's already started. I was in there longer than I realized. I settle down in my seat, sinking so low I hope no one can see me here.

"Did you meet his grandson?" Bee asks absently, her gaze fixed on the screen.

I hesitate. "Unfortunately."

A hideous silence settles between us.

"Again?"

"I didn't mean to," I say, as though that's a defense.

Bee folds her nervous hands in her lap. "It's all right," she says. "It'll pass. It always does."

These words hit me hard in the chest. *It always does.*

This has happened before, and Bee knows it. She knows what I'm capable of.

For the next two hours, I stare at the screen, seeing nothing, feeling nothing except for him. Michael's scent clings to my body, and even from here I can hear his heartbeat inside me, sweet and strong and faster than before. I have to bite down to keep my teeth from sharpening.

The movie ends, and I don't wait for the lights to come up. The Buick lurches over the gravel and overgrown grass, but when we get to the exit, a shadow darts in front of us. Michael. He comes around to the driver's side, holding something.

"You forgot these," he says.

He passes me a box of popcorn and the two Cokes I left on the counter. The drinks are piss warm by now, but he probably thinks they're fresh. His eyes still glazed over, he's been in a haze ever since I left the lobby, floating on cloud nine where I put him.

"You'll be back tomorrow night, won't you?" he asks, leaning a little closer.

I wet my lips, the echo of Dracula stirring inside me. But before I can move, before I can do anything I'll regret, Bee puts a light hand on my arm.

"Sure, Michael," she says, smiling. "We'll see you tomorrow."

And that's it, enough of a reprieve. I press the gas pedal hard, and the car jolts forward, warm Coke spilling in my lap, buttered popcorn tumbling like confetti over the upholstery. Bee adjusts the rearview mirror, watching Michael wave goodbye behind us.

"He's cute," she says as we turn onto the state highway.

"I didn't notice," I say, and though it's a lie, she doesn't call me on it. We head home, one taillight burned out and Dracula whispering on the wind. He's laughing, too. He always has a good chuckle when he gets to see me acting like him.

The house is waiting sullenly for us, dark as always and colder too.

"Don't worry, Lucy," Bee says as we cross into the parlor. "It'll all work out. It always does."

Smiling, I pretend to believe her as I open the drawer on the rolltop desk in the corner. An unlit candle in my hand, I'm looking for a matchbook, but there are other things in here too. Things I'd rather forget.

A silver letter opener, a gift from Mina that's no longer safe for me to touch.

A pot of nearly dried ink and withered paper, for letters we never write.

And a single antique necklace strung with rubies the color of fresh pomegranate seeds. The last of my long-ago dowry. Bee and I have almost no money to our names, but that doesn't matter. We keep this in case we need to run. In case these men force us to run.

That was how we got here in the first place. We'd never wanted to leave England, but we didn't have much choice. The war came, and then another, and we couldn't stay. Especially not when Rochester was closing in on us. He tracked us to London in the middle of the Blitz, and I wasn't sure what scared us more: the hellfire of bombs or him.

"He'll never stop," Bee had whispered as we cowered in the dank basement of the semidetached house we were renting in Blackheath.

It was Bee who chose Hollywood, pointing to it on a map.

"We can hide there. We can be anyone we want," she'd said, and she was right. In the blink of an eye we became California girls, even shedding our accents, anything to blend in. It's easy to play make-believe in a city cobbled together from it.

And we had just enough to get us here. My mother had always called it a hope chest, and that was exactly what it gave us. We bartered two brooches for third-class passage on a freighter. A black velvet band with a diamond buckle for cross-country seats in the back of an ice truck, quiet and gloomy as a tomb. An emerald bracelet for this very house, long past its prime anyhow. When at last the journey was over, and the unforgiving California sun was sneaking in through every window, this was the only piece of jewelry we hadn't used up.

"Let's keep it for a rainy day," Bee had said, tucking it in the back of the drawer. That's where it's stayed ever since. Where I hope it stays forever.

My hands shaking, I finally find the matchbook and turn away from the desk.

After the candle burns out, Bee heads to bed early,

but I can't sleep. My door locked, I sit up, my knees pulled into my chest, my sheets crumpled around me like a discarded love letter. The coyote from last night returns, scratching again in the garden, howling loud enough to set the floorboards rattling, but I keep the curtains closed.

Friday comes, sneaking in sly as a thief, and it's hotter than yesterday, the heavy swelter settling in by noon like an unwanted houseguest. I'm halfway through checking on the urns when there's another knock at the door.

I roll my eyes. More empty threats about city council, no doubt.

With Bee down the hall in the kitchen, I cross to the front door and fling it open, ready to surprise Tyrone, maybe even make that empty heart of his seize up in his chest.

But he's not the one standing on the other side.

It's a girl, her hair damp and stringy. She stares at me, not saying a word. I've never seen her face before, but there's something off about her, something I can't quite place. She isn't one of the neighbors here to complain about the state of the house, that's for sure.

"May I help you?" I ask, and that's when I realize what's wrong.

I can't hear anything. There's no heartbeat inside her.

I back away. "Who are you? What do you want with us?"

"Lucy?" Bee's voice lilting in from the next room. "Is everything okay?"

Before I can tell her no, tell her to run, she materializes in the archway behind me.

Instantly, the girl's face brightens. "Hi, Bee," she whispers, and at the sight of her, Bee goes completely gray. Dread coils through me, my gaze shifting back and forth between them, fully aware that something terrible is happening, even though I'm not sure what.

One final, weightless moment, like a free fall before you hit the ground.

"Jane," Bee says at last, and the whole world unravels around us.

three

Jane Eyre.

I've seen the name more times than I can count, on bookshelves and marquees and splashed across posters in bright red letters. With all that fanfare, you can't help but expect the legend. Instead, you get the girl, slouching on our front step. Her feet are bare, her pale hair's tied back with a ragged yellow ribbon. Something in her gaze looks wild, almost feral, like she's just wandered in from a long, thorny year in the wilderness.

Bee can't take her eyes off her. "I thought I'd never see you again."

Jane's cheeks redden. "I should have written. I should have told you I was coming."

They keep staring at each other, and I fidget between them, feeling somehow like I'm witnessing a secret that isn't mine to share. Then all at once, I remember my manners. Or what's left of them.

"Come in," I say, motioning Jane toward the parlor, as though we actually entertain our guests there instead of just our ghosts.

The three of us sit in a haphazard circle, me in the winged-back chair, the two of them side by side on the fainting couch.

Nobody says anything. No niceties, no introductions. I was never a very good Victorian, but I suppose I'll have to do my best imitation today. Shoulders back, chin up, a polite smile plastered on my face.

"I'm Lucy," I say, and hold out my hand.

Jane doesn't take it. "Nice to meet you," she says without inflection. Bee's still watching her, but Jane won't look at her now.

Silence settles around us, the invisible guest in the room. Near me, in the corner, an urn of Dracula's ashes is sitting in its glass case, but it's the quietest one of the bunch, so even it has nothing to add. For once, I long for small talk, for something to cut through this strange stillness.

I lean forward suddenly, thinking of a question. "Are you living in Los Angeles?"

Jane shakes her head. "San Francisco."

That's it, all she says. Not where in the city or for how long or why in the world she's materialized on our front step after more than a century. For her part, Bee says nothing at all. She just keeps watching Jane.

I sigh. They're not making this easy. My hands tightening in my lap, I try again.

"So Bee tells me you're a governess," I say brightly, but immediately regret it. Of course, she's not a governess anymore. It's 1967. Nobody's a governess these days. That kind of job doesn't even exist. It'd be like asking her if she's a chimney sweep or a leech collector.

Jane forces a smile. "I used to be a governess," she says. "I guess you could say I'm retired now."

"So what have you been doing?" Bee asks, a twinge of pain in her voice.

"Traveling, mostly."

A long, ugly moment.

"With him?"

"Yes."

"And how is he?"

"The same." Jane studies a small splotch on the carpet. "He's always the same."

My skin prickles, my mouth goes dry, and here it comes. More silence. It feels like there will always be silence now. Unending bouts of miserable silence. This house was scarcely bearable before. Now I'm starting to consider just staking myself and joining Dracula in the urns. It could hardly be worse than this.

"Would anyone like tea?" I ask.

Bee's eyes flick up at me, a quizzical look twitching across her brow, but Jane lets out a small, grateful sigh.

"Yes, that would be wonderful," she says, and without another word, I bolt from the parlor and into the kitchen. Then I stand there next to the empty icebox and realize what I've done.

Tea. I'm supposed to get them tea. I don't know why I even offered. We have no running water, no tea bags either. In a moment, I'll have to walk back into the parlor, red-faced and empty-handed.

In the wall, an urn of ashes snickers at me, and I shoot it a glare. Now that I'm out of the room, though, Bee and Jane are talking at last, their voices seeping through the crumbling plaster.

"And that book with your name on it?" Bee's asking.

"Not my words," Jane says. "Or at least not all of them. He got hold of it first."

There's a familiar lilt in her voice. Unlike Bee and me, Jane's never lost her accent. It sounds like home, like somewhere I've nearly forgotten.

I don't know what to do here. How to entertain. How to pretend I actually like people. I was a socialite once, but that was a long time ago. I don't remember any of the rules anymore.

Faint footsteps in the hall.

"Lucy?" Bee appears in the doorway. "What's wrong?"

I give her a tight smile. "We're out of tea."

Bee chuckles. "I know," she says, and throws up her hands. "I'm sorry about this. I never expected her to show up here."

I stand back, waiting for her to say something else, but she goes quiet, the two of us staring at each other across the empty kitchen.

"So," I say, fidgeting next to the counter, "that's Jane Eyre."

"That's her." Bee exhales a thin sigh, a sudden urgency in her eyes. "She needs to stay with us awhile. Just until she gets back on her feet."

The notion sticks in my throat like glue. Someone living with us. Someone asking questions I don't want to answer.

"Are you sure that's a good idea?" I say, my voice splitting in two.

Bee nods solemnly. "After everything he's done to her, I want to help. I want . . ."

She trails off, that familiar faraway look on her face. I hate it when she gets this way. So melancholy, so strange.

"We have plenty of room," I say, trying to be helpful.

Bee brightens again. "Thank you, Lucy. I knew you'd understand."

And with that, she's gone again, returned to Jane in the other room.

Except she's wrong. I don't understand this at all. Why would she ever want to help the woman who replaced her, the second wife who let her burn to death in that attic? Someone I always thought was no more than a stranger to her.

But they're not acting like strangers. Late afternoon whispers in, and the two of them are still together in the parlor.

"How many people were in the house in San Francisco with you?" Bee asks.

"Too many." Jane heaves out a tired laugh. "You know how Edward always loved a party."

I try not to listen. Instead, I concern myself with the decay. It follows me everywhere I go, the rot of me leeching into the plaster. Without Bee to help, it comes quicker than usual.

A blot the color of cancer swirls on the wallpaper in the hall, and I pursue it with a broom, eager to beat it from existence. But it's faster than I am, slithering along the crown molding, hiding in the cracks, taunting me.

"You can't stay up there forever," I say, glowering, but I'm wrong, because it hovers there for hours until nightfall. When it finally starts to drip down in the corners, thick as tears, rank as roadkill, I chase it farther down the hall, crushing it with the bent bristles of the broom. Over and over until there's nothing left. Triumphant, I look up, and my cheeks flush. I'm standing in the doorway of the parlor, and Bee and Jane are both watching me.

"Lucy," Bee says, as though she hasn't seen me in years. "Come sit with us."

But I don't move, the broom drooping in my grasp. The rot hasn't settled in the parlor today. Everything around the two of them looks gleaming and new. Jane's curled up on the fainting couch, watching Bee as she hums along to the Victrola.

"I've always loved your singing," Jane says. "I could recognize you from anywhere."

Unease shifts inside me. "Is that how you found us?" I ask. "By listening for Bee?"

By eavesdropping, I mean.

Jane goes rigid, her face gaunter than before. "Yes," she says finally. "Once I left him, I knew this was the only place I could go."

I look to Bee, but this revelation, this blatant intrusion, doesn't seem to bother her.

"So long as you're away from him," Bee says, leaning over the couch, entwining her hand with Jane's. They gaze at each other for a long moment, the air buzzing with possibility, their secrets leaving no room for anything else.

With the Victrola still bleating out old love songs, I leave them alone, propping the broom next to the statue of Venus and slipping out the door.

On Santa Monica Boulevard, I fill up the Buick at the Union 76 station, using my last five-dollar bill. The gas tank's almost rusted shut, my decay slowly settling in every crevice of the car. Soon we'll be lucky if the engine starts at all.

At the next intersection, I seize up, trying to decide where to go. I could head alone to the drive-in. Michael's waiting for me, lingering behind the counter, his heart twisted with longing, twisted from what I've done to him. This thrall, a silvery tether between us, thinner than a spiderweb, tougher than titanium.

Even from afar, I can sense him. He buzzes in my blood, his scent like pine, his skin warm, and I suddenly can't help myself.

"I'm right here," I whisper, but my voice dissolves

on the restless wind, as the Cadillac behind me blares its horn. With a rueful sigh, I head the other way. Toward the other man in my life.

The Hollywood sign shimmers in the moonlight, and I kneel beneath it, my hem soaked in earth. It only takes a few fistfuls of dirt until I find it.

The urn, only inches beneath the ground now.

"You've been busy," I say. In just two days, Dracula nearly dug his way out. If I hadn't come back, he might have been free by tomorrow.

The city gleaming below me, I nestle down in the over-grown grass, watching the moon shift in the sky. I can't go home, not yet. I'm not welcome there, not so long as we have company.

Here's what I know about Jane Eyre: She's quiet. She's loyal. Sanctimonious, even. She was an orphan, then a governess, and finally a wife. That's the CliffsNotes version, of course, but here's the thing: Bee never told me any of that. I learned most of those details from the movie, the one with a purse-lipped Joan Fontaine and a bellow-ing Orson Welles.

(I wanted to read the book, but Bee forbids it in the house. "Bad luck," she always said, and I couldn't blame her for that. We don't keep a copy of that *other* book either.)

In fact, Bee never mentioned Jane at all. "That awful story," she'd always call it, like she couldn't even say her name. Until today at the front door, I wasn't even sure they'd ever met.

"It's bad enough having someone in the house," I say, the urn resting in my lap. "But why is she *here*? And why now?"

I stare down at what's left of Dracula. He's watching me. He's always watching, those invisible eyes peering into places I've never been able to go.

"Is there something you see that I don't?" The words nearly catch in my throat. "Why is she running?"

I wait a long, empty moment, but there's no answer. I don't know why I'd expect anything different. Dracula never told me the truth before. Why start now?

With my head heavy, I wish for this night to be over, but the night's not done with me. A rustle in the nearby sagebrush, and I'm suddenly not alone.

"Hello, Lucy."

Michael, standing in the dark, his soft heartbeat threading through me.

"What are you doing?" I gape at him. "Did you *walk* here?"

A sheepish shrug. "It's not too far," he says, but that's a lie. It's at least five miles, up a dusty highway and over rocky terrain. He must have started more than an hour ago, as soon as he realized I wasn't coming to the drive-in.

As soon as I called out from the car, luring him to me.

He's here because he's the only thing I'm hungry for tonight.

Dracula stirs within me, his words from years ago echoing through my mind again. *Take what belongs to you, Lucy.*

Michael edges a step closer. "What is that thing?" he asks, nodding at the urn.

My hands tighten around it protectively. "Ashes."

A small scowl twitches across his face. "From a person?"

"Not exactly."

With the urn under my arm, I brush the dirt from my dress and start to stand, and Michael reaches out to help me up. But the moment he touches me, he recoils.

"You're so cold," he whispers.

Humiliation bubbles up in me. "That's what happens when you're dead."

He exhales a sharp laugh. "That sounds like a terrible problem to have."

He probably doesn't believe me. And why should he? Here in the California moonlight, I just look like an ordinary girl. Not a monster, not his would-be murderer.

But maybe I'm not the only monster in town tonight. There's a smear of movement behind the sign, and Michael jolts toward it, his eyes wide.

"What was that?" he asks, and I stare into the darkness, at the shape drifting there.

An animal. The same one that was below my window.

Except this isn't a coyote at all. Not a stray dog, either. It's a wolf, his eyes glowing red, his fur the color of shadows. And he's not alone.

In a flash, they're everywhere. A dozen of them, their bodies a blur of teeth and tails and gnarled claws.

A lonesome howl pierces the night, followed by another and another after that, right down the line, all of them serenading us. Michael's heartbeat quickens, urgent and throbbing, and a flush of desire, of unrepentant hunger, surges through my body. In this moment, I can't decide if I'm more afraid of the wolves or afraid of myself.

"Where are they coming from?" Michael asks, his breath ragged, but I already know.

Dracula. He always attracted wolves, whole packs of them, swarming around him like common houseflies. They were his harbingers, warning him of what was to come, protecting him from the world.

One by one, the wolves slip between the letters of the Hollywood sign, weaving in and out. I dart in front of Michael, worried they'll go after him, that they'll rip that beautiful body of his to pieces, but he hasn't even caught their eye.

They're only watching me.

Michael exhales an uneasy chuckle. "They sure seem to like you, Lucy."

Of course they do. I've got what they want, the urn clutched to my chest.

The wolves advance another step, but I don't flinch, my muscles going rigid as iron, my teeth elongating, until they sense it in me. Something primordial. Something powerful. My skin hums—everything about me is humming—and for the first time in years, I feel almost alive. And I don't feel afraid.

"Go away," I seethe, and the wolves apparently aren't as brave as they look. A final mournful howl before they withdraw and skulk off into the night.

Michael's heart slowly eases back to normal. "That's strange," he says. "I thought wolves were extinct in California."

"They are," I say, and my eyes are on him. "Come on. I'll drive you home."

It's Friday night, the streets of Hollywood bursting to life, and I take the long way to the drive-in. Michael leans back in the passenger seat, the glow of neon lighting up his face. He tells me about himself, and I listen, even though I shouldn't. After all, nobody goes into a five-star restaurant and asks the prime rib for its life story.

"I was discharged from the army four weeks ago," he says. "Went back home to Ohio, but it didn't work out. My mother told me I needed fresh air and sunshine. I told her I'd gotten plenty of that already. She bought me a ticket and put me on a plane anyhow."

He hesitates before adding, "Nobody knows what to do with me anymore."

His hands shaking, he cranks up the radio dial, as if to end the conversation he started. The speakers crackle with DJ Dave Diamond. KBLA in Burbank. It's all Donovan and Dylan and the Doors, and though it isn't my kind of music, I leave it on, as Michael reaches out and entwines his fingers with mine.

"Let's not go back." He gazes out at the skyline, glinting like shrapnel in the moonlight. "We could run away together."

He means it too, the poor fool. I could take him anywhere tonight. Drive him to the ends of the earth or down some dusty lovers' lane. Tear off his clothes, tear out his throat. Drain every last drop of his blood and welcome him into me, holding him in my veins where he'll always be mine, where we'll always be together.

The urn quivers on the floor at my feet, encouraging me. Dracula wants me to do this. And he wants to watch.

But I won't give him the satisfaction. I take Michael home instead, to a little shotgun house behind the drive-in. I shift the car into neutral, stopping right beside Walter's rusted Ford pickup, the robin's-egg blue paint job flecking off into the grass. I wonder what he'd do if he knew what I wanted from his grandson. Bring out a Winchester and put a fistful of lead through my heart? As though that would do any good. It would have to be silver, and even then, I wouldn't stay dead, not for long.

Next to me, Michael smiles, his hand still wrapped around mine. "I had fun tonight," he says, the glimmer of the thrall dancing behind his eyes.

Shame blisters through me. "Listen," I say. "You need to stay away from me."

Michael's face contorts, as if in pain. "Why?"

"Because if you don't, I'll probably kill you."

This should be enough to scare him off, to scare anyone off. He only shrugs. "You wouldn't be the first person to try."

This knocks me off-balance. I hadn't thought of that.

"But can't you feel it?" I stare at him, at that golden boy face of his. "Can't you tell I've done something to you?"

"Sure you have." He grins. "That's why I'm falling for you."

I roll my eyes, ready to bite him on principle. "No, you're not," I say. "You don't even know me. You don't even have a choice in it."

He lets out a strident laugh. "Choice," he says, rolling the word around on his tongue, grimacing like he'd rather spit it out. "Since when do any of us have a choice?"

His question sits in my belly like buckshot.

"Get out of the car." I reach across his lap and flick open his door. "*Now.*"

He does as I tell him—of course he does, that's the problem—but at the last moment, as he closes the passenger door, he looks back. "Can I see you again tomorrow night?"

The Buick peels out of the lot. Even without glancing in the rearview mirror, I know Michael's watching me, waving goodbye, as though this was an ordinary date instead of a failed crime scene.

"Stay away," I whisper, and hope he hears me.

At home, I stagger past the statue of Venus, the night heavy in my bones. I'm ready to head to bed, but Bee's waiting up alone in the parlor.

"Where have you been?" she asks brightly.

"With him." I hold up the urn, still dirt-caked around the rim. "Where's Jane?"

"Asleep upstairs," Bee says, as I check on the urn in the cabinet. It's quiet as usual. No movement, no cracks.

I light a candle, and Bee follows me into the kitchen. With the urn from the Hollywood sign under my arm, I reach into the wall behind the icebox. In the darkness, Dracula shivers softly against me.

I recoil from him. Then I turn to Bee, a question boiling inside me. "Why is Jane here?"

Bee hesitates, as if she's been waiting for me to ask. "Where else could she go?"

"Maybe anywhere?" I start toward the cellar. "At the very least, she shouldn't expect her husband's first wife to provide room and board."

Downstairs, Bee and I huddle over the last urn of Dracula, his rage burning into the stone floor.

I grip the candle tight. "I don't understand why you'd even want her here."

A look of certainty flashes across her face. "Because," Bee says finally, "I love her."

In an instant, it falls into place. The abiding loneliness in Bee. All those faraway looks. I always figured she was thinking of Rochester. But he wasn't the one who broke her heart. It was Jane. All this time, Bee was thinking of her.

"She and I talked about running away together," Bee says as we trudge up the cellar stairs, the heat of Dracula wafting after us. "But she was still in love with him then."

My gaze shifts to her. "What makes you think she isn't still in love with him?"

"She left him, didn't she?"

Together, we reach the hallway, and Bee watches me, the flame burning down faster.

"Lucy, can you please give Jane the benefit of the doubt? For me?"

A gleaming, hopeful look in her eyes. This is it, her chance to reclaim the life Rochester stole. A chance I won't spoil for her.

"Of course," I say, and mean it.

The next morning, my decay is draped like an ancient wedding veil over the house. Bee's helping me clean off all the records and the shelves when Jane tiptoes into the parlor.

"Can I help?" she asks, and on instinct I scowl, wanting to send her away. Then I remember my promise to Bee.

"Sure," I say, and pass Jane a broom. "Just clear out any cobwebs you find."

"That shouldn't be hard," she says cheerfully, and off she goes, deeper into the serpentine halls of the house.

Bee beams at me from the Victrola. "Thank you, Lucy."

The rot is thick today, the thickest we've ever seen, and we're both squashing splotches of black mold on the antique rug when Jane wanders in from the kitchen.

"Where does this thing go?" she asks, and my whole body goes numb.

She's holding an urn of ashes.

"Don't move," I whisper, starting toward her, but Dracula's too quick for me.

In her hands, he shivers, and I can almost hear him laugh as Jane's eyes go wide. She lets out a small, strangled gasp, and I don't even have time to scream before the urn slips away from her.

With a dull thud, it shatters on the parlor floor.

four

He's everywhere, the remnants of him like stardust in the air. A cloud of him emerges from the bits of broken urn, sluggish at first and then swirling faster, until he's a dizzying sight to behold.

Bee wheezes next to me. "What do we do?" she asks, but I don't know. This has never happened before.

The curtains flicker in the breeze, and I know that's where he's headed. An escape, a way out of this house. I lunge for the nearest window, yanking it closed. He goes for the next one and the next one after that, and I have to keep stumbling across the floor, locking each window before he can sneak out into the morning.

It doesn't help that every time I shove aside the curtains, sunlight slices into the room, knocking us both back, the memories of what we were seeping into us. In my mind, I see him, the way his hands used to move over my body. Around my waist, caressing my cheek, pressed into my throat until I couldn't even rasp out a scream. I see Mina, too, how he went after her when he was done with me. Her face is faded, crescent moons the color of thunderstorms beneath both eyes, her lips parted but making no sound.

I wonder what Dracula sees. What are the things that haunt a monster?

The ashes slither across the ceiling and into the hall-way, and I'm running now, desperate to keep up. Bee lags behind me, the closed windows in the parlor suffocating the air from the room, making it feel like a tomb. Like the attic that imprisoned her.

Meanwhile, Jane's no help. She's standing there in the doorway, utterly dazed, her mouth slack, and I want to shake her, to tell her to move, to do something to fix this, but I just push past her instead.

Dracula slips into the kitchen next, looking for the nearest way out. My feet in a knot beneath me, I stagger in front of him and close up the room. He swirls over-head, and I sneer at him.

"You're not getting away from me," I say, and appar-ently, he's eager to prove my point, because all at once, the cloud of ash churns faster, and he rushes toward me. In an instant, he forces his way between my lips, filling up my mouth with him, snaking down my throat.

He's inside me, crawling his way in deeper, and all I can taste is him. Bitter as decay but almost sweet, too, like a whiff of marzipan. My head spinning, I fold at the waist and gag him up. He comes out in wet, sticky clumps, writhing on the stone floor where I spat him. As I wretch up the last of the dust, I'm sure I hear him laugh, sharp and strong and cruel. Then he's off again, the bits of him moist and heavy, though it doesn't slow him down. He winds up the steps and down the hall.

My bedroom. I charge upstairs and push my way through the door, and there he is, whirling over my mattress, twining through the sheets, his scent permeating everything that should be mine.

"Get out of here," I growl, and I hate myself for saying it, because once again, he obliges. The ash darts toward the open window, billowing through the heavy curtains and dissolving into the day.

My hands curl into fists. He won't get away that easily. Not now, not after all these years. I don't have time to go back downstairs and do this the civilized way. My heels kicked off, I climb onto the sill and toss myself out the window after him. Sun on my face, breeze in my hair. For a moment, it almost feels like flying.

Across the street, Tyrone is watering his bungalow's lawn. He sees me as I hit the earth, my body landing with a heavy thud on the shriveled grass. An ache's already blooming in my bones, but I'm up again, searching the sun-drenched sky, trying to follow the ashes like vapor trails across the clouds.

Unfortunately, this is a perfect California day, bright and bold and merciless, and the sunlight ricochets through me. I shouldn't be out in this. Neither should Dracula. Daytime whirls his mind as much as it does mine, so he won't stay outside for long. He'll find a dark, quiet place to hide. I need to get to him before he disappears.

He's floating higher, snaking through the serrated leaves of a palm tree, too far up for me to catch. I reach for him anyhow, my long arms stretching until my joints pop, but it's not enough. The sunlight sinks deeper into me, and I can't focus, a face from my past creeping closer. Mina, my first friend, my lost friend.

Lucy, the ghost of her whispers. *Don't leave me.*

"I'm sorry," I say, my legs giving out as I collapse at the edge of the yard.

"Are you on drugs?" Tyrone hollers from across the street, never taking a single step closer to help me. He probably thinks my reefer madness is contagious or something.

I don't answer him, my throat raw with ash, my muscles soft and useless. The last remnants of Dracula glimmer across the sky above me, as everything fades to black.

WHEN I OPEN MY EYES, Bee and Jane are hovering over me, the ground cold and hard beneath my body. We're in the vestibule. They must have dragged me back in here.

"Look what you did," I practically spit at Jane.

She can't stop trembling, her eyes red with grief. "I'm sorry, I'm so sorry, I don't understand," she keeps saying, her words slurred together.

Bee does her best to explain it, the two of them sitting together in the parlor. I stand sentry nearby, guarding the urn in the cabinet, guarding it from Jane.

"Lucy's lived and died the same as us," Bee says. "But she did it a different way. And she's got different needs now."

Bee, always very careful not to use the V word.

"But what was that dust?" Jane's still shaking. "And why did it move like that?"

Bee hesitates. "It was a man. Once. Now it's just a monster."

And this is Bee being very careful never to use the D word. I wonder if Jane even knows who he is. Maybe she's lucky. Maybe she's never heard his name once in her very long life.

Either way, she's listening quietly to Bee, finally starting to understand.

"Why the urns, though?" Jane turns to me. "Why are they so important?"

"Because," I say, my voice like steel, my eyes on the wall, "they're made from his native soil."

It's a familiar sight in the movies. A vampire towing boxes of dark earth, a remnant of his homeland, a way to keep himself safe. What those films never tell you is that you don't need the earth, not really, not unless you want to be at your peak, at your most violent and glorious. There's a power in the places we come from. They sustain us, give us strength.

But there's a catch, one that Dracula never realized

until he met me. The earth is stronger than he knew, even stronger than him. Rest on a mound of your native soil, and you preserve your power. Sealed inside a vessel fired from it, and your power's still protected all right, but you can't escape, either. It holds you in on all sides. The same thing that shelters you becomes your prison.

That's why I built the urns myself, knee-deep in the wet earth of the Carpathian Mountains, over a bonfire that burned brighter than the moon.

Seventy years, and not one iota of him, not a single piece of ash, ever escaped. Not until the moment Jane Eyre arrived.

Dizzy with rage, I gather up the urns from around the house and retreat to my bedroom. I hate it when they're all together, but right now, they're safer here than anywhere Jane might find them.

I'm separating them in the room—one in my closet, another in the vanity, the third under my pillow like a morbid keepsake—when Bee's suddenly in the doorway behind me.

"Jane didn't mean to."

"Of course not," I say, rage coursing through me.

"It was an accident," Bee insists, falling back a step, lingering in the hallway. "She's been through a lot, Lucy."

I whirl around to face her. "And we haven't?"

Bee only sighs. "You could have told her about the urns. *Warned* her."

"I didn't want to tell her," I say, "because I don't trust her. And maybe you shouldn't either."

We stare at each other through the doorway, not moving, not saying a word, and I sense it. A stalemate. Bee's not going to change her mind, and neither am I. She finally shakes her head and turns away, disappearing down the unlit hall. With my heart in my throat, I shut the door, sealing out Bee, sealing out everyone.

All day I stay locked in my room, the urns murmuring around me. I tell myself at least we're together. At least they can't get far.

It's late afternoon when someone else finds me. The echo of Renfield.

Where are you, Miss Lucy? he calls, his voice warbling from afar, but before I can scream or sneer or even hide my face, he drifts away, as though he's been plucked from the ether.

"Stay gone," I say, as I curl up in bed and close my eyes, letting the hours pass me by. Night comes and goes and then comes back around, Saturday slipping into Sunday, the hours evaporating around me. When I look again, the shadows press closer, and everything's changed. The decay's no longer a thin shroud of dust and cobwebs. It's a sarcophagus, thick as a cocoon, clinging to every wall. There's too much death in this place, all the urns in one room, me alongside them. That's why the decay is getting worse.

"Go away," I seethe, and a tiny blot of mold inches away from me.

I watch it go, something building in me, the same thing I felt beneath the Hollywood sign with the wolves. Something strange, something primordial.

With my skin humming, I reach out into the darkness. "Come back," I say, and the spot of mold obeys.

It's never done this before, never listened to my whims, never cared about me at all.

The rot is getting more powerful. But maybe so am I.

It's morning again, Monday now, and I'm still training a blotch of yellow decay to wiggle across the carpet when I hear her. Bee down the hall in her bed, having another nightmare.

"Get it out of me," she wheezes, as I rush into her room.

That thing inside her is moving fast, stretching her skin taut and translucent. She scratches at her own arms, again and again, raking her nails across her flesh, until she's raw and bleeding.

But no, bleeding isn't the right word. Whatever's inside her isn't red and flowing. It's gray and crawling, viscous as oil, and when a drop of it hits the marble floor, it tries to escape, tries to dart across to the wall. I chase after it, stomping on it again and again until it's crushed to dust on the hardwood floor.

Bee perches on the edge of the mattress, tears streaking her cheeks. "Thank you," she says, her arms already scabbed over, holding back the rest of what's inside her. Her own sort of decay. The only alimony Rochester ever gave her.

It's taken me years to piece it together from the things Bee let slip in moments of grief. How the Rochesters were a family of bitter landlords, counting every shilling and every grudge. Generation after generation, wringing the life out of the land, out of the people. And if you couldn't keep up with them, couldn't keep up with the rent and the grueling work and the grueling hours, then one day you'd return home to find the locks changed and everything you ever owned whisked away, a final payment for your debts.

That was what the Rochesters used the attic at Thornfield for, to store all the things they repossessed from the dispossessed. Cradles for babies too sick to see their first birthdays. Wedding veils and mourning veils and funerary shrouds with yellow stains too terrible to fathom. Heirloom jewelry and silverware and little trinkets that meant nothing except to the people who once cherished them. Hopes and dreams left to rot in the dark. Left for years to ferment into something else, something sentient.

Something vengeful.

Poison the world long enough, and the world will figure out a way to poison you back.

When Rochester finally discovered it there, that writhing thing his family had inadvertently created, he should have been afraid. He should have begged for mercy. But that was never his style. He welcomed it instead, letting it seep into his skin like rancid oil, and when he felt its power, the way it was eternal and made him eternal too, he decided it wasn't a monstrosity at all. He decided it was a gift. Something worth sharing. Something worth tricking his new bride up into that attic.

"We'll be together forever now," he told Bee as he held her down on the dusty floor and let it crawl inside her.

When it was over, her heart quiet in her chest, Bee couldn't stop crying, couldn't stop screaming, couldn't stop threatening to tell the world what he'd done to her. That was when Rochester accused her of being a mad-woman.

"So ungrateful," he growled, and left her in the attic, forgotten like a crate of moth-eaten clothes, while he went and wooed Jane. After all, he needed someone who would appreciate him.

A shadow in the doorway, and Jane's suddenly with us. "Are you all right?" she says, rushing to Bee's side, embracing her. That's when I see it.

Her arms, crawling and restless. The same thing that's in Bee is inside her.

Jane buries her face against Bee, hiding like a child. "We'll never escape him, will we?"

Bee gazes upward, a steel resolve budding in her eyes. "Not unless we do something," she says. "Not unless we stop him ourselves."

The house goes quiet, and I'm suddenly chilled. This is the first time she's ever said anything like that.

"How?" Jane asks, her voice no more than a wisp.

"I don't know yet," Bee says, and pulls Jane closer, their limbs in a tangle, everything about them looking so comfortable, so intimate. Standing here, I feel like a prying little sister, so without a word, I slip out into the long hallway.

Back in my room, the rot is waiting, wriggling in my presence. It seems almost happy to see me. I sprawl out on the floor and whisper to it, making it flick this way and that. On the carpet, on the walls, across the threadbare comforter on my bed.

"You're mine," I say, and the cobwebs on the ceiling dance in refrain.

It's almost night again, the urns chattering in their hiding places, when Bee knocks on my door.

"We should go out," she says. "All three of us."

I'm ready to tell her no, to stay here commanding the decay in the dark, when she adds, "To the drive-in, maybe?"

My hunger stirring within me, I glance up at her and smile.

Tonight's a double feature of *The Dirty Dozen* and an early screening of Roger Corman's *The St. Valentine's Day Massacre*, both of them bloody spectacles, which isn't even fair. Why do the movies always have to remind me of what I'm missing?

My stomach somersaults, and I gaze at the lobby. I pretend I don't care if Michael's working tonight. I pretend he isn't the whole reason why I'm here.

In the front seat, Bee and Jane are curled up together. They look like a pair of pristine debutantes, the two of them in Bee's best dresses, Jane in blue satin and Bee in red silk. I sprawl out in the back, still wearing the same thing from two days ago, the scent of Dracula's ashes, the scent of roses leeched into the seams.

Over at the next screen, the family-friendly one that's playing *Mad Monster Party*, a mother and father are sitting on the hood of their station wagon. Next to them, their little girl in pigtails keeps turning around, her eyes wide and eager. She wants to get a peek at the gore on our screen.

Jane glances up at her. "Do you still remember being that young?"

I sit back, shaking my head. "Not really."

"Me neither," Bee says. "I barely remember my own mother anymore."

Sorrow seeps marrow-deep into me. Bee hasn't told me much about her past, but she's told me that much. Her mother, packed away to a sanitarium in Spanish Town where the family left her to die. And then Bee, packed away to England with Rochester, where she was left to die in a different way.

"You know, he hated my mother." Bee's nervous hands smooth a wrinkle in her silk dress. "They never met, but he hated her anyway. He would always call her my 'infamous mother' or 'the Creole.' He never said her name."

I gaze at her. "What was her name?"

Bee hesitates, as though she never expected anyone to ask her again. "Antoinetta," she says. "The same as my middle name. It's the only thing of hers I carry with me."

My heart clenched, I want to ask her more, but Jane reaches out and takes Bee's trembling hand, the two of them so close now, so content, and that's my cue to leave.

I'm crossing the lot when the little girl breaks away from her family and skips toward me. She flashes me a gap-toothed grin, her pigtails wagging in the breeze. Then she passes by, arcing back to the station wagon. I don't listen for her heartbeat. I can't even hear it. I might be hungry, but there are things I'd do, and then there are things I'd never do.

Of course, that's not what people said. The men who claimed to care for me once—my fiancé and his friends and that awful doctor back in England—wrote all about me in their journals. The "bloofer lady," they called me. Out for blood, out for children. That was what they said to prove I was a monster deserving of a mouthful of garlic, my heart cut in two. None of it was true, those rumors they invented as though they were scribbling on a bathroom wall. But that didn't matter. Their words are the ones everybody remembers, not mine. That's the way it goes. The best story becomes reality, and the truth becomes an afterthought.

In the lobby, Michael's waiting at the counter, and all at once, the past washes away as I look at him, my own private daydream.

"You know," he says, leaning closer, "I can't avoid you if you keep coming to me."

My cheeks flush, and I want him a little more. "That just means you should probably run."

But he doesn't listen. Instead, he motions me through the back door. I already know where we're going.

To the little shotgun house behind the drive-in.

Inside, the rooms are dark, and everything smells of mothballs and regret. He takes my hand, guiding me past a splintered dining room table, his stainless steel dog tags hanging on a rusted nail on the wall.

He glances at me, smiling. "Are you still thinking about killing me?"

"Always," I say, and pin him in the corner. "Doesn't that worry you?"

"No," he whispers. "I'm just glad you came back. Before this place is gone."

A knot tightens in my throat. "Gone?"

"Those are our last movies," he says, nodding through the smudged picture window at the shapes on the screen. "We're closing the place up."

I should have expected this. Nobody ever comes here anymore. My whole world is becoming obsolete.

"Don't look so sad," Michael says, and his body's warm and getting warmer, his heart throbbing fast. There are no wolves this time. No distractions. I have him all to myself. The tether between us, this thrall, goes taut, and he drops slowly to his knees. I brace for what comes next, wanting him. Pitying him a little too.

But he does something else, something I don't expect. He puts his ear to my chest and listens to the emptiness there, the harsh silence within me.

He's silent too, carefully working up the courage for what he says next.

"What does it feel like to die?" he asks, his breath hot and frayed, and I know what he really wants—to hear what it would have been like if *he'd* died, to know what happened to the boys he fought alongside and the boys he fought against, the ones who never made it to California or to anywhere else except the inside of a zippered-up body bag.

I should lie to him. Pretend it was nothing, pretend it was like falling asleep. I tell him the truth instead.

"It's cold," I whisper. "And slow. So much slower than you'd expect. Time just stops, and you're standing both inside and outside of yourself."

His fingertips slide carefully down my body. "Were you afraid?"

"Every damn time."

Michael hesitates, inspecting my face in the dark. "How many times have you died?"

"Too many to count."

Enough that I don't want to count. And I don't want to remember, either. I draw him toward me and flick at the buttons on his shirt, popping them open one by one.

"This way," he whispers, disappearing into a narrow bedroom at the end of the hall.

I stand here, frozen. It would be so easy to follow him. Just a few more steps, and we'll be together. He'll give me whatever I want, even if I ask for everything.

And that's exactly what I need from him. If I walk into that room, he won't ever walk out again.

I'm back outside in an instant, my knees weak, Michael calling out my name. I try not to listen.

My head spinning with hunger, I stagger across the gravel lot until I'm suddenly leaning against the doorway of the projection booth. It's a tiny shack built of peeling cinder blocks, junk piled along every wall. Rolled-up posters from long-forgotten movies moldering in corners. Stacks of metal tins filled with nitrate film stock.

Cigar stub in hand, Walter peers out at me. "The heart of every theater," he says, the projectors whirring softly behind him. "This is where it all happens."

And where nothing will happen now.

I peer at him, his face craggy as a lunar landscape. "I'm sad to hear about this place closing."

A sudden flicker of despair in his eyes, even as he waves me off. "None of that now. Don't want nobody feeling sorry for me."

"Maybe I'm just feeling sorry for myself." I've loved this place, found solace here, and soon it will be gone. Just one more ghost blighting the landscape of Hollywood.

Walter takes a long drag off his cigar. "I'm happy you came back tonight," he says. "My grandson's very fond of you."

My guts twist. "That's a shame."

"Why?" he asks, one gray eyebrow twitching up. "Are you going steady with someone else?"

I cough up a jagged laugh. "You could say that."

I bid Walter good night, maybe even goodbye, and I'm starting back to the car when a strange whisper ripples through the hazy night air. For a moment, I'm sure it's Renfield, sniffing around again like a loyal retriever. Then I hear that familiar lilt in her voice.

Jane. She's left Bee in the Buick, and she's pacing small circles on the other side of the projection booth.

"I'm doing my best," she keeps saying, and at first, I figure she's talking to herself. Then a small smile curls on her lips. "I love you too, Edward."

Rochester. She's talking to Rochester.

A bolt of rage sears through me. "Even after what he's done to Bee?"

The sound of my voice is sharp, like the unexpected slamming of a door, and Jane chokes out a quiet, surprised cry. Then she stares at me, a wave of shame melting over her.

"You don't understand," she whispers. "You don't know what he's like when he doesn't get what he wants."

An excuse. And a meager one at that. In this moment, I'd wish her dead if it wasn't already too late for that.

I charge back toward the Buick, Jane desperate to keep up with me. The second film hasn't even started yet, but I ask to go home.

"What's wrong?" Bee asks, but my chest constricts, and I won't tell her. I won't be the one to break her heart.

Meanwhile, Jane doesn't say anything at all. Not in the car, not when we get home, not when I sneer at her and head up the stairs, her pensive gaze tracking me, wondering what I'll do.

I wonder what I'll do too. I drift back and forth in my rot-draped bedroom, the urns still safely tucked away. Maybe Jane will do the decent thing and confess it herself. If not, I can't keep this from Bee, not for long. No matter how much it will hurt her.

It's a couple hours until midnight, and I'm still pacing the room when I hear them. Wolves in the distance. They're everywhere, their howls like the strangest lullabies. Like a message I can't quite decipher. I stare out the window, listening to them.

They sure seem to like you, Michael said to me at the Hollywood sign.

Something rises inside me, a startled realization. Dracula attracted wolves because he's a vampire. But so am I.

What if they're not his harbingers at all? What if they're mine?

"What do you want?" I whisper to the night, and the floor creaks beneath me. There's someone downstairs.

The parlor's dark, and as I rush in, I'm expecting chaos, the house unraveling around us, but Bee's alone, perched by an open window.

I light a candle on the mantel. "Where's Jane?"

A strained silence, heavy as the grave. "Gone," Bee says, not looking at me. "When I woke up, she'd already left."

So that's it. Rather than tell Bee the truth, Jane just ran. Took the coward's way out.

Bee doesn't know that. "What happened tonight at the drive-in, Lucy?"

I hesitate, everything a jumble inside me. "I caught her," I whisper, "talking to Rochester."

A ripple of grief crosses Bee's face. "So she went back to him," she says slowly. "I was afraid that might happen."

I wait for something more, some kind of devastation from her, but that's it. There's no rage, no indignance, barely a hint of surprise.

I gape at her. "Aren't you mad?"

"At him? Sure. But at her?" Bee shakes her head as she drifts across the room, past the rolltop desk. "This is how they are. The back and forth. He's been doing this to her for decades now." A long moment passes before she adds, "You know what that's like."

My chest tightens. "What's that supposed to mean?"

"You and Dracula," she says, and instantly I bristle.

"This is nothing like me and Dracula."

"Really?" Her gaze turns sharply toward me. "You're telling me you never talk to him when nobody else is around?"

She lobs the question at me like a grenade. I stare at her, stunned.

"No," I say finally. "Never."

"Lucy," Bee says, something softening in her, a flicker of understanding in her voice. "I've *heard* you. All those one-sided conversations. All those times you honestly hoped he'd answer."

My cheeks burn with shame. "That's different," I say, though I don't know how.

Bee's pacing faster now, her eyes wild. "He can't keep doing this to Jane. He can't keep hurting her." Resolve hardens on her face. "I won't let him, Lucy."

There it is again, that newfound fire to go after Rochester. All these years we spent tucked away from the world. Bee doesn't want to hide anymore.

"So what now?" I ask, but then I hear it. Another distant howl like a warning shot. My head snaps toward the sound, the night breeze whispering in through the open windows.

Then something else whispers too, a voice that cuts through the dusty air.

"Hello, Miss Lucy."

Renfield, back again. I sneer, ready to ignore him, but when I glance at Bee, her eyes are wide, her face gone wan. She hears him too. He isn't speaking from afar this time.

He's speaking from the doorway behind me.

five

Bee backs against the far wall, a pile of records splayed at her feet.

"What *are* you?" she asks, and I turn and see Renfield in the flesh for the first time.

After all these years, he looks so much worse than I expected. The decay that follows me, that follows Dracula too, has nestled over Renfield, veiling him in cobwebs and dust and pale spots of mold, a stark sheen of gray enveloping him. He takes a wavering step toward me, and his whole body creaks, his bones half-rotted beneath his skin. He isn't built for immortality. Dracula was never that generous, never bestowed that parting gift. Instead, Renfield's trapped between life and death, and somehow, he got the worst of both worlds.

"I've missed you," he says to me, a musty smell rising off him, his crinkling flesh thin as tissue paper.

"You've never even met me," I say, and it's true. We're

strangers, always have been. He shouldn't have been able to find me.

But then Renfield drifts another step forward, his body illuminated in the candlelight, and I realize there's someone else with us. A faint blot of ash hovers along the ceiling. The remnants of Dracula that escaped two days ago.

That's how Renfield knew where I was. From across thousands of miles, Dracula beckoned him here, his freed ashes strong enough at last to call out.

Renfield parts his desiccated lips and asks the only question that matters to him. "Where's the rest of him, Miss Lucy?"

"The rest of who?" I ask, feigning innocence.

But Renfield's waited a long time for this, and he won't wait any longer. His head down, he darts across the parlor, skittering like a snake past the fainting couch. His shadow envelops me, and we're suddenly entwined, my fingers digging deep into his arms. Pieces of his flesh peel off in my hands, stiff as worn leather.

"That's terribly impolite of you," he says, and makes a quick swipe at my face. Something primordial flares up in me again, and I shove him hard toward the mantel, where he collapses in the corner, knocking the taper candle to the floor.

One candle, one flame. That's all it takes for the fire to catch on the frayed carpet. Our house, our dubious sanctuary, has been hungry for destruction for years. We've tried to hold it at bay, but it was always a losing battle.

Now I barely have time to blink before the whole room is alive and blazing.

The smoke thickening around us, I stumble toward the doorway. Bee doesn't follow. She stands frozen next to the Victrola, the flames reflecting in her eyes, vacant as tide pools.

Fire. This is what happened to her before, how Thornfield Hall crumbled into cinders. How she lost Jane all those years ago. The past is crashing over her, stopping time, stopping everything.

"Come on," I cry out, and my voice is enough to break the trance. Her eyes swirling again, she races toward me, and we dash together for the hall, as the blaze wraps its long fingers around the room. The Victrola, the stack of records, the fainting couch, everything melting and crackling and turning to nothing.

We've spent years hiding in this place, and it only took Renfield minutes to destroy it.

And he's not done yet. His filmy eyes set on me, he gathers himself to his feet and steps through the flames, his skin hissing like old wood set on an autumn bonfire.

Everything in me wants to run, to escape all of this, but I can't leave, not yet.

"I'll meet you outside," I say to Bee, then rush up the stairs to my bedroom.

The decay's waiting to greet me, swirling on the ceiling. With Renfield bellowing on the steps, I lock the door and start collecting the urns. First, the one beneath my pillow, dirt from the Hollywood sign still caked around the rim.

"Lucy!" Bee's voice through my window. She's standing below on the lawn, reaching up her hands. "Drop the urns down to me."

I gape at her, wanting to tell her no, but I don't have many choices left. I toss it through the window to her, and she easily catches it.

"The next one," she says, and I go after it. The quiet urn, stashed in the vanity drawer. It's barely moved, barely done anything at all, as though it's been waiting for me. I'm starting back to the window when Renfield knocks on the door, like he's a gentleman.

"Miss Lucy," he wheezes, as he scratches at the other side, his gnarled fingernails screeching against the splintered wood. Dracula's ashes are already starting to seep in through the cracks, as Renfield presses hard against the frame, the lock ready to give way.

I try to ignore it, try to pretend this is all a bad dream, but I barely manage to drop the second urn to Bee when the door collapses and Renfield's suddenly at my side. He grabs me by the throat and shoves me across the room, my body bouncing off the wallpaper.

"Lucy!" Bee calls out below, but I can't reach her. The flames are climbing through the floor, my bedroom curtains catching fire, the window closed off to me. Everything in the room is about to disintegrate, me and Renfield along with it.

But he doesn't care. Near the vanity where I cast no reflection, Renfield corners me. Embers float like fireflies all around him, and I stare into what's left of his face.

"You don't have to do this," I whisper, but he shakes his head, flashing me a sad smile.

"You know I don't have a choice, Miss Lucy."

This twists like a blade inside me. Renfield moves toward me slowly, his every step looking like agony. I want to help him, to save him from what Dracula's condemned him to, but I know it's too late for that.

Instead, my hand presses into the wall behind me, searching for it. The closet door, the place where the last urn's hidden.

Renfield's shadow drapes over me, his ragged arms reaching out, but at last, I manage to yank open the door and shove him through it. He topples into the dark, right past the very thing he wants most in the world.

I scoop the urn off the floor, the heat of it searing into my hands. This is the one from the cellar, the worst urn. I wrap it in the hem of my dress and slam the door, flipping the latch and sealing Renfield inside.

He drums on the wall, desperation setting in. "Please don't leave me, Miss Lucy," he cries on the other side, the flames burning brighter, and a sob lodges in my throat, because he's the same as me. A victim in all this, collateral damage from a monster who never gave a damn about either of us.

Above me, the ashes of Dracula churn in the grimy air.

"I'd like to kill you a thousand more times," I seethe, and I swear I hear him laugh again.

I won't listen. As I stagger across the hazy room, I glance up at the decay, all the beautiful bits of mold and cobwebs I've been training. They'll burn here, they'll turn to ash, and there's nothing I can do. Everything's disintegrating faster than I can fathom.

"I'm so sorry," I whisper, and vanish into the hall.

Downstairs, the flames are devouring everything. The kitchen's already collapsing inward from the heat, the icebox thick with dust. Even with all the windows open, the house is blooming gray.

"Lucy?" Bee is somewhere nearby. She came back for me. "Where are you?"

"I'm here," I say, my voice nearly dissolving in the rush of flames.

In the smoldering hall, Bee and I find each other, the blaze singeing our dresses, our hair, our skin. The rooms are lost to us, everything here is lost. We stumble past the parlor, and I can't help but look back. Inside, chunks of horsehair plaster crumble from the ceiling, crushing the rolltop desk, burying Mina's letter opener.

And my ruby necklace. Those jewels were supposed to be our rainy day, the thing we'd been saving for a night like this. We've got nothing left now. We're the heirs to oblivion.

"Forget it," Bee says, and together, we keep going, the smoke clogging up our throats.

In the vestibule, the statue of Venus is already crumbling in the heat, her body breaking apart, her chest split down the middle. I whisper a useless goodbye to her, as Bee pulls me through the door.

Outside, the air tastes stale and chalky. There are sirens in the distance, drawing closer, wailing like eager banshees. We need to get out of here. We certainly can't stick around and answer questions from the police about who we are and what happened to us. Nobody would understand. Hell, I barely understand it.

Bee grabs the two urns off the lawn before scrambling behind the wheel of the Buick and turning over the croaking engine. I wilt on the seat next to her, bruised and aching. I always forget how much a body can break without just doing the decent thing and dying. The weight of the decay heaves through the house, flames billowing out all the windows, a fault line cracking across the center. Through the chasm, Renfield lurches out of the darkness, the shadow of Dracula swirling over him. They spot us here, but from across the yard, they're not fast enough to catch us.

As we screech down the driveway, neighbors we've never seen before are pouring out of their houses, clutching their robes and their pearls, shocked at the spectacle we've made of ourselves.

Tyrone's standing on his front stoop, his striped flannel pajamas sagging around his shoulders.

"I told you that place was a fire hazard," he calls out, and my last regret as the rest of the house collapses into cinders is that I don't have enough time to charge across the street and snap his reed-thin neck.

Bee twists the wheel hard, and we burst onto the road, rocketing in the opposite direction of the sirens. I put the last urn on the back seat, and the three of them murmur to one another, speaking a language I can't decipher.

Shivering, I turn away. "We need to find somewhere to hole up."

Bee's dark eyes glint in the moonlight. "But we've got nowhere else, Lucy."

My gaze shifts to her. "You know that's not true."

If she wants to go after Rochester, if she doesn't want to hide anymore, there's only one place left.

Her face like stone, Bee doesn't answer me, doesn't argue either. My head lolls back, a smear of palm trees above us, the streetlights glinting like distant stars. The world fades to black for a while, and I relish it, the escape from everything.

When I open my eyes again, it's still dark, and Bee's hands are steady on the wheel, her jaw set, a flinty determination flickering across her face. A road sign flashes past the Buick. We're headed north on the 101, and I already know where we're going.

Up the sinuous highway, straight toward the heart of San Francisco.

six

We're past Santa Barbara when Bee flicks on the radio, her nervous hands searching for something to do.

"I've never been this far north of L.A.," she says, the shadowy hills closing in around us.

"Me neither," I say, my throat raw from smoke. I haven't been much of anywhere, not in years. Neither has Bee. We abandoned London during the Blitz, practically crawled our way to Hollywood, and then never left. Until now, anyway.

In the back seat, the urns are still whispering, louder than before but still just as arcane. Dracula wants it this way. He likes it when I know he's here, and he likes it even more when I can't understand a word he's saying. This is such fun for him, a bit of foreplay, a way to keep me guessing.

Gritting my teeth, I reach into the back and nudge

the urns apart. I hate it when they're this close. The way they're always colluding with each other. The way they seem to enjoy themselves a little too much.

I settle down in my seat, but after another mile, I look again. They've skittered back together. I never see them move. That's part of their game.

Three urns. That's all I have left.

The quiet urn from the parlor.

The one from beneath the Hollywood sign.

And the worst urn, the one from the cellar, the rage in him as hot as a July boardwalk. I feel him behind me, slowly searing a hole straight through the upholstery, the stench of melting leather filling the air, even with the top down.

I look up at the sky, listening to the time on the radio. It's midnight on Tuesday, and we've been on the road for two hours already. That should put us in San Francisco around five in the morning. Just in time for sunrise. I only hope we get there first.

"It's such a big city," Bee says, her eyes still on the road. "I don't even know where to start once we get there."

A long moment, the rush of the pavement beneath the wheels almost deafening in the dark. Then she asks the real question, the only thing that matters to her right now.

"How are we ever going to find Jane?" She looks at me, her face twisted, panic seeping in. "Or Rochester?"

Without a word, we both understand it, the hopelessness of this. It's not like Jane left a forwarding address. She could be anywhere. So could he.

But I won't say that. Instead, I reach across the seat and squeeze Bee's hand. "We'll figure it out," I say, and hope I'm right.

The miles pass by slowly. Just outside of Salinas, the gas gauge dips toward empty, and Bee pulls off at the first service station we find. It's a lonely place, the kind the world forgot. There are no other cars in the whole lot, and only one lamppost that flickers from time to time like even it can't decide if it wants to be here. The rickety sign's got no logo on it, though from the looks of the place, it used to be a Mobil or a Shell, back before progress breezed through and left it in the dust. Now it seems almost unreal, like a cheap movie set ready to collapse at the edges.

We idle up to the first pump, a rusted-out number that's probably been around since the Great Depression. The engine cuts out, and Bee and I dig through the glove box and between the cushions and underneath the seat, searching for gas money. We each hold out what we've scrounged up, counting it carefully, counting it twice. Eight dollars. That's it, every penny to our name. It'll have to be enough.

From inside the station, a man lumbers out to the car. "What'll it be?" he asks, a wad of chewing tobacco tucked in his bulging cheek. He leans a bit too far into the Buick, his skin stinking of sweat and motor oil and something else, something I'd rather not get too strong a whiff of. Her face pinched, Bee turns away from him and holds out the money like a ticking bomb.

He takes it from her, his eyes sliding over us, slowly, like he's memorizing every curve of our bodies for future use. His faded overalls slouch around his chest, and as he starts to pump our gas, he wipes his fingers on himself, the front of him smeared with splotches of grime. Not that I have any right to judge. I'm covered in soot, my nails caked thick with dirt, my whole body reeking of smoke. Bee and I look like we've been through a war, and in a way, maybe we have.

In the back seat, the urns murmur to one another, never tiring. Even from here, I can see them starting to split apart, tiny hairline fractures forming along the sides. They won't last much longer, not when they're this close together.

My hands shaking, I reach into the back, taking hold of the urn from the cellar. Its heat has fused into the leather, and it takes a moment to peel it free. Bee tosses me the key, and I unlock the trunk, leaving the passenger door open behind me. As I set the urn inside, the farthest I can move it from the others, I swear I feel Dracula glaring up at me. Here I go again, ruining all his fun.

I look up at the attendant, and his eyes are on Bee, studying the places he likes on her body. He's leaning too close again, one hand on the pump, the other in his pocket. I try to imagine what we'll do if he keeps leaning in, if he just won't stop. I could take care of this, of course, that uneven heartbeat in his chest more than eager to give out. I could leave him in a shallow grave or no grave at all. I could satisfy every urge brimming in my blood and not even break a sweat.

Except the last thing we need is to leave a body count up the coast of California. And the last thing I need is to give Dracula exactly what he wants. A killer made in his image.

With the trunk closed, I'm busy watching the attendant when something darts suddenly off the highway. A figure, thin and sprightly, moving past the open passenger door. Dark hair, turned-up nose, eyes that flash deviously in the moonlight.

Mina. I'm certain it's her, come back to me.

But then a pair of dim headlights from the highway pass over the figure, her face shifting, and when I look again, she's just a girl, some little flower child in a buckskin vest, a crocheted bag slung over her shoulder, her tangled hair in her eyes.

"Is this yours?" she asks, and there's something in her hands.

An urn. One of *my* urns.

I lunge forward, my legs liquid, and snatch it away from her, clawing at her fingers, ready to shatter her bones to dust. But I don't have to. With a wince, she gladly surrenders it.

"I'm not a thief," she says, backing away from me.

I clutch the urn closer than a prized heirloom. "Where did you find it?"

"Right here." She motions indignantly to the crumbling pavement next to the Buick. Next to where I left the passenger door open.

Bee braces against the steering wheel. "How did it move so fast?" she asks.

"He's getting stronger," I say, and it's true. It used to take Dracula hours to budge a single inch. Now, with his ashes free and the urns gathered close together, he's learning how to scurry quicker than a centipede.

I peer into the back seat at the other urn, the quiet urn. It's still there, right where I left it. It's the only one that doesn't cause me grief. My arms crossed over the urn, I move toward the passenger door, past this little hippie girl.

"Who's Renfield?" she chirps.

I turn back sharply. "How do you know that name?"

"From that bottle or whatever it is," she says, pointing at the urn I'm holding. "It was whispering when I picked it up. Calling out for somebody named Renfield."

My stomach heaves. "You can *understand* it?"

"Sure," she says, a bewildered look on her face. "Can't you?"

"No," I say, and part of me almost wants to laugh. I've been desperate to decipher Dracula for decades, and here he goes, giving himself away to the first girl with a heartbeat who puts her hands on him.

She waits for me to explain it, why the urn's speaking to her, but when I don't, she doesn't seem too bothered. "I'm Daisy," she says brightly, as though she's expecting me to return the favor.

"That's nice," I say, and climb back into the Buick,

pretending not to see her, even though I'm sitting in a convertible and she's loitering two feet away.

"I'm headed to San Francisco." She smiles at me, and she looks so impossibly sweet. Like a little lost lamb headed for the slaughter. "Any way I could hitch a ride with you two?"

I shake my head. I hate everything about this. Her trusting face, her impeccable hearing, her gentle heartbeat that won't stop thrumming inside me. I could break her in two in an instant, and she wouldn't even have time to whimper.

The man finishes pumping our gas, his eyes still wandering over all of us. I pass Bee the car key, and Daisy's face starts to crumble, because she knows she's losing her chance.

"You're looking for . . . Jane, aren't you?"

Bee's head snaps toward her. "How did you know that?"

Daisy gives her a sheepish shrug. "I can still hear that bottle whispering."

I roll my eyes. Of course she can. More foreplay from Dracula, him spilling all our secrets to strangers. I cover the urn with both hands as if that might keep it quiet.

"I know a lot of Janes." Daisy gnaws her bottom lip. "I could introduce you to all of them if you'd like."

The offer lingers in the air, the possibility of it.

"No thanks," I say, and the engine sputters to life.

As we pull away, the man at the pump gives Daisy an ugly grin, and I don't like anything about it. Neither does

Bee. The Buick gets to the edge of the parking lot but stops suddenly there.

I hesitate. "You're wondering if she could help us?"

"Maybe," Bee says. "If nothing else, she could show us around the city." A long, strained moment before she adds, "And she can tell us what those urns are saying."

"*If* he tells us the truth," I say. Dracula could always whisper lies instead, throwing us off his trail. Either way, I'm not too eager to take on another passenger. Look how well things turned out the last time we welcomed a new guest. A broken urn, a broken heart, a burned-down house. Honestly, when we find Jane, she should probably pay us restitution.

I glance in the rearview mirror. Daisy's still back there, and that man's standing closer to her now. I don't want to think about what he might do to her, or what the next trucker who offers her a ride could try, the bargain he might force her to make in the dark. I don't like to think about what I could do to her either.

It would be better for us to leave her here. Probably safer, too. She's a stranger to us, dead weight, a nobody. But I was a nobody too, and I remember what it's like for everyone to forget you, just because it's easier that way.

With a sigh, I wave one hand in the air. "Hurry up," I call to Daisy, and with a childish whoop, she comes running.

"I was at a music festival in Monterey all weekend,"

Daisy tells us, as the Buick ricochets up the 101. "But then my ride ditched me, and I've been hitching along the highway ever since."

Daisy keeps on like this, giving us answers to questions we haven't asked, barely stopping to take a breath. We pass through a eucalyptus grove, pungent and earthy, and I sit back, imagining somewhere else. Imagining Michael. He's back in L.A., searching for me. The thrall tightens between us, and I close my eyes.

"Here," I whisper, drawing him closer.

Bee glances at me. "You all right?" she asks, and I nod, not looking at her. Not wanting to admit what I just did.

Daisy droops suddenly over the front seat. "Give me your hand," she says to me.

I sneer. "Why?"

"Because," she says, "I read palms. People tell me I'm really good."

That's all I need, some hippie girl peering into a future I wish I didn't have. But Daisy seizes my hand anyhow, inspecting every crevice.

"You'll find love," she says, "but it won't last. You'll survive it, though, because that's what you do. You keep going, no matter what."

"She's right so far," says Bee, her eyes still on the road. "What else does it say, Daisy?"

"You think you don't need anybody, but that's silly. We all need each other." A strained pause. "Your lifeline, though—"

I scoff. "Does it go on forever?"

"No, that's just it," she says. "It's barely there. Like it's been cut in half or something. See?"

She points at it, a vague line etched into my palm. It's thinner than I remember, and shorter too. As though I don't have forever after all.

I pull away from her, as the urns shift restlessly again, one in my lap, the other at my feet.

"They're talking about daylight now," she says. "How we don't have much longer before sunrise."

They're not wrong. The night starts to snake away, the horizon glowing gold, and in the gathering light, Daisy inspects our faces, still smeared with smoke.

"What happened to you two?" she asks.

"House fire," I say, not looking at her.

She sucks air through her teeth. "Far out," she says, and sounds almost impressed.

Part of me wants to tell her about us, what we really are. She can already hear Dracula, so why not? We might as well give her our side of things. I start to say something, to try to explain, but Daisy leans forward again.

"There it is," she says, and the city materializes through the fog.

San Francisco. It's like sailing into a dream. Even in person, it looks like a postcard, so bright, so toweringly perfect. Glittering buildings and highway spirals and a blood-red bridge that could take your breath away.

I want to keep looking, but the sun's eager to catch a glimpse for itself. It rises up out of the clouds like an eternal curse, and I brace against the dashboard, because there's nowhere to hide. The light spills across my body, and my vision flashes in and out, my muscles weakening to porridge. In my mind, Mina's face surfaces again, and I want to reach out for her, to retrieve her from the ether, but she's already long gone.

"Lucy?" Bee's voice, tinged with panic. "Stay with me."

Daisy peers over the seat, her soft eyes pitying me. "You've got some sort of condition?"

I heave up a thin chuckle. "You could say that."

Bee turns the wheel hard and veers off the next exit. "We need to get her inside. *Now*."

"That's no problem," Daisy says breezily, as though she's met plenty of girls with an inexplicable allergy to sunlight. "I can take you somewhere."

I part my lips to ask her where, but the street pinwheels around me, and all at once, I fade to nothing.

The next moment, I'm moving, my body weightless, the air hanging heavy around me. Bee and Daisy are on either side of me, helping me up steep concrete steps, my arms slung over their shoulders. I blink up at the bright building looming over us. It's a skinny Victorian with a pointed spire like a witch's hat, painted in shades of mauve and royal blue and baby pink. There are voices within, so many of them, and heartbeats by the score.

"Why are we here?" I wheeze.

"Because this is my house," Daisy says. "And it can be yours too."

She's inviting me in, the poor little fool. She doesn't know who I am, what I could do to her. I want to tell her,

I want to warn her, but before I can argue, the front door swings open, and she and Bee carry me inside.

The house is nothing like I'm expecting. Everywhere I turn there are people, spilling out of rooms, pushed into corners, leaned up against windows. Hand-painted murals array every wall, not that it matters, since you can't see them clearly. Only a petal of a flower here or the tuft of an acrylic cloud there, the rest of the images concealed behind figures moving in and out.

Daisy shows us into the living room, past a group of men sitting cross-legged in deep meditation, girls flung on couches, toddlers waddling around barefoot. The sunlight still boiling in me, I collapse in an old oak rocking chair in the corner.

"The urns," I murmur.

"They're fine," Bee says, two of them clutched under her arm. The last one must still be in the trunk of the Buick. That's good. Keep them apart for as long as we can.

Laughter rises and falls around us, smoke in the shape of mushroom clouds floating to the ceiling. The crowd of faces looms closer, their heartbeats overlapping.

"How many of you live here?" I ask, my mouth watering.

Daisy grins, blissfully oblivious. "Too many to count. The more the merrier, you know?" she says, and that's when they descend on us. A whole gaggle of girls, all long hair and gauzy tops, their skin scented like peppermint and lavender.

"What are those things?" they ask, pointing at the

urns in Bee's arms. "And why are they chattering on like that?

"Isn't it *wild*?" Daisy says, and my heart corkscrews in my chest. It's not just her—they can all hear him. Dracula's talking to every girl here but me. Pretty young things with rosy cheeks and heartbeats, the kind who could make him a nice dinner.

They all lean in and listen. "It's talking about Lucy," someone says. "Who's that?"

My stomach jumps, and I raise a shaky hand, like a guilty schoolkid about to be scolded.

One of the girls giggles. "It's claiming you're not very nice," she says. "Is that true?"

I think for a moment of tearing out her throat and wearing that sweet smile of hers for a necklace. "Yeah," I say. "It's true."

Even though we're inside now, the sun's still pouring through all the open windows. My skin burning, I coil against the rocking chair, daylight streaking my body.

Daisy glances at me, her brow furrowed. "Come on," she says, motioning Bee and me through a doorway draped in dark, iridescent beads. "I'll show you where you can crash for a while."

We follow her up a winding staircase and past a line of rooms, their splintered doors closed. We pass another stairwell too. It leads up to an attic, no doubt. A place we won't go. A place Bee can't go, not with the memories she has.

Fortunately, that's not where Daisy's taking us. At the end of the hall, she ushers us into a tiny bedroom, a sea of thin mattresses spilling across the floor, rusted springs exposed, everything stained yellow with sweat.

"You'll be safe up here," Daisy says, and I do my best not to burst out laughing. As if we're safe anywhere.

A jubilant voice calls up the steps, and Daisy rushes to answer. That leaves me and Bee in the doorway, no more tour guide, no more anything. This isn't much different than the first floor, the room smelling of stale cigarettes and remorse. It's too enclosed for Bee and too bright for me, but we can fix that. The crook of one arm over my eyes, I struggle along the perimeter of the room, yanking open all three windows. They're narrow and cracked, but they'll be enough. Even a little air will calm Bee, make her remember anything besides that rotting attic.

When I'm done, I back against the wall, and Bee closes the ragged curtains after me.

"Thanks," we say to the other at the same time. Our ritual. I open the windows, she blocks out the sunlight. We're in this together, or not at all.

Exhausted, Bee and I collapse in a corner, bits of drywall flaking off in our hair. After last night, we need to rest, but we're not alone here. There are a couple guys strewn about the room, lifeless as rag dolls, their heartbeats lethargic in their chests. They're not dead, probably not even close, but they're so listless they don't even tempt me. It's like sleeping next to roadkill.

"Why are all these people hanging around here?" I nudge the nearest one with my foot. He barely moves.

"Jane told me it was like this in San Francisco," Bee says. "People just live where they live. Simple as that."

"I don't like it." I scowl at the wall. "I'm not sure I like that Daisy either."

Bee shrugs. "I think she's sweet."

"I think she's a fool."

"You think everyone's a fool, Lucy." Bee lets out a small laugh, the sound of her voice clear and calming, and I can't help but smile. Nearby, one of the guys sprawled out on a ratty mattress grunts and turns over on his belly.

Bee situates an urn next to her and passes me the other one. I shove it behind me, where I wish I could forget it.

"Renfield was in England, wasn't he?" Bee murmurs, her eyes closed. "How do you think he got all the way here?"

I stare up at the ceiling, conjuring his haggard face. "I don't know," I say finally. "He must have smuggled himself into cargo."

Years ago, Dracula did the same, concealed among boxes of earth aboard the *Demeter*. The only difference is Dracula got a schooner, and Renfield got Pan Am. I imagine him hidden behind towering stacks of Samsonite luggage, tucked away in the womb of a Boeing 707. It probably wasn't even hard for him to hide. He looks like a bundle of cobwebs and shadows, something that could disappear in plain sight. After all, people always peer straight through the forgotten.

Voices seep up through the floorboards, rattling in my bones, but Bee doesn't mind the company. Next to me, she's already asleep.

I tell myself I shouldn't stay here. I should get out before these heartbeats eat me up alive and then I do the same to everyone else. But last night still sits heavy inside me, and with my body numb, I close my eyes as the morning falls away.

seven

It's nearly sundown when my hunger jolts me awake.

Through a gap in the curtains, the last bit of day-light spills golden across the horizon. Dracula must be getting closer now, his own ashes calling out to him.

My head heavy, I reach behind me to check on the urn, but it's gone. Nothing next to Bee, either. I'm on my feet now, searching the room, searching everywhere.

It doesn't take long to find them. The two urns have made it all the way to the door. With a quick lunge, I scoop them both up into my arms. Obstinate as children, they try to slither away, but I hold them tight.

"You're not going anywhere," I seethe, but that's not true. Another few minutes, and they could have gotten to the top of the staircase, and then god only knows who would have found them. Maybe one of those doe-eyed girls downstairs, come to play rescuer to the man who'd murder her.

"They're getting more restless, aren't they?" Bee's standing next to me, her arms crossed over her.

"It'll be okay," I say, and wish it were true.

Voices float up the stairs like ghosts. Daisy and the others, their laughter lilting through the smoke-drenched air. It's been a long time since I've been in a house with this much mirth, this much possibility. How lovely it all sounds. How quickly I could spoil it.

They're downstairs in the living room, only about a dozen of them now, all long legs and bare feet. Daisy looks up when Bee and I creep in.

"I'm glad you're awake," she says, creaking back and forth in the rocking chair. "I'm heading out soon. You should come too. Maybe we'll find your Jane tonight."

Then Daisy glances down at our tattered dresses, a whiff of soot and decay in the air. She crinkles her nose. "You might want to change first."

In the bathroom, frayed washcloths in our hands, Bee and I scrub the remnants of last night from our faces. Daisy's left a couple dresses on the sink for us. I don't know if they're hers, I don't know where they came from. Everything seems to be shared here, a primordial vat of scrappy hand-me-downs and secondhand treasures.

"Do you think they really know her?" Bee flicks a cinder from her shoulder. "That they've met Jane?"

"Maybe," I say, not wanting to disappoint her, not wanting to lie, either.

We shed our worn clothes, these gowns we've owned for longer than some of the kids in this house have been alive, and slip into the outfits Daisy gave us. Bee looks at home in her embroidered frock, stitched meticulously with tiny pink flowers, but I just stand here next to her, fidgeting. My dress is shorter than hers, the pale fabric gauzy, practically see-through, the neckline dipping down.

The Victorian in me can't help but blush.

This isn't me. None of this is, not the house or the clothes or the bohemian company. We've only been in this city a few hours, yet I already feel like I'm dissolving, becoming someone else.

Not that I know what I look like in this dress, not really. I'm right in front of a mirror, but I can't see my own reflection. There's only a gray shadow, an impossibly hazy outline where my figure should be. After all these years, I don't even know who I am anymore.

Bee leans against the sink, her reflection right there where it belongs. She won't look at herself.

"Can you drive tonight, Lucy?" she asks, and her hands won't stop shaking. She's terrified we won't find Jane, and also terrified we will.

"Of course," I say, forcing a smile, pretending everything is normal. Nearby, the two urns whisper on the floor. The fractures in the clay have widened again. They can't stay like this. They're too strong together.

I scan the bathroom. There's a hole near the ceiling, an old furnace vent where somebody removed the metal grate. I wrap an urn, the quiet one, in our discarded clothes, muffling the sound of his voice, before stuffing him into the dark.

"Is that safe?" Bee purses her lips, wincing a little. "What if somebody else finds him first?"

I grip the other urn, the one from the Hollywood sign. "And what if Renfield finds us?"

Downstairs, the front door is already open, and Daisy is waiting outside on the sidewalk, her crocheted bag slung over her shoulder.

"Ready?" she asks brightly, and we all pile into the Buick.

From the back seat, Daisy directs us to the party, accidentally leading us astray three times, circling the Haight until we're almost dizzy. When we finally arrive at our destination, it turns out we didn't even need to bother with the Buick at all, since the place is only about five blocks over, and it takes as long to find a parking place as it would have if we'd walked.

"I used to ride in carriages," I mutter, struggling into a narrow spot next to a dingy lamppost. "Nobody worries about parallel parking a fucking horse."

At last, the Buick slides into the space, and we all file out. It's not even nine o'clock, and I'm already exhausted.

The party's got an open-door policy, and we walk right in. This place is bigger than Daisy's, but it's just as bare-bones. A few pieces of humdrum furniture—a stained sofa, a couple of rusted metal chairs, a coffee table loaded with rolling papers and tin cans for ashtrays. There are people everywhere, standing, sitting, leaning, smoke in the air, bottles of Southern Comfort passed around like golden collection plates.

I freeze up in the doorway, the urn quivering in my hands. I don't know what to do here. I used to go to parties all the time, but not like this one, and besides, it's been so long that I hardly remember how to speak to another human, let alone socialize.

But Bee's ready for this. "Come on," she whispers, and I follow her, the two of us moving along the perimeter of the room, closest to the open windows. We ask around, we ask everyone, but nobody recognizes the name of Jane Eyre. They're more than eager to offer us suggestions, though.

"Up at the Presidio, there's some chick named Jane."

"No," someone else chimes in. "That's a June."

"That Jane over on Clayton might be your girl."

"She's a Joan," somebody corrects them.

This goes on for an hour, the minutes ticking away, as everyone tells us they can help, even though nobody can.

"What's this Jane like anyhow?" one of the girls asks, and Bee takes a long moment to answer.

"She's a little younger than me," she says finally. "Quiet. Blond. British."

That should give it away, but still, none of them recognize her. Meanwhile, the place just keeps on getting more crowded, people pushing through the front door, the back door, even a rickety side door. This is too much for Bee, too cramped.

Together, we retreat to the end of the room where I pry open a narrow window. Bee leans against it, inhaling the sticky summer air, breathing though she doesn't need to.

"Thanks," she says, giving me a strained smile. This isn't going how she'd hoped.

"We'll find her," I say, even though it might not be true. Jane might not be in the city at all. Hell, by now, she might not even be in the state.

Across the room, someone calls out our names. Daisy, elbowing her way through the crowd. "I just met a girl," she says, breathless. "A Jane. Do you want to come and see if she's the one?"

In her exuberance, Daisy doesn't even give Bee a chance to answer. She seizes her by the arm and drags her away from me, the two of them vanishing into the crush of bodies. Bee looks back once, and I want to go after her, but my head whirls, all these heartbeats thrumming inside me.

Still clutching the urn, I stumble through a beaded curtain into the next room. It's quieter in here, and darker too, the windows blocked out with cardboard, the overhead bulb flicked off. Somebody's got a liquid light show going, a small projector on the floor beaming splotches of color across the cracked plaster. Navy blue and daffodil yellow and a deep juniper green, the shapes pulsing and churning, a kaleidoscope so bright it'll make your eyes numb. When it gets to the color red, it looks like rage incarnate.

There's one other girl in here, smudged cheeks and long blond hair, smoking a joint. She starts to breeze past me but turns back suddenly.

"What's the deal with that thing?" She glares at the

urn, jabbing her finger accusingly in its direction. "And why's it keep talking at me? Is it like a magic trick?"

My hands tighten around the urn. "You could say that."

The girl raises an eyebrow. "Does it grant three wishes?"

"No," I say. "It takes away all your wishes instead. Your hopes and dreams, too."

At this, her face goes strangely blank.

"Bummer," she says, and passes me the joint like a consolation prize. I take a long drag off it but feel nothing. Of course I don't. I'm dead. That means you don't get to have any fun at all.

The projector cycles through its colors again, and I watch, a little mesmerized, as the red returns. A couple guys with headbands, their pulses slow and steady, wander in and cross over the projector beam, and for a moment, the splatter of light looks like a crime scene across their bodies. I like it more than I should. I need to get out of here before I do something that I'd like even more.

I sneak back through the beaded curtain, the urn pressed tight against me, as Bee returns, entirely deflated. The girl across the room turned out to be an ordinary Jane, not the proper Jane.

Daisy shrugs, undeterred. "There's another party over on Waller," she says. "We could go there next."

And that's precisely what we do. One house after another, we shuffle in and out of front doors where everyone's invited, into crowded rooms packed to the brim. Plenty of pot smoke and not nearly enough furnishings.

But even after half a dozen parties, nobody's heard of Jane Eyre.

"They should have at least read the book in school," I mutter.

In one place, nobody speaks at all. They're all too busy sitting cross-legged on the hardwood floor, listening to young men with long hair strum songs on Silvertone guitars. Some of the boys are rather good. Some of them aren't. Regardless, they all seem convinced they're geniuses.

"I don't think I can take another wannabe Bob Dylan tonight," I say, as we walk to the next party down the block.

Daisy snaps her tongue. "You're too cynical," she says, as though she's old enough and worldly enough to decide such things.

I scrunch up my nose. "I'm not cynical," I say, and Bee chirps up a laugh, as if to say I am.

At the next house, we're barely through the door before we're separated, Daisy blithely showing Bee around, explaining her odyssey to locate this mysterious Jane.

"Can you help us?" she asks, and everyone closes in around them.

I back away into a corner, the only place I feel safe, but it doesn't take long until someone else joins me. A young man, no older than Michael, in buckskin and fringe, his scent like sandalwood and sweat. He's standing too close, but then again, everyone here is too close for my taste.

"We could go upstairs," the guy says, as though he's finishing a conversation we weren't even having.

I scowl. "Why would I want to do that?"

"Because it would be fun." He sucks his cigarette down to the filter and then nods at the urn. "Is that an ashtray?"

My whole body goes rigid as he moves toward me, his hand on the lid, ready to unscrew it and flick the butt of his Winston into Dracula's remains.

"No," I say and bare my teeth. They aren't even sharp, but he recoils anyhow.

"I was just asking," he says. "Jesus Christ."

Cursing to himself, he charges off, slipping back into the sea of partygoers. I settle against the wall, grateful he's gone. A moment later, though, I see him talking to Daisy, his arms flailing, his eyes wide and bewildered. Tattling on me like a child. I count to ten, and Daisy's already starting toward me.

"Lucy, darling," she says, "I want you to feel free to be yourself and everything, but could you maybe not growl at my friends?"

I shrug. "Maybe your friends shouldn't bother me."

"If you keep growling at them, I doubt they will."

"Then we'll all be happy, won't we?"

She inspects my face for a long moment. "How old did you say you are?"

I tilt my head and smile. "Almost a hundred."

Daisy lets out a throaty laugh. "Aren't we all?" she says, passing me her crocheted bag. "Put that bottle thing in here. That should muffle it enough that nobody bothers you about it."

I seize up, the urn in one hand, the bag in the other, thinking how that's not a terrible idea. Daisy's a clever one, I'll give her that.

I drop the urn in the crocheted bag, slinging it over my shoulder. "Why are you doing this?" I ask her. "Why are you helping us?"

She hesitates, as if it never occurred to her not to. "You helped me," she says finally. "Plus, that's what we do here. We help each other."

And with that, she wanders back into the party, her frame so slight that she looks again like a lamb headed to the slaughter. Those bright eyes, that eager face, the way she never stops smiling. The world's going to eat her up alive. The same way it did to me.

Another hour, and the night's lazing into a nervous slumber. Most everyone's gone by now, and the ones left behind are curled up on the hardwood floor or slouched in a heap on the piss-yellow couch, passing around the last joint. None of them are any help anyhow. We've already asked them. They don't know Jane Eyre.

We head to the door, Bee with that familiar faraway look on her face.

"We'll try again tomorrow," I say, even though we shouldn't. It isn't safe for us in this city. Dracula's ashes must be even closer now. He could be anywhere. So could Renfield.

We're almost to the front step, when that same guy in

buckskin and fringe puts his hand on Bee's shoulder. She recoils from him, and on instinct, I feel my teeth sharpen.

"I was just thinking," he says in a slow drawl. "There was a girl once."

"A Jane?" Bee asks, hope rising in her voice.

"Maybe," he says, "I don't remember. All I know is she lived across the bay in an odd little house. A house like a dream." He whistles, as if remembering something. "They had some *wild* parties there."

Daisy hesitates. "You mean that place up in the Marin Headlands?" She looks at us now, all the color leeching from her face. "You don't want to go there."

Bee stares back at her. "Why not?"

"Bad vibes," Daisy murmurs, something frantic in her eyes, but Bee won't listen. If Jane's there, that's all that matters.

It takes us twenty minutes up Route 101, across the Golden Gate Bridge, Alcatraz in the distance. Daisy passes me a dollar to pay the toll, and we keep going, past the county line, the darkness creeping closer.

It's strange up here in the Marin Headlands, so close to so-called civilization and a whole world away, too. I remember hearing about this place on the radio back in L.A. The land's alive and wild now, but not for long. Gulf Oil is planning a development here. Marincello, they'll call it. A new city next to the bay city, complete with sky-scrapers and a mall and a mountain of concrete. A rich place for rich people, the kind who level everything that came before. Soon there will be no more untamed ridges or clusters of bishop pine trees or silver lupine wildflowers sprouting up between stones. That's the way it goes. Nobody wants the old things anymore.

At last, we take a curve around the sinuous highway, and Daisy shudders.

"There it is," she whispers, and a barb twists deep in my chest.

The house is like a phantom nestled back from the road. It's made of glass, all the walls transparent, as if to say it's got nothing to hide. From the driveway, there are cars snaking around in a long line, and a drone of music seeps out into the night.

I park the Buick off the side of the road, and we just sit here for a moment. I don't want to go in, dread bunching up inside me for no good reason, but this is Bee's choice. I won't abandon her to do it alone.

Daisy, however, does the smart thing. She waits in the car. "Good luck," she says, not looking at us.

At the front step, the door creaks open, another house where you need no invitation. I've never been in a city where I can walk around so freely, a vampire welcomed everywhere she goes. Bee and I slip inside, vanishing into the crowd. We look the same age as everyone else, even though we're old enough to be their great-grandmothers. It's a good disguise.

On the trip here, Daisy wouldn't tell us why she's afraid. "I just don't like it there" was all she'd say, and now that we're inside, I'm starting to understand why. All night, we've been in houses that made do with next to nothing, while this place can't seem to get enough. Everything's gleaming and polished, the colors bright, garish even, demanding your attention. Blaze-orange lamps and teal curtains and a chartreuse love seat, the stone floors painted a brilliant crimson.

The décor's got a slapdash quality to it, modern and nostalgic in a jumble together—an egg chair next to an antique tapestry on the wall, a chrome end table topped with burnished candleholders—like someone trying to assemble a life in a hurry and not caring that nothing fits together.

But it's the people who really make my stomach whirl. Back at the other houses, everyone was winding down for the night, but the party's only starting here. If this is a party at all. It seems more like a funeral. The women all dressed the same, in long billowing frocks, the cotton bleached white, their bare feet peeking out beneath hand-stitched hems. They huddle together in small groups, and they smile sometimes, and they laugh too, very suddenly, as if on cue from an unseen director, their whole lives a dress rehearsal for a performance that might never come.

I don't spot a single guy in the whole place. Maybe they're all out back on the patio. Or maybe they weren't welcome for some reason.

Bee doesn't notice any of it. She's too busy asking everyone near the door about Jane. I go on ahead of her, drifting through the room. There's no upstairs, probably no basement either, which should at least make this easy. If Jane's here, we should find her quick enough.

The house is laid out in a boxy rectangle, one of those art deco numbers, only weirder, everything designed on sharp, indecent angles. Like Frank Lloyd Wright on acid.

A ceiling that cuts down sharply in the middle like a razor's edge.

A fireplace, sullen and cold, in the dead center of the room, the brickwork around it in the shape of an obtuse triangle.

A slim hallway, stretching down to a vanishing point, the walls narrowing, as if devouring you whole. I hesitate at the mouth of it. There are heartbeats at the end of the corridor, soft but clear. I shouldn't follow the sound, but I can't help myself. The melody draws me nearer, so sweet it makes my teeth ache, and when I get to the last door, I quietly nudge it open.

Inside, three girls are sitting on a king-sized bed, not moving, not speaking, not even looking at one another. They're the same as the other women in the house, arrayed in plain cotton dresses, their hair a mousy brown.

The ceiling's vaulted over them, violet curtains cascading down the wall like a thunderstorm, and the girls look almost comically small in this giant room. I gape at them from the doorway, but they don't seem to notice me. They don't seem to notice anything.

"What are you doing in here?" I ask, and the sound of my own voice startles me.

One of the girls looks up, her face etched with sorrow. "Waiting," she says.

"For what?"

"For him," says the second girl, her jaw set, her lips barely moving when she speaks.

"And who exactly is *he*?"

The third girl, stock-still until now, turns and eyes me up, surveying me like a piece of property. Or a piece of meat.

"He's out by the pool," she says, and motions to a sliding glass door on the other side of the room. "You should say hi. I think he'll like you."

Something twists inside me, tighter than a screw. I don't want him to like me. I don't want to meet him at all. But whoever he is, he might know about Jane, and right now, that's all that matters.

The party buzzing outside, I cross the bedroom, still watching the girls. Their faces are blank as fresh canvas. It's like they're expecting someone to step in and finish them, to put the color in their eyes, a pink swirl on their cheeks. Are they here because they want to be? Or because they have to be?

I'm at the glass door, flicking open the lock, but at the last moment, I turn back.

"Do you need help?" I ask, and it's a ridiculous question. I'm a vampire who could devour them in an instant. But I was also a wide-eyed girl once, just like them, sitting around waiting for the world to break my heart.

The three of them stare up at me from the bed, the expressions on their faces never changing.

"We're fine," they say without inflection, but they keep looking at me, right through me, and my flesh tightens on my bones.

"Suit yourselves," I say, and with my hand unsteady on the door, I wrench it open and step into the night.

Outside, the air is sweet with summer, the pungent scent of chlorine leaking in at the edges. The pool glitters in the moonlight, the shape of a teardrop, blue and spotless as a phony lagoon from a movie set. There are girls everywhere, the same as inside the house, but I see him immediately, the man they're all performing for.

He's standing at the rim of the pool, next to a row of plastic lawn chairs, each one filled with another vacant-eyed girl. Where does he find them all? Or worse yet, do they simply find him?

He's older than the rest, maybe thirty-five, with thick eyebrows, a square jaw, hair the color of midnight. A stern face like a military father, a face without pity. He's holding a drink, a bourbon on the rocks or some other nostalgic man-in-the-gray-flannel-suit nonsense. As I move toward him, he turns to look at me, seemingly pleased with what he sees.

I smile, even as I wish him dead. "They tell me you're in charge."

He waves me off. "Nobody's in charge here," he says, his dark gaze piercing into me like a blade. "We're in this together."

"Really?" I nearly laugh in his face. "Because I met your girls in the bedroom. They don't seem to be in charge of much."

"Are they still waiting for me?" he asks, and I can tell by the curl of his thin lips, how pleased he is about that.

They're not the only ones waiting on him. Nearby, a couple of girls in lawn chairs are watching me, their eyes darting up when they think I'm not looking. All these women, they're flocking to him, competing with the others, each of them trying to prove they're worthy of his attention. There are no other men here but him, and I wonder if this is an audition of sorts, a strange kind of cattle call.

And maybe he wants to screen-test me too, because he won't stop looking at me. "I don't think we've had the pleasure of meeting yet," he says, and extends his hand like a gentleman. I don't take it.

"I'm only passing through," I say. "We're looking for someone."

He scoffs. "Who isn't?"

The girls from the lawn chairs are standing up now, their willowy figures creeping closer. A few partygoers are climbing out of the pool as well, their faces obscure in the moonlight, and though they dry themselves off with fuzzy towels, everything so cool, so nonchalant, they're getting nearer, too.

I try to track all of them at once, but there are too many. My chest constricts, and I hold Daisy's bag a little tighter, gripping the urn inside, and that's my mistake, because he notices.

"What is that you've got there?" he asks, closing the distance between us.

I wrench away. "No," I say, a word he isn't used to hearing. Instantly, the crowd goes quiet, and they don't pretend anymore. They're all openly watching me now, their eyes faded and unblinking, waiting on a command from him.

But he doesn't give one. He just shrugs. "All right," he says, and his voice is all hard edges, cold as steel, jagged as thorns. "I won't force you."

With a sneer, he starts to turn away, but I can't let him go. Not yet.

"One more thing," I say, and he glances back at me. "Where's Jane?"

His body heaves a moment. "Who?"

"Your wife," I say. "Your *second* wife. Where is she?"

He feigns an innocent look, though it doesn't suit him at all. "I don't know who you're talking about."

"Sure you do," I say, and we hold each other's gaze for a long time. Too long. He wants to make me uncomfortable, but I won't give him the satisfaction. I won't say his name, either, though I know it anyhow.

Edward Fairfax Rochester.

I've never met him before, but I would recognize him anywhere. From what Bee's told me, from what the movies have told me too. He's kept his accent, the same as Jane, and he's kept his old habits too. This is exactly what he used to do at Thornfield—hold lavish parties, invite everyone he knew. There was music on pianofortes and people pretending to be civilized. Now it's music on high-fidelity turntables, but otherwise, it's all the same.

There's another dead giveaway too. The silence in

his chest, the emptiness within him. Though to be fair, I doubt a man like him ever really had a heart.

Behind me, the patio door creaks open. Rochester barely looks up.

"Bertha, my love. How are you?"

"It's Bee," she says, but he already knows that. He just doesn't care.

"I've been trying to reach you." He grips his highball glass tighter. "Been calling and calling. You never answer."

"That should tell you something," Bee says, and she's standing next to me now, near the rim of the pool. Something's shifting in her, her gaze like fire, her voice like stone. This is a side of her I don't know. A side that maybe he alone has seen.

"Well," he says, and finishes his drink in one ragged gulp, "we're glad to have you both here. Welcome to Dahlia Hall."

I stare at him, incredulous. "You named this house too?"

"Why not?" He exhales a harsh laugh. "If it's mine, don't I deserve to claim it?"

At this, his eyes shift to Bee, watching her in a way that makes me squirm. It never ceases to amaze me how obscene some men can be without ever lifting a finger.

But Bee's used to him by now, and she doesn't miss a beat. "Where's Jane?"

Rochester flashes her a slimy smile, and at last, he's found an expression that looks good on him. "She's not here," he says. "Anyhow, I thought she was on her way to find you."

Bee doesn't answer, her lips pursed, her face looking ready to crumble, and though she doesn't say it, Rochester guesses the rest.

"That girl just can't make up her mind, can she?" He shakes his head ruefully, as his acolytes draw closer. There are more of them now, some even shifting outside through the main patio door to join the throng. These girls in their flowing cotton dresses, their backs stiff, their mouths rigid and downturned.

We're outnumbered by a mile, and Rochester knows it. He's got nothing to worry about. Men like him never do.

Still grinning, he rattles the ice in his glass. "I'm sure Jane will be back soon, Bertha. In the meantime, why don't you make yourself at home?"

Then he waits a long, hateful moment, his grin tightening, before adding, "Pity we don't have an attic. I know how much you love those."

Her hands curled into claws, Bee starts toward him, but the others are right there, flanking him in an instant. They're everywhere, they're unrelenting, and in the dark, their eyes are all I can see.

I put a hand on Bee's arm. "Jane isn't here," I whisper, and though the rage is still quivering in her, every muscle in her body constricted, Bee nods.

We back away from the crowd, edging toward the side of the house. That's the only chance we've got—to shortcut around, not through. It isn't safe to walk back into that party. But as we pass the side door, it jerks open, and the three girls from the bed emerge, blocking our path.

"Leaving already?" they ask, their voices in unison. They smile at me, everything about them so serene, as they refuse to budge an inch. Their heartbeats flutter a little faster, and I fall back a step, not because I'm worried about them, but because I'm worried about me. I might be able to hold them back, to hold everyone here back, but with my hunger burning brighter, I'm not sure I can hold myself back.

Rochester watches us before shaking his head. "Such a shame," he says.

Bee glares at him. "What is?"

"You." His eyes are on her. "I'd always hoped you'd turn out differently."

A rueful laugh. "And how did I turn out?"

"Exactly like your infamous mother."

Something in Bee's face cracks, just a little, just enough that he sees it. He knows her, knows the thing that will hurt her most.

She scoffs, trying to play it off. "You haven't changed a bit, Edward."

"But you have, Bertha." He crosses toward her, closing the distance in a flash, his long shadow draped over both of us. "Do you remember when we met in Spanish Town? The way you dazzled me?"

A memory flickers in Bee, as he reaches out and runs his fingers softly through her hair, before whispering, "How did you ever get so old?"

And there it is again: that rehearsed laughter, all the girls pretending he's so very funny. I hate them for it, for how they're mocking Bee, but Rochester's reveling in this moment, reveling in his power, so this is our chance. I squeeze Bee's hand, and together, we run.

Back at the car, Daisy barely glances up at us. "Was she there?"

"No," Bee says as we slide inside and I crank the key in the ignition. The Buick doesn't hesitate tonight. It roars to life, and we squeal out onto the highway, not turning back.

"So," Daisy says, picking at a piece of yellow foam through the leather seat, "did you meet *him*?"

She doesn't say his name. She doesn't have to.

My mouth goes dry as I glance at her in the rearview mirror. "We did," I whisper.

"I'm sorry for you," she says, all the joy drained out of her face. "I made that mistake already."

An aching silence breaches the car, as Bee and I digest what this means.

"I'm not special," Daisy says, as though we're judging her for it. "He's seduced half the girls in the Haight."

This realization sticks in my throat like glue. All night we were asking for the wrong person. We inquired about Jane Eyre, but almost nobody knew her. She was just another conquest, another anonymous face in the crowd. If we'd wanted to find her quicker, we needed to ask about him. It's the same as it's always been, the same as the movies, the same as with Dracula: he's the one everybody remembers.

We drive down the 101 for miles, nobody saying a word. At a stoplight, I give Daisy back her crocheted bag and clutch the urn in my lap, just to have something solid to hold on to.

"We need to go back to that house," Bee says at last. "Tomorrow night. Jane might be home by then."

I shake my head. "I don't know if that's a good idea."

"But that's where she'll go, Lucy. Back to him. And who knows what he'll do to her?"

Bee's hands clench into fists, her eyes going vacant with rage. I've never seen her like this.

I park on the street in front of Daisy's place. The house is quieter now, and inside, all the lights are out. It's late, almost four in the morning, and most everyone is away at parties that never end or curled up in one of the bedrooms, resting up for parties about to begin.

The engine cuts out, and I turn to Bee. "Did you see those girls with him? How devoted they are? How dangerous?"

She stares off into the sky. "I don't care."

"Well, *I* care," I say, my voice splitting apart. I squeeze my eyes closed, but all I can see are their terrible faces, the way they were watching us. The things they'll gleefully do to Bee if she goes back to that house. The way they'll take their time with her.

"They're just kids," Bee says. "We're stronger than they are. *You're* stronger."

Without a word, I know what she's asking me to do.

"I can't," I whisper.

"Then you don't have to come with me," Bee says, as if that's a solution.

We climb out of the Buick, the two of us arguing all the way up the front steps and through the front door, Daisy dragging her feet behind us, like a child caught in the middle. We're still arguing when we reach the living room, silent and dim. Along the wall, Daisy fumbles for the light switch, and a single bulb flickers on, its naked shape painting our faces jaundice yellow.

"She's headed back to him," Bee keeps saying. "It's the only place she'll go."

I shake my head, ready to tell her I don't want to fight anymore, when I notice something different in the room. There in the corner, the oak rocking chair is in a haphazard heap, broken into serrated pieces. I gape at it, the truth settling over me, too slowly to matter.

A bit of dust in my eyes, and it happens in an instant. Renfield, emerging from the shadows, a splintered piece of wood gripped tight between his battered fingers.

"My apologies, Miss Lucy," he says, and buries the stake in my heart.

eight

Dying is always the worst. I hate it almost as much as being alive.

My head spins, and the sound drops out first, as if someone's turned down the volume on the whole world. Time slows to nothing, just like I told Michael, and as Renfield stumbles back a step, grinning, my body starts to retreat into itself, my skin sizzling, my guts going soft.

It feels like hell on earth, and it must look like that too, because Daisy collapses in the corner, her hands over her eyes, her mouth gaping. She must be screaming, but I can't hear her. I can't hear Bee either, even as she growls something at Renfield and then charges at him, her hands gnarled, her eyes flashing. All the rage in her is unfurling at him, her hatred of Rochester, her heartbreak over Jane. Between me and Renfield, I'm not sure which of us has it worse. I might be dying, but she just scratched out his eye, a thick, pale ooze dripping from the cavernous orifice where Renfield used to peer through the darkness, scrying into the beyond, searching for Dracula. Searching for me.

A twinge in my heart, and part of me feels sorry for him. Part of me wants to help finish him too. I certainly don't want to leave Bee to do this alone, to clean up the mess I've accidentally made, but I don't get a choice.

Daisy's screams must be louder than I thought, because others are staggering down the stairs, roused from their heavy dreams. They peer into the living room, and their faces twist at the sight of me. I wonder what they see.

Another moment, and I don't have time to wonder. The rest of me turns to dust, and I can't hold on to the urn anymore. It falls through my crumbling fingers, shattering into a thousand pieces on the floor. Overhead, Dracula's muddy form smears across the ceiling before dripping down to meet himself, the parts of him mingling together, his body becoming stronger, while mine becomes nothing at all.

I won't watch him now. I close what's left of my eyes and let the darkness rush in to greet me.

IT'S BEEN A WHILE since I died. Seventy years, give or take. Back then, I did it all the time, as though it was a sport, a diversion, my favorite hobby. There were so many different ways it happened. A stake through my heart, a blade across my throat, a silver cross that bisected me.

But I don't want to remember any of that now. I don't want to remember what they did to me. What he did to me.

The world stops spinning, and I open my eyes, already knowing what I'll see. This same place from all the times before. What it is, *where* it is, is anyone's guess. It might be heaven or it might be purgatory or it might simply be an odd sort of waiting room. Because that's what it looks like—a tiny space, four walls, an antiseptic quality lingering in the air, as though even the afterlife doesn't want to reek of death.

And, of course, there's them. Hands pushing through the walls like taffy, the outlines of writhing fingers that are never quite strong enough to break through. Instead, the plaster just keeps contorting at their touch.

I don't know who they are. I can't see their faces, and I can't hear their voices, either, only raspy whispers that fade out like a song at the end of an old record.

This is what I've come to expect when I die. A hundred hands here to greet me, reaching out, desperate to take hold, their bodies nowhere to be found. There's only one difference now.

This time, there's someone inside the room with me.

"Hello, Lucy," a small crystalline voice says behind me.

I whirl around to face her, those familiar eyes, that curtain of dark hair, that turned-up nose.

"Hello, Mina," I say.

This is the first time I've seen her since she died, and I can't stop staring at her. She's the way I remember her, the way we were when we were only girls who didn't know any better.

She stands across from me, no more than a half dozen

steps away, but it feels so far in this room. Everything feels far, and neither of us knows quite what to say.

"How are you?" I ask at last.

"Dead," she says. "And you?"

"The same." For a moment, I want to laugh, and I want to cry, too. "How long have you been in this room?"

She crinkles her nose. "It's hard to tell," she says, and I know exactly what she means. Time passes differently in this place, everything wrapped in an instant and an eternity.

We keep watching each other, and I think how strange it is, how after all these years, she's the ghost, and I'm the one who can't help but stay among the living.

Another hand pushes through the wall and takes hold of Mina's arm. A strong grasp, but not an unkind one. She pulls away, shaking her head.

"Do you have any idea who they are?" I ask.

"I'm not sure." Mina presses her fingertips into the wall, and a small hand presses back. "But I think they're like us, Lucy."

Like us. The other girls, the ones he's bitten. The ones the world has forgotten.

I inch forward and put my hand to the wall, too. "Have any of them ever gotten through?"

Mina turns to me, her eyes gray. "Not yet."

I look back as something rolls across the floor nearby. It's the stake Renfield buried in my heart. That's the one thing I can carry through, other than myself. A morbid little souvenir of what got me here.

Not that I get to stay. My body coils into itself, my skin pulling like it's on too tight. I feel whole, I look whole, but it's only an illusion. I never stay dead for long. That means we don't have much time. Mina and I inch closer, tentative at first, almost like strangers. Then we sit together on the floor. There are no chairs in the afterlife, no amenities at all, but maybe that's not so terrible. At least we have each other.

Our heads down, as if in prayer, we listen to distant voices. They're coming from Daisy's house, no more than whispers, too far away to matter.

"Can you hear me when I'm over there?" I ask.

"Sometimes," Mina says, and blushes. "I try not to eavesdrop, though."

I smile back at her. Of course she doesn't. That would be rude, something that's anathema to Mina. She was always so much better at being a well-behaved Victorian than I was.

Mina was better at a lot of things. She did what I never could. Thanks to Van Helsing coaxing her back from the brink of death, she lived out her life, one careful day at a time, through matrimony, through motherhood, finally passing away quietly in her sleep, crow's feet around her eyes, a murmur in her heart. I don't envy her for it. The thing about making it to old age is that not everyone else will. That means you get to sit back and watch the world slip away from you, one tragedy at a time. First it was her friends, the Texan and the laudanum-loving doctor and that odious lord I nearly married (sometimes, death is a mercy). Then it was her husband, Jonathan, his body frail, his spirit broken. And finally her only son, lost on the Western Front in a war the world said would end all wars, as though that could ever happen. People love slaughtering each other far too much to ever give up their favorite pastime.

Her face wears this grief like a luxurious veil, and she looks at me through the shadows that seem a little closer now. Then with a small, devious grin, she reaches out and entwines her hand with mine. Everything about this feels like home, like an innocence we never deserved to lose. This is what we used to do, me and Mina, how we used to cure our ills. It didn't matter what it was—a thunderstorm, a nightmare, a heartbreak. We'd just take the other one's hand and wait it out together. If only we could wait this out too.

"You're colder than I remember," she says with a laugh, and I laugh too, because I realize just how much I've missed her. Mina, my childhood friend, my first friend, the only one who ever came to visit my grave, always leaving me a bundle of wisteria tied neatly with Queen Anne's lace.

"For you, my Lucy," she would whisper, and sometimes, I was sure she saw me watching from the shadows. I wanted to go to her then, to tell her we could still run away like wayward schoolgirls, that it wasn't too late to dream, but she never lingered in the cemetery. The darkness always frightened her away.

Voices leak into the room, so much louder now, Bee's voice and Daisy's too.

Mina gives me a sad smile. "It's almost time, isn't it?"

"I'm sorry," I say, everything in me aching. I'd rather stay here with her. Away from Dracula, away from the world.

But then I hear her. Bee, calling out my name, doing her best to beckon me back. She's singing, too, to steady herself, her voice too beautiful to bear. I won't leave her behind, abandoning her in San Francisco without Jane, without anybody.

My hands turn soft and ashen, Mina's fingers slipping right through me. I'm dying in reverse, and there's nothing we can do except sit here and wait for it.

"Daisy's right, you know."

My skin goes translucent. "About what?"

"You're too cynical. You never used to be."

"Things change," I try to say, but my voice evaporates first.

Mina shakes her head, as if arguing with fate. "Don't let him win, Lucy," she says, and that's it. I'm gone, pulled back into the world against my will, my body cracking, my bones stretching taut against fresh skin.

It's always more painful than I remember.

WHEN I OPEN MY eyes, it's already evening, the sun vanishing from the sky. Bee is sitting next to me, her face splotchy with tears.

"Welcome back," she whispers.

She'd never seen me die before. I wonder what it looked like to her. I wonder what I look like even now, my body not quite finished. My skin's settling over my rib cage, my hair still curling into place. Everything about me is brand-new, and I don't entirely feel like myself. I'm more like a prototype, like a Lucy that hasn't been broken in yet.

Quivering, I lie on my side, facing a wall, barely able to move. Bee watches me, as though she can't believe I'm real.

"I wasn't sure you'd come back," she says, and my chest tightens, part of me convinced she knows the truth. That I wanted to stay there with Mina. That I wanted to stay dead.

"Renfield?" I ask, my lips parched.

"I chased him away," Bee says. "And that other thing too."

That specter, that shadow. Dracula. With the daylight dissolving into nothing, he'll be back again soon enough. That means I can't be here waiting for him.

I struggle to sit up, everything in me weak and brittle and so terribly hungry. I always come back from the dead famished.

And there's something else that happens every time I come back, one final insult from the afterlife—I return without a stitch of clothing on. Bee's done the polite thing and wrapped me up in an old quilt, which is better than nothing, but I need to get dressed before anyone else sees me.

I finally manage to prop myself up on my arms, but when I turn away from the wall, I realize I'm already too late. Bee and I aren't alone. The living room, so empty last night when we returned, is filled to the brim with people. They're cross-legged on the floor, sprawled out on furniture, even standing room only. All of them patiently gazing at us. At me.

Daisy's at the forefront, smiling. "Good to see you again, Lucy."

I gape at her, trying to fathom why I'm sitting naked in front of dozens of strangers. "What is this?"

"They've been here all day," Bee says, impatience edging into her voice. "Apparently, they have a lot of questions for you."

I tug the blanket tighter around me. "About what?"

"About everything," Daisy says brightly. "Life. Death. What's in between."

The yellowish light flickers above us, and I sit here, dumbfounded. They think I can explain this. Who I am, what's happened to me. There must be fifty of them, maybe more, and they won't stop watching me, their eyes so eager. They saw my body turn to dust, and then they witnessed me slowly put myself back together. They must think I know everything, even though I know nothing at all.

My stomach convulses with hunger, and I gaze back at all these hopeful faces. This would be so easy. I could pluck any of them from the crowd, and they'd follow me. Upstairs to the bedroom with the dirty mattresses or outside into the darkest alley I can find. And I'd give them the answer to eternal life all right, just not the way they want to learn it.

There's someone else who could teach them the same thing. His familiar scent like roses still wafts around me, the echo of him lingering in the air. My heart twists in my chest, and I suddenly remember the urn upstairs. The one we left unattended last night. The one I haven't checked on since.

I drag myself to my feet, still clutching the quilt. Bee tries to help me, so do Daisy and all the others, but I pull away from them and stumble up the steps and into the bathroom where I peer inside the wall. My stomach seizes. The old furnace vent is empty now. Renfield must have gotten this one too. That leaves the urn in the trunk of the Buick, and that's it. And what if that one isn't there either?

On the bathroom floor, someone left behind a dress. Maybe for me, maybe not, but I slip into it anyhow. It's even shorter than the last one, sheerer too, more like a nightshirt than a proper gown, but I can't complain. I was just naked in front of fifty people. This is certainly an improvement.

I retreat into the hall, past the narrow stairwell leading up to the attic. Apparently, not everyone has gathered in the living room. There are girls giggling behind a closed bedroom door, the melody of their heartbeats leaking through. I drift closer, imagining how sweet they'd taste if I could get hold of them. How they'd revive me in an instant. How at last I could take the very thing Dracula has always said is mine.

"Lucy?" Bee's voice floats up the steps, incriminating me without even meaning to.

I back away from the door, my cheeks burning with shame. "Be right there."

Downstairs, the others are flocking around the foyer, waiting for me. "Can't you help us?" they ask, their desperation marrow-deep. "Can't you tell us what you've seen?"

They watch me, innocence in their eyes, hope in their hearts. This is why they're here, why they ended up in this city, living together in spartan rooms with strangers. They're looking for something, and they think I can help them find it.

"I'm sorry," I say, slipping between them and out into the night.

The Buick waits solemnly on the street. I rush to it and put both hands on the locked trunk. Relief washes over me. The last urn's still there, the heat of him seeping through, his rage so potent it burns straight down to my bones.

He's not free yet, not completely.

Bee's standing with me now. "We should go," she whispers, "before Renfield comes back."

I peer at her. "What about Jane? And Rochester?"

She shakes her head. "We've tried," she says, defeat cutting sharp lines in her face.

I start to argue with her, to tell her it's not too late,

when a crush of bodies pushes past us. At first, I think it's the kids from inside the house, but no, they haven't followed us. These are all people we've never seen before, moving down the white line in the center of the road, not worried about traffic, not worried about anything.

"They're headed to Golden Gate Park," Daisy says, appearing next to us like a specter. "Today's the Summer Solstice Festival."

The summer solstice. The longest day of the year. And the shortest night. That doesn't give us much time.

Bee instinctively knows this. The car key in her hand, she slides into the driver's seat, the look in her eye as grim as a funeral. "Come on, Lucy," she says.

I trudge toward the passenger door, my hunger pressing into me, slowing my every step. Daisy follows close behind.

"Take me with you?"

I turn back to her, my jaw slack. "Why?"

She gives me a sheepish grin. "Because you two are the most exciting thing to happen here since Leary."

More people keep moving by, an endless exodus, but Daisy just stands there in the street, that smile of hers never fading. She's the same as her friends. She thinks we can help save her from herself. That Bee and I have some arcane insight into the universe. That just because we're dead that must mean we're wise.

I climb into the Buick, and though the top is still down, I lock my door anyhow. Daisy catches my hand, turning my palm upward.

"Look," she whispers. "Your lifeline."

I gaze down at my changed body, at the vague crease in my skin. It's only half of what it was yesterday, and I think I know why. I wanted to stay there with Mina. I wanted to stay dead.

Maybe I've only got so many lives in me after all.

"Listen," I say, wrenching my hand away, "I promise you don't want to come with us."

Daisy scoffs, her nose crinkled like a spoiled child. "Why do you get to make that choice for me?"

There's that word again. Choice. It's the one thing I've always wanted, and the one thing I've always been denied.

Bee cranks the engine, a warning shot for Daisy, but this only makes her edge closer, her face softening now.

"Please," she says, those keen eyes watching me. Everything about her is so familiar. Daisy and I aren't so different. She just wants people to see her, to *really* see her. I remember what that's like.

I want to tell her I'm sorry, to tell her I wish things had turned out differently, but Bee shifts the Buick sharply into gear, and we surge down the street. Away from Daisy, away from everything.

The night settles like tar over us, and I don't look back.

We're at the edge of Golden Gate Park, the streets clogged with red taillights, kids in bell-bottoms spilling off the sidewalk in waves. There are so many people, cramming every available space, bodies nearly tumbling atop bodies. It seems like everyone in the world is here.

Bee does her best to ignore them. "You want to go north?" she asks, and I start to answer her when the breeze changes, and someone else is with us. Someone we know.

Bee. A thin voice, so small I barely hear it. It isn't Rochester this time.

Bee and I see her at the same moment. Jane. She's at the top of a sloping hill, that yellow ribbon in her hair, still wearing the same blue dress she borrowed from Bee. The Buick screeches suddenly, Bee jerking the wheel hard, as we skid to a stop at the mouth of the park. This is the farthest we can go in the car. Now it's on foot down the dirt path or nothing at all.

I expect Bee to leap out and run to Jane, but she doesn't. We've come all this way, yet now she's frozen, her hands tightening on the wheel, regret leeching into her. That faraway look, the one I know so well, casts a shadow across her face as she remembers it, remembers everything. How they were together, then how they weren't, and how many days there were in between. The past is always so much heavier than you ever expect it to be.

Bee, is that you? Jane's voice again, desperate and pleading, but Bee doesn't look at her. She looks at me instead.

"What should I do?" she asks, and this catches me off guard. I stare back at her, terrified I'll say the wrong thing.

"Do whatever you feel is best."

That must be the right answer, because in an instant,

her door flicks open, and she's rushing to Jane. Across the sidewalk and up the hill, past hundreds of people, their faces blurred in the night. Her figure collapses in on itself, smaller and smaller, until I lose sight of her altogether.

Now here I am, alone in a crowd, wilted in the passenger seat like a hothouse flower. Music rises in the air like honied elegies, and figures push all around me, brushing against my door, their pulses quickening in the heat, their bodies smelling of sweat and smoke and the first promise of summer.

Everything in me crawls with want as I watch them. All these jubilant kids, their faces smeared with tempera paint, the outlines of stars and moons and sunshine on their cheeks. Somebody's brought a giant inflatable globe, and the crowd punts it back and forth, as though the whole world is theirs for the taking. You always believe that when you're young. If only the feeling could last.

I search again for Bee, but she's long gone now, vanished into the mass of bodies. She and Jane must have found each other. After a whole night of searching, Jane ended up being so close to us. Maybe she heard Bee singing to me today. Maybe that led her right to us.

And I've led someone else right to us too. Michael, wandering through the throng, like a phantom in chains. Of course he's here. I've been drawing him to me ever since we left L.A.

He's at the edge of the park, so close I can breathe him in, his scent like pine, like home. Bright-eyed girls with flowers in their hair are watching him, their eager gazes sliding over his body, but he never sees them. He's only searching for me. With a whisper, I could make him look right at me. I could lure him into the back seat, our bodies tangled together as I devour him by the mouthful. In the gathering dark, nobody would even notice. We'd be just another amorous couple in the middle of a lovefest.

I turn away, sinking deeper into the passenger seat, letting him drift past on the sidewalk.

"Go away," I whisper, and hope he'll listen.

Besides, there's something else here now. A flash of gray in the corner of my eye, and dread spirals through me. I scan the crowd as more bodies pour across dirt paths and untrimmed fields, everything gone muddy with a thousand restless footprints. I tell myself maybe it wasn't really there. Maybe I'm imagining ghosts where there are only smiling faces.

Then I smell it. That rank pelt. That hot breath. Another streak of gray, and those familiar red eyes are peering out through the shadows.

There's a wolf in Golden Gate Park, and no one can see him but me. He's good at hiding, slipping behind wild roses and tiger lilies, settling down in the coastal scrub, always out of sight. He doesn't want anybody else to notice him. That's because he's mine. My omen, here to warn me about something.

Only, he's already too late. A dulcet laugh echoes right through me, down into my aching veins, into a body that still doesn't feel like my own.

"Hello again," they say, their voices in unison. Three girls in plain cotton frocks, their faces hard as concrete. These are the same ones from Rochester's bed last night. The girls that tried to stop Bee and me from leaving.

And maybe they'll get their wish tonight, because with their eyes on me, they're surrounding the car.

nine

The girls circle me, slowly at first, as calm and determined as vultures. Or sharks.

"Are you all alone?" they ask, their breath smelling of Marlboros and something sweet, something cloying like gumdrops.

"Apparently not," I say, as they slither around the Buick, grins on their faces, their hearts beating faster. They draw a little closer to me, and for once, I'm grateful I don't need to breathe, because they'd suffocate the air right out of me.

I sit back in the car, these strange girls swarming all around me. This is the first time I've really looked at their faces. At a distance, it's easy to mistake them as the same, in their identical dresses, their long hair frizzed and lifeless at their backs. But there are tiny differences in them, differences enough to matter.

The one with a splash of red freckles on her cheeks.

The one who can't make eye contact, who simply follows behind the others.

The one with an old scar on her jaw, an imprint of a fist perhaps, of a class ring once promised to her like a keepsake. Like a weapon.

They're young, the same way that I guess Daisy's young too, but I can't figure out much beyond that, the girls lost at sea in that interminable gulf between nineteen and all the years thereafter. When you've been alive as long as I have, every age starts to feel the same.

Another laugh, as lovely and unnerving as a church bell at midnight, and it sets my skin buzzing. The girls say something else, all of them speaking at once, their lips barely moving, but a motorcycle blares past, a thick stench of exhaust and old leather, and their words dissolve in the air like dishwater bubbles. I only hear the last word they say.

"Lucy."

I stare at them, part of me convinced I misheard. "How do you know my name?"

The girl with the freckles smiles. "From Edward," she says, like there could be no other answer. "He knows everything about you. All your secrets."

"I feel sorry for him then." After all, even I don't want to know my secrets.

The girls are leaning over the edge of the topless car now, their bodies nearly melting into the Buick, their thin fingers pressing into every corner of the torn upholstery. They reach around me and past me and even under me, and though they don't say it, I know what they're looking for. *Who* they're looking for.

They shouldn't even know about him. No one should. But maybe they're right. Maybe Rochester really can see things nobody else can. In that way, he and Dracula aren't so different. A couple of Peeping Toms who are always so impressed with themselves about all the places they keep peeping. As if their lack of dignity is a badge of honor.

The girls keep moving, keep searching, which means they'll find it soon. The last urn. Once they realize there's nowhere else to look, they'll figure out where I'm hiding him.

I squirm in the passenger seat. It's too late to run, even if I wanted to. Even if I could. My vision fades in and out, and for a moment, all I can hear are heartbeats I can't have.

"So you know me," I say. "But what about you? What are your names?"

At this, they seize up, their faces pinched, their shoulders rigid, each of them measuring me, what I'm up to. My chest constricts, and I wonder if this was the wrong thing to say, if they're liable to stake me too, the same as Renfield, sending my body back into oblivion before I've even had a chance to heal. But then all at once, they're smiling again. The kind of smile that seems to be laughing at you, even if you don't know why.

"I'm Bellflower," says the one with the freckled face, the one who must be the leader since the other two girls keep hanging on her every poisoned word. "And these are Vervain and Rowan."

She points first to the one with the scar and then to the one who still won't look at me or anybody else. Not that I'll remember which is which. In ten seconds, they'll look mostly identical to me again, their faces, rosy-cheeked and sun-kissed, bleeding together. I doubt Rochester can tell them apart either. They're just those girls waiting in his bed. No more, no less.

Only I don't want to be like him. I don't want to treat them as if they're alike, as if all girls are simply interchangeable.

"Bellflower, Vervain, Rowan," I repeat, already trying to remind myself. Then I hesitate. "Are those names you gave yourselves or names he gave to you?"

Bellflower's dark eyes flick up at me. "Is there a difference?"

"You know there is," I say, and another motorcycle revs past us on the crowded street. A Harley-Davidson probably. A Hells Angel. They're common as ants around these parts, their brows always knit, their fists always ready, each of them convinced they have all the reason in the world to be angry. But then, every angry man always thinks that, doesn't he?

Rowan leans against the passenger door, her cotton frock sagging around the collar. "It's not here. He said it would be here, but it's not."

Vervain shoots her a look that could stop time. "You always give up too easily."

"Yes, you do," Bellflower says, her smile never fading. "Besides, we just haven't looked hard enough."

At that, she reaches around the steering wheel and snatches the key from the ignition. I lunge for her, but I'm not nearly quick enough, everything about me as sluggish and hazy as the bay fog. Death always makes me like this, hungry as hell, but a little dizzy too. Like sipping one too many glasses of champagne.

The three girls dart toward the back of the car, their giggles rank as garbage. The sky tilts above me, as I heave open the door and stumble out. Across the nearby field, I search for the wolf, for Michael, for any ally at all, but they're long gone. I'm alone in a crowd of a thousand people.

The girls have gathered like euphoric pagans around the tail end of the Buick.

"I can already hear him," Vervain marvels, as Bellflower fumbles with the key, shoving it hard into the lock.

The trunk flips open, and as I stagger toward them, we all see it at the same instant. The interior has turned to ash, the upholstery curled away into nothing, the heat of him nearly melting through the chassis. Smoke in their eyes, the girls reach in and yank him from the darkness, fighting one another for who gets to hold him. Bellflower wins. In all their fights, I bet Bellflower always wins.

But not this time. I pounce at her, and we tumble together toward the sidewalk, both our hands wrapped tight around the urn. The clay's still as hot as ever, maybe even hotter. He's searing off our flesh, yet neither one of us will let him go. This is what he does to women. It's exactly the way he likes it.

As Bellflower tries to pin me down, Rowan and Vervain are right there next to us. They're crowded around me, but nobody stops to ask what's wrong. The three of them look like they've got it covered. Like they're helping a friend, some girl on a bad trip. Which in a way, I suppose that's exactly what I am.

I've still got hold of the urn, but so does Bellflower, and she's starting to yank it away from me. But I won't let her. With one quick twist of my hips, I wrestle Bellflower beneath me, pressing my knee into her chest, my fingers wrapped around her throat, feeling the gentle throb of her heart. So eager, so enticing.

All at once, the buzz of the crowd falls away, and Dracula's in me again, those familiar words echoing in my bones.

Take what belongs to you, Lucy.

The urn falls away from both of us, as I lean closer, her eyes slowly turning dark and vacant.

Rowan backs away. "I want to go home," she murmurs, but no one hears her. Vervain is too busy trying to pull me off, but she's barely a gnat, barely worth noticing. My hand tightens around Bellflower's throat as she squirms beneath me, her body already starting to go limp at my touch.

This isn't my fault. She did this to herself. She tried to steal what was mine, a monster that could unravel the world. As my teeth elongate, my skin humming, I tell myself I have no other choice. In a way, this is only self-defense.

"Lucy?" A voice calls out in the distance. It's Bee. From across the park, she sees me here, and instantly she knows what I'm about to do. The mistake I'm about to make.

With the girls' sweet heartbeats still ringing in my ears, my head lolls back. I won't do this. It's the one thing, the only thing, that separates me from Dracula.

My jaw set, I wrench away from Bellflower, falling back against the pavement, and she convulses for a moment, desperate to catch her breath. My vision blurs again, my hunger curdling in me, even worse than before, and I reach out for the urn, for something to steady me. But it's gone.

Already halfway across the street, Vervain's got it, and she wraps it up in the hem of her dress, the fabric smoldering against the heat of the urn.

The color returned to her face, Bellflower lets out a final laugh, sharp as dog rose thorns. "See you around, Lucy," she says, and in a flash, she's joined the other girls, the three of them skipping together to a cream-colored Volkswagen bus parked across the street.

Tittering, they climb inside, and I already know where they're going. Headed up the 101. Headed back to him.

I dodge toward them, but the crowd is too thick, the restless bodies pushing me back a step, just enough that I can't reach the girls before they start up the creaking engine.

I rasp out a scream and nearly dash out into traffic, when a hand suddenly catches my arm and pulls me back. Bee, standing at my side. Jane's with her too, and together, we watch the girls in the van vanish from the Haight.

"Do you know them?" I ask Jane, testing her.

She hesitates. "Yes," she says finally, as though she hardly wants to admit it to herself.

Bee helps me back to the car, my muscles like sludge, nothing in me bouncing back the way it should. I'm too hungry, too tired. But I know what we need to do, and with one look at Bee, she knows too.

The Buick roars to life, and we're off, crisscrossing through traffic, following them. Bee's behind the wheel, Jane up front next to her, me curled in the back seat, almost too exhausted to move.

"You shouldn't have come back for me," Jane keeps repeating, her voice splitting apart, her entire body shaking.

Bee grips the steering wheel tighter. "Please stop saying that," she whispers, but I'm starting to wonder if that's what Jane really wanted. To be left alone.

It's long past rush hour, but traffic's thick tonight, and we've already lost the pale Volkswagen on the highway. It doesn't matter. We just keep going, across the Golden Gate Bridge, the ocean obscure in the evening mist.

It takes less than an hour to get there. It might as well be an eternity. Up ahead of us in the dark, they could have already broken the urn. They could have done anything.

"Those girls are toying with you." Jane's wheezing now. "We should just disappear. Forget about them."

I grit my teeth, my cheek pressed against the crumbling leather seats. "It's not that simple," I say.

On a narrow back road, we take a sharp corner, and the house materializes before us.

Dahlia Hall.

I'm expecting another party, another serpentine line of cars twisting down the driveway. Only, there's no one here. No music seeping through the glass walls, no voices either, everything quieter than a graveyard at dawn. If we hadn't been here just last night, I would think this whole place had been abandoned for months.

But maybe not quite so abandoned. As Bee pulls off to the shoulder, I spot that pale Volkswagen parked at the top of the driveway. It might not be too late.

"Please," Jane says as we clamber across the lawn. "We don't need to do this."

She's grasping for us, desperation setting in, but I won't listen. With Bee at my side, I twist open the front door and step inside. It's dark, except for a small blaze in the fireplace casting strange outlines on the wall.

"I'm glad you could come." Rochester. He's waiting for us, stoking the flames with a brass poker. "I started this for you, Bertha. I know how much you love fire."

The blaze dances higher, and all at once, the strange outlines around us start to move. The shadows in the dark are girls, *his* girls: Bellflower, Vervain, and Rowan at the forefront, others looming behind them. There are fewer of them than last night—six, maybe seven of them total—but they're more determined than before. Only the most devoted must have gotten an invitation this evening. That's why they were so eager to prove they were worthy last night. It was an audition after all.

"I'm so sorry, Bee," Jane whispers, and the truth finally settles deep in my bones.

A trap. Jane let us walk right into a trap.

Rochester motions to her, and with her head down, she goes to him, not looking back, not even when Bee reaches frantically after her.

"My Jane's been a wonderful help," he says, and runs his hands through her hair, never noticing when she winces a little. "We couldn't have done it without her."

Bee gags up a sob, as we both finally understand it. That's why Jane came to us, why she was talking to Rochester back in L.A., why she was waiting in Golden Gate Park to separate me and Bee while the girls got the urn. This was always about Dracula.

Behind us, the front door is gaping open. We could turn back right now and run, but the fire dances, the light in the room shifting, and I see it there. The urn, wrapped in a silk handkerchief and clutched tight to Rochester's chest.

"How did you even know about him?" Bee asks, her voice like sandpaper on stone.

Rochester beams, and I've never seen anyone so smugly impressed with himself. "You see," he says. "I don't just call out to you, Bertha. I listen too."

These words boil in my bones. I was right. All this time, he's been eavesdropping on us, the same as Dracula.

There are no secrets these men won't steal, no private conversations they don't invite themselves to.

Grinning, he leans against the fireplace, Bellflower clutching tight to his shoulder, Vervain clutching tight to Bellflower, and Rowan clutching tight to herself, her eyes downcast. Jane cowers behind them, still not looking at Bee, standing back like a statue. Like a decoration.

I suddenly feel so very sorry for her. For all these girls. For what Rochester's done to them and what he still plans to do.

But one thing he doesn't understand: he might be a prophet in this house, but he's no vampire. And he's no Dracula.

I stare at him. "You really believe you can control him, don't you?"

"I don't want to control anyone," Rochester says, and snaps his tongue. All his acolytes mimic the sound, the whole room clucking at me at once. "Besides, you're the one who wants to control him."

"That's right," Bellflower says, as she reaches out and caresses the urn. "And we're going to help him. Then if we're lucky, he'll help us."

My throat closes up as I see it there, the promise of eternal life flashing in her eyes like wildfire. It's in all their eyes. This is what Rochester's offering them, how he's turned them pliant in his hands. They're just like Daisy, like all the others back in the Haight, like everyone, really. They're looking for something, and he's pretending he can give it to them.

Rochester's condemning all these girls to immortality, and he honestly thinks he's doing them a favor.

A sharp fury rises within me. "Monster," I say, and lunge toward him, but he's all the way across the room, and he's already expecting this.

He gives me that ugly smirk and passes the urn to Bellflower, letting her do the honors. She looks practically giddy about it, her delicate hand unscrewing the lid I so meticulously built all those years ago, not at all bothered as the hot clay burns away her flesh. With her gaze on me, she flips over the urn. Such a simple gesture, one that's so quick. So irrevocable, too.

The ashes spill into the air, and when she's sure it's empty, she lifts the urn above her head and thrusts it down hard onto the stone floor. It breaks apart into nothing, into less than nothing. Into something I can never repair.

I part my lips to scream, but no sound comes out.

Bee and I back away, the two of us slumped against the wood paneling, gazing through the glass walls. Dracula's coming now. I can feel him shivering through my body, the rest of his freed ashes rushing across the darkness toward us. Drawing nearer to himself, nearer to being whole again. I want to flee, to cry out, to go as numb as the dead, but then my rage bubbles up in me, and because I just can't help myself, I turn toward the others.

"He's going to murder all of you," I say, "and he's going to enjoy it."

At this, the girls chortle, their throaty laughter like

knives against my skin, but Rochester doesn't join in. He won't even look at me, something strange flickering across his face. Regret perhaps, a crawling realization that I might be right, that he might have made a terrible miscalculation.

Only it's too late. Dracula's here, the shadow of him draping over the front wall, obliterating the moonlight, as complete and unforgiving as an eclipse. He leaks into the room through the open door, one fistful of dust after another, and he does it slowly, like he knows he can take his time. After all, I can't stop him now. Nobody can.

Rowan looks directly at him, at the place where his face ought to be. "What *is* that?" she asks, as he swirls across the ceiling, his silhouette broader than before.

"That's what I promised you," Rochester says, and grips her hand, tight as a vise, pretending it's to comfort her, even though it's just to keep her from running away.

I wish I could run too. Instead, I stagger forward, desperate to stop this, but the dust from the last urn rises up higher, eager and ready. Above us, the two parts of Dracula join together, like ink blots bleeding across a crisp white page, and there it is, his body emerging, bit by bit. His cruel arms, his muscular thighs, his bare feet landing on the stone floor. And that face. That handsome and hideous face, watching me the way he always has.

"Hello, Lucy," he says, his voice like a most glorious requiem, and everything falls apart.

ten

I want to close my eyes. I want to scream. I certainly don't want to look right at him, looming there at the front door like a maelstrom, blocking our way out.

But even as I turn toward the wall, I can't escape. There's a strange gravity he brings with him, tugging you closer, the shadows growing longer, as though his very presence conjures its own atmosphere.

The girls are gathered around him, their voices growing to a fever pitch.

"What can we do?"

"What do you need from us?"

"What can you tell us about where you've been, what you've seen?"

They haven't even been properly introduced, but they're already eager to worship him, their hands pressed together as if in prayer. They're probably convinced that he's God, that everything Rochester told them is true.

And in a way, who can blame them? Dracula's material-ized in their midst, seemingly summoned from nothing. If that's not a god, then what is?

The dust settles around us, and I gaze right at him now. Dracula looks back at me, and it takes an impossi-bly long moment for me to realize there's not a stitch of fabric on him.

A flush of heat surges through me, and I avert my eyes again, but I can feel him grinning at me.

"Come now, Lucy," he purrs. "Don't pretend you've never seen me like this."

Their faces flushed, the girls draw closer to him. "Is this what you want from us?" someone asks, maybe Bell-flower, maybe Vervain. Whoever it is, they rally the oth-ers, all of them taking his naked body as an invitation, an encouragement. One after another, they cast off their clothes, their white cotton dresses fluttering to the floor, these uniforms Rochester commanded them to wear.

His arms crossed, Rochester doesn't join in. He just stands back and watches.

It's a tangle of skin and sweat now, everyone knotted together. On their knees, the girls are kissing Dracula's feet, his hands, his thighs, and I twist away and stare at the floor, at the heap of discarded clothes, not wanting to see where they'll kiss next. My cheeks keep burning, and I'm starting to cry, but I'm starting to laugh too, because here I am, trapped in a house with my resur-rected nightmare, and I don't know if I'm more terrified or embarrassed.

On the other side of the room, Jane's tucked back in a corner. She's the only one who hasn't joined them, her hair in her eyes, her shame at her feet. I want to call out to her, to tell her to come back to us, but Rochester looks up first, finally noticing his second wife is missing from the fray.

"Hurry up," he says, impatience blistering in his voice, and I hear Bee stir beside me.

"You don't have to do this," she whispers to Jane, but it's too late for that.

"*Now*," says Rochester, and with her hands trembling, Jane looks away from us and strips off her clothes, piece by aching piece.

Her blue dress, borrowed from Bee, from a life that no longer exists.

Her pale underwear, frayed around the elastic waistband.

Even the yellow ribbon in her hair.

She does it quietly, as if this is the last thing she'll ever do. Like a woman shuffling up to the gallows. When she's finished, her body bare, she shivers a little and joins the rest, vanishing into the throng until I lose sight of which one she even is.

Bee chokes up a single sob, and at last, I manage to reach out to her, grasping her hand. The front door is still blocked, but there's more than one way out of this house. Down the narrow hallway that never seems to end, the ceiling dipping below us, the house swallowing us whole.

"I'm not finished with you, Lucy," Dracula calls out, and they're following us now.

Bee and I get to the bedroom, slamming the door closed, but there are too many of them, piling against us on the other side. The polished hinges give way, and we tumble backward, the Buick key skittering out of Bee's hand, as the girls pour into the room, past the violet curtains and the oversized bed that's been put to use more times than anyone should count.

Gripping tight to each other, Bee and I rush across the floor, as Bellflower and Vervain flank Dracula, their bodies coiling around him, tighter than pythons. But he shakes them off and advances on me instead.

Dread tightening in my throat, I back against the wall, letting go of Bee's hand, hoping she'll get to the patio door, hoping she'll get away. At the back of the crowd, Rochester's giving us that ugly smirk of his. No Jane, though. Maybe she doesn't want to see this part.

Dracula inches closer to me, and everything about this is horribly familiar. His shadow envelops me like an abyss, and in a flash, he seizes my arm, pulling me into him, pressing my palm hard against his bare chest.

His touch is the same as I remember it, cold and impersonal, like the caress of a spider.

I try to wrench away, but he holds me there, forcing me to feel his body. I gag on air, but then something happens, something new. My fingers slip right through his skin. Again and again, I find them, scattered in a constellation across his chest.

Tiny spongy holes, pieces of him that are missing.

He tips his head down, his mouth gaping, and for the

first time in years, I see his teeth, sharp and ready. "What have you done with the rest of me?"

I stare back at him, at those bottomless eyes that never stop watching me. "The rest of you?"

"The last urn," he says, as my hand plunges deeper into him, grazing the spot where his heart should be. "The one from the parlor. Where is it?"

I pull away. "I have no idea," I say, shuddering, my fingertips still damp from being inside him.

"Liar," he says, and I hate him a little more. His eyes still on me, he backs away and whispers something to Vervain, and she brightens, motioning the others to follow her. They gather in a circle around the door they just dismantled, and even from here, I can tell it's built of wood. Walnut probably, or maybe redwood. Either way, they know what to do with it. At least a few of them have seen the movies. After all, these days, everybody knows how to kill a vampire.

With their bare hands, they tear the door apart, plucking the splintered pieces from the wreckage, weapons they can use against me. As they work, frenzied and determined, Dracula beams at them like a proud father. He knows this won't vanquish me for good, but that doesn't matter. He so dearly loves to watch me die.

Except he won't get the satisfaction. Bee's at the patio door, flipping the latch, wrenching it open, the night breeze whispering in.

"Lucy, this way," she calls out before darting into the darkness.

I sprint across the room after her, but when I reach the door, I turn back. As the others start toward me, their makeshift stakes in hand, Dracula takes hold of Bellflower, his arm looped around her waist, their bodies pressed together. They sway across the stone floor, dancing to music no one else can hear. She lolls back in his embrace, under his thrall already, and he guides her to the bed, his gaze flitting up at me.

He wants me to see this part.

His mouth on her throat, that look of ecstasy on her face. That expression will fade soon enough, once she realizes what he's really doing, how deep the pain can go, how long it can last. How she'll never be able to return to this moment and reverse it. How many times she'll relive it anyhow.

"Don't," I wheeze, but Bee reaches through the open door and grasps my hand, pulling me out into the night.

Together, we dash past the edge of the electric-blue pool, taking the same sinuous path around the house we did last night. The others are right behind us, their footfalls heavy, their laughter like venom.

Bee and I get all the way to the bottom of the driveway, all the way to the Buick, before we realize it.

The car key. We lost it inside.

I turn, ready to run back to the house for it, but they're coming faster now, a sea of wooden stakes quivering in their calloused hands. Just how many times are they planning to kill me?

Bee climbs inside the car and sags against the steering

wheel, her fingers fumbling with the ignition, trying to will the engine to life. Trembling, I put one hand on her arm.

"Leave it," I say, and the words ache inside me.

Our bucket of rusted bolts, the taillight we never fixed, the upholstery we tried duct-taping into place until even that seemed pointless. But this belonged to us, *our* Buick. Now we have to abandon it, just one more thing these men have stripped away from us.

Our hands wrapped together, Bee and I disappear into the canopied hills where the overgrowth is thick as shadows. Briars cut into our bare legs, but we don't stop, and we don't let go of each other.

Distant laughter ricochets through the trees. The girls are still tracking us, the wild foxes in their hunt, but Bee and I keep climbing, through heavy brush and past towering pines.

Together, we reach the top of a sharp ridge and look down at the other side of the hill. The Pacific Ocean shimmers diamond-bright below us, San Francisco glinting like a daydream just beyond it, but it's still miles away. It's the shortest night of the year, and we've got nowhere left to go.

"I really don't want to die again." Bee stares down at her arms, at that thing slithering inside her skin. "I was entirely gone, you know, when it pulled me back. But even when I was dead, I could feel it from far away. Crawling inside me, filling up my body like a limp balloon."

This is the first time she's ever talked about this.

I peer at her in the dark. "How many times for you? Dying, I mean?"

"Only once. From the fire."

That fire, the moment that changed everything. All of Rochester's power was in Thornfield Hall. In that land, in that attic. When Bee scorched it to cinders, he lost it all. His chance to bestow immortality on whomever he chose. Now he's got to settle for the next best thing. He's conjured Dracula to do the job for him. When this is over, Rochester will have a houseful of wives and a party that never ends.

At least that's his plan. I wonder what Dracula will have to say about that.

"How about you?" Bee asks. "How many times have you died?"

I shake my head. "I don't remember anymore."

"That many?"

"Yeah."

Bee gazes across the water at the glittering skyline. "So I guess this is it," she says. "We've got nobody left, Lucy."

I hesitate. "That's not entirely true."

Bee turns sharply, studying my face in the gloom. "Is Michael even around?"

I nod, my throat going dry. "I saw him at Golden Gate Park tonight," I say. "While I was waiting on you and Jane."

Bee winces at that name, as if I spat fire at her.

A long moment, the locusts bleating in our ears, a coyote howl in the distance, before she asks it, the question that's haunting her.

"It was all an act with Jane, right? She was just pretending to still love me back in L.A.?"

A tremor in her voice, so soft, so small, and it nearly cuts my heart in two. This is what she wants to believe, what will make everything so much easier. That Jane doesn't love her and never has.

"I don't know, Bee," I say. "Maybe it's complicated."

She scoffs. "It was never complicated with you and Dracula."

I rasp out a laugh. "It's *always* been complicated with me and Dracula."

A heavy silence cuts between us. Bee and I have never discussed this. We promised we wouldn't ask questions the other didn't want to answer. But after all these years, there are things we barely know about each other. Things we should know, things we should have talked about, screamed about, not held inside us like malignant tumors.

A rustling in the nearby coastal scrub, and Bee's face goes wan. "Maybe you should call Michael."

We creep farther along the ridge and down to the nearest road. When we reach the potholed shoulder, all the white lines worn away, Bee stands back, and I close my eyes.

Even from miles off, I can hear Michael's heartbeat, slow and steady. I envision him, alone behind the wheel of Walter's rickety Ford pickup. Where did his grandfather think he was going when he asked to borrow the truck? Not to pursue a vampire, that's for sure.

I hold him in my mind, hold him close. "I'm here," I say.

This is an imprecise art, and we don't have much time

left. Michael might not make it before sunrise. If he's still back in the city, it could take him an hour to find us, maybe longer, and that's if he even heard me.

He's here in less than ten minutes. The truck idles up beside us, that familiar robin's-egg blue, the passenger door flicking open.

"Need a ride?" he asks, smiling. Bee clambers inside, but I seize up, Michael's heartbeat threading through me.

I don't want to do this. I don't want to use him, and I certainly don't want to sit right next to him, not when I'm this famished. Nothing about me is safe.

But what's coming up behind us isn't safe either. Their voices echo in the shadows, that faceless crowd, their bloodlust rivaling my own.

Bee turns back to me, the dome light bathing the interior of the pickup in a sallow yellow. She senses it in me, the way I'm frozen again.

"Come on, Lucy," she says, her voice soft, her hand outstretched to me.

I reach back, and she pulls me inside the truck, yanking the door closed behind me. The bald tires squeal on uneven asphalt, and the last thing I see before we vanish down the road are those terrible eyes peering out from the brush at the top of the ridge. I wonder how long they've been watching us.

We drive a little ways, maybe a mile, maybe ten miles, the trees bleeding past us, everything bleeding past.

"I wasn't sure I'd find you," Michael says, but of course he did. He must have already been nearby, north across the Golden Gate Bridge and detoured off the 101, cutting down these back roads, searching for me. Searching because I haven't given him any other choice.

We're back on the highway now, and Michael's hands are steady on the wheel. "Where do you want to go?"

I watch the horizon, daylight leaking up over the edges of the world. "Anywhere indoors."

He takes us back to San Francisco, to a no-tell motel where he's been staying. It's a tacky little joint in the Marina District, all the doors painted butter yellow, a red neon sign with half the letters burned out.

We trudge up to the third floor and down a corridor with too many corners, where anybody could be lying in wait. Beneath a fluorescent light, the bare bulb flickering, Michael fumbles with the room key, his hands shaking, everything about him nervous as a schoolboy. I remember suddenly how young he is, all of twenty-two, and how he's probably never rented his own motel room, let alone invited girls inside.

Not that Bee cares a bit about him. Once he finally unlocks the door, she files in like a weary warrior and collapses on the first bed she sees. She's out in a minute. I envy her for it.

Across the room, Michael tugs all the curtains closed. Then he wavers at the edge of the second bed where I've stretched out, my shoes kicked off.

"I can sleep on the floor if you want," he says, even though he knows that isn't what I want at all.

"It's fine," I say, and he slides beneath the blanket next to me, his body warm and inviting, his heartbeat thrumming faster.

I curl against him, and I'm so tired, so hungry. He'd let me have a taste if I asked. He'd let me have anything I want. But I won't. Because it's not his choice. Because Bee's in the next bed, and I don't want a witness. I don't want them to know what I'm really like.

Thin fingers of daylight seep in at the perimeter of the curtains. They're not near enough to be a danger, but I watch the light anyhow, desperate for something to focus on, wondering where Dracula and Rochester and their followers are now. Wondering where Renfield is too. A fragment of hope blooms in my chest as I remember what Dracula said. The last urn. It's still out there somewhere. Renfield must not have found it.

I think again of the furnace vent upstairs in that house, that strange and busy house where people come and go, hidden behind closed doors.

A sudden chill seizes me. The urn's not just somewhere. I already know exactly where it is.

At dusk, Michael drives Bee and me across town. Back to Haight-Ashbury. Back to Daisy's house.

She greets us at the front door, her eyes bright. "I knew you wouldn't leave for good," she says, but I'm not looking at her now.

There's a piece of cardboard tacked to the outside of the door, with skull and crossbones drawn in magic marker and a simple message scribbled in cheerful, bubble letters.

> *German measles*
> *KEEP OUT*

Apparently, the sign's worked, too, because as Bee and I edge inside, Michael lagging behind us, everything's different, the downstairs quiet as a tomb. This party house with nobody around to party except for Daisy.

"I'm not sure they're really sick," she says, her worried eyes flitting up the steps. "But they sent everyone away anyhow."

"Who sent them away?" Bee glances between us. "Lucy, what's going on?"

"Come on," I whisper, taking her hand, leaving Michael behind.

Together, we tiptoe upstairs to the bedroom at the end of the hall. The one that was closed yesterday. Even now, girls are still giggling inside.

Without making a sound, I nudge open the door, and there they are. Five of them, the same girls Daisy introduced us to that first morning here. They're sitting cross-legged in a circle, reverent and wide-eyed, the urn in the center of the room. It's limned in a ring of flowers, the stems all knotted together, the petals wilted from being so close to him, to his decay.

An altar. This is their altar to him.

And that's not all the girls have done. The outside of Dracula's urn is practically Technicolor now, nearly every bit of surface area arrayed in colorful tempera paint. Tulips and peace signs and—my personal favorite—at least three different dandelion-yellow suns. The girls have turned the clay into a canvas for their own tiny mural, and I've got to admit, it doesn't look half-bad. If nothing else, Dracula would hate it, which makes me like it even more.

The five of them blink up at me, their cheeks flushed. These girls are sick all right, but it's not with measles. It's something different, something no doctor could diagnose. A lovesickness of sorts, a thrall in the making. They want Dracula all to themselves—that's why they put that sign on the front door, anything to keep others away.

"Show's over," I say, and start toward the urn, but the girls scramble to their feet.

"Who says it's yours?" they ask, frowning, and honestly, it's a fair question.

"I made it," I say. "That should give me some kind of claim."

They snap their tongues. "You didn't make what's inside," they say, and they're not wrong. I stare at them, at the whole line of girls, thinking how they might not be the worst people to take care of him. They clearly haven't tried to free him, and let's face it, they've kept this urn intact longer than I probably would have.

"Listen," I say, "you don't know what you're dealing with here."

One of the girls rolls her eyes. "That's what the other woman said too."

I squint at her. "What other woman?" I ask, and they all nod behind me.

Her shadow passes over us, even before I turn around, the shape of her emerging from the dusty corner behind the door.

Jane Eyre, with tears in her eyes and a stake in her hand.

eleven

Jane doesn't move. She just stands there in the shadows, backed against the wall, like a still life, like a dour wax figure from Madame Tussauds.

Bee stares back at her, her gaze fire-bright. "Get out of here. *Now*."

"Bee, please." Jane's voice is spiderweb-thin. "I came to help."

"Really?" I gape at her, edging back a step, half tripping over the ring of flowers. "Then why the hell do you have that?"

I point at the stake gripped in her hand. She looks down at it and lets out a little squeak, as though she's as surprised as we are, before tossing it away like a cherry bomb. It rolls quietly across the floor, stopping sullenly beneath an open window.

"That's not what it looks like." Jane winces, flushing

with embarrassment. "It's not for you, Lucy. It's for him. In case he followed me here."

I nearly laugh aloud at this. It's something I hadn't even considered. There's more than one vampire in this city now. And by the time Dracula's done, there's going to be a whole lot more.

I take another step back, inspecting Jane, her eyes downcast, and I'm curious if she really wants to help, or if this is just another of her tricks.

"How did you know the urn was here?" I ask finally.

"I didn't." She clasps her hands together in front of her, a girly flourish, and for a moment, she looks every bit as young as she was when she died. No more than a child, no more than twenty. "I wasn't looking for him. I was looking for you."

Her eyes are on Bee now, and they watch each other, their stares naked, the years taut between them. Once again I fidget, feeling like an invader.

I must not be the only one who doesn't want to be here, because there's a creak of the floor and a tiny giggle, and when I look behind me, the other girls are gone. So is the urn.

I roll my eyes. "Of course." I say, and I'm back down the stairs in an instant, my head still woozy, the hunger drilling deeper into me.

Downstairs, Michael's waiting in the living room, right next to the spot where I died. Daisy's sidled up beside him, her hand on his arm, trying to coax him into letting her read his palm.

"They say I'm really good." She's smiling up at him, sweet as spun sugar, and even though he doesn't seem to notice her, a pang of jealousy sears through me anyhow.

I try to shake it off. "Where did those girls go?"

"Out the back," Daisy says, motioning brightly. I dart through a beaded curtain into the kitchen, past a Formica table with a hot plate nobody bothered to turn off and a sardine can for an ashtray.

"Lucy, wait," Michael says, and they're all following me now. Him and Daisy. Bee and Jane, too.

"Please," Jane keeps pleading. "Let me explain."

They keep in step with me, and all I can think is how this is ridiculous. I should be alone. Tracking down Dracula's remains shouldn't be a spectator sport.

Across a scraggly lawn, we cut down an alley behind a long row of narrow houses, Daisy pointing out every shortcut, until we finally emerge on the main drag.

Haight Street in all its scrappy glory.

Screen-printed posters are plastered in every storefront window, colorful graffiti sprucing up the crumbling white facades. At the corner of an old building, we pass a green bumper sticker that says BE A PUBLIC NUISANCE in big block letters. Next to us, there's a pay phone that's got a different kind of message. DON'T SAY ANYTHING ON THIS PHONE THAT YOU WOULDN'T SAY TO A COP.

I see the girls up ahead, and I want to break into a sprint, I want to run with everything left in me. But that's the problem: there's not much left besides my hunger. I'm still famished from yesterday, from when I returned like a phoenix from the ash. My head spinning, Michael does his best to help me along, Daisy right next to him.

"It'll be all right," she whispers to me, and I wonder if that's true.

Behind us, Bee and Jane are still arguing.

"I didn't know," Jane's saying.

"You didn't know what?" Bee's voice, sharp as barbed wire. "That you shouldn't conjure a vampire back from the dead?"

I struggle ahead, trying to outpace them, the street reeking of exhaust. There are people everywhere, kids walking past us, frayed sandals on their feet, rolled-up sleeping bags on their shoulders.

There are tourists too, some of them behind the windows of chartered buses, others free-range on the sidewalk, all of them openly gawking at us. They snap quick pictures on their Polaroids and their Dianas, the flashbulbs so bright in the dark they nearly blind you, and when they're sure they've got the shot, they give us smug smiles, daring us to do anything about it. I imagine what they'll say when they retreat home to their precious picket fences in Iowa or Indiana or the rolling plains of Texas.

"Hippies in their natural environment," they'll tell the blue-haired ladies at Sunday school, as they pass around the pictures of us like contraband.

If only they knew what we really are.

We're out of the Haight now, passing over trolley tracks, headed toward the bay, Daisy narrating merrily as we go.

"I used to stay at a place right over there on Larkin for a while," she says, "but then it became a bad scene."

I shake my head. "Isn't everywhere with people a bad scene?" I ask, and all at once, my legs give out, and I nearly crumple to the pavement.

Michael catches my arm just in time. "You all right?"

"Sure," I say, but we both know it isn't true. The decay stirs within me, stronger than before. It sits in my belly like lead, it pools beneath my fingernails, black as a malignant growth. My hunger's taking me over from the inside, hollowing me out, and it won't stop. It'll keep gnawing away until there's no more me left.

We lose the girls in the crowd and find them again a block later, though they're always just out of reach. I don't know their names, but even if I did, it wouldn't do any good to call out to them. They're not going to do the polite thing and bring back the urn.

At a dusty corner, a streetcar whizzes past us, and I turn to Daisy. "Did you know they had one of the urns upstairs?"

She shrugs. "Sure," she says. "I thought you left it behind for them. Like a souvenir or something."

I gape at her. "Why would I do that?"

"How should I know?" She takes a step back, her brow knit. "I don't know why you have those things in the first place. Or even what they are." She shakes her head, looking wounded. "You and Bee are all about your secrets, aren't you?"

This hits me dead center. She's only known us three days, and she's already figured that out.

A giggle ricochets through the air, and up ahead, I spot them again. Those five girls, darting across the street. They're rushing toward a towering stone building, slipping between a group of people on the sidewalk and disappearing inside.

"What is that place?" I ask, and Daisy peers over the bobbing heads of the endless crowd.

"That's the Fillmore," she says. "A music hall."

I exhale a ragged sigh. Of course it is. Somewhere loud and crowded and hard to find them.

We dodge across the street, everyone following my lead. There's a line beneath the marquee, but Daisy cuts to the front and sweet-talks the bouncer, some guy she apparently knows from a house over on Van Ness. I can't hear what she says, but it must be the right thing, because with a grin, he waves us on, and we all slide right through the front door like a knife in butter.

"Have fun, Daisy," he calls after her, and she tosses her head back and laughs.

Inside, it's dark and cramped, the air unbearably moist, the ceiling cloud-high. There's a band onstage, a group I think I've heard before, and a liquid light show behind them. The whole wall's immersed in splotches of color, like we're standing inside a giant lava lamp.

Daisy bops back and forth, trying to get Michael to dance with her, trying to get me to dance too. Even when we shrug her off, she doesn't stop, nothing cracking that smile of hers.

She's the only one having a good time, though. Behind us, Bee and Jane are still going at it.

"He only told us you two were imprisoning somebody," Jane's saying. "That you'd been holding him hostage for years."

"Because we had no other choice."

"I didn't know that."

A long moment, the crowd pulsing closer, before Bee finally asks it, the question that's been haunting her. "Is that the only reason you came to L.A.?"

Jane doesn't miss a beat. "You know it's not."

They fall back now, Bee overwhelmed at the throng, at how claustrophobic a ballroom can feel. But I keep going. The speakers crackle with static, and onstage, a singer with a fringe of dark hair over her eyes croons about pills and rabbits and a girl named Alice. With everyone pushing nearer, my hunger gnaws at me again, raw and cruel, and I glance around at the anonymous faces, their bodies swaying, all loose limbs and relentless heartbeats.

How long would it take me to murder everyone on the dance floor? A minute? An hour? Some of them would surely get away first, fleeing through front doors and back doors, any doors that will have them. But at least a few of them would stay, huddling behind one another, frozen like our statue of Venus, unable to move, unable to scream. The same way I was when Dracula came for me.

How many people has he murdered at once? A whole

kingdom's worth, or is it far fewer than that? And even if he only seduces a single victim at a time, does that make him any better? Or does it just make him more methodical?

I snap to attention, afraid I've lost the girls, but there they are, threading through the crowd, passing the urn between them like it's a game. I keep moving after them, past kids who stare back at me like they know me, their gazes sliding over my face. Sometimes they whisper, and sometimes I hear them.

"That's her. The one they're talking about."

"The one who doesn't die."

"At least not for long."

My cheeks burn. I'm a walking freak show, an urban legend in the flesh. Something that has no right to exist.

A few of them start to follow me, desperate to be faithful disciples.

"What do you need from us?" they ask, nipping at my heels, impatient as puppies, and I cringe, since that's the same thing those girls asked Dracula last night.

What do they expect me to tell them? How they can be immortal too? Or how the afterlife is a real drag, like a bad trip that never ends?

But I envy them a little, because I remember what it was like to be them. To want something better. I'd given up on that years ago. I'd given up on everything because of Dracula.

I manage to break away, pushing between bodies, everyone twisted together. At last I stumble upon the girls, and they look startled to see me. That gives me an opening, my chance.

I put both hands on the urn. "He's mine," I say, and something surges inside me, something dangerous. Something like him.

The girls must sense it in me, because all at once, their grasp on the urn goes slack, and they start to back away.

"He warned us about you," one of them says. "You're not as nice as you pretend to be, are you, Lucy?"

My hands quivering, I press the urn to my chest. "I never said I was."

I should run now, but I don't even make it two steps before my head goes dizzy, and I wilt in the middle of the dance floor, still clutching the urn. Instantly, a crowd gathers around me.

"She needs air," Daisy says, and even though that's not true, it's not a terrible idea. Fresh air would be outside, and outside would be closer to escape.

Michael helps me up, and I cling to him, one arm wrapped around his neck, the other clasping the urn.

"This way," Daisy says, our eager tour guide as we slip through a service door, all of us stumbling into an alley. Bee and Jane are already here, lingering out in the open, still at each other's throats.

"Lucy's sick because of you." Bee glowers at Jane. "She died when we were looking for *you*."

Jane purses her lips, on the precipice of tears. "I didn't do this."

"You sure didn't help."

They keep on like this, but I can't hear them. The world spins around me, their voices bleeding into static, everything bleeding together.

I sag against Michael, and he pulls me closer. "What can I do?" he asks, his heartbeat ringing in my ears, his scent like pine, like home.

It only takes a moment for it to happen.

"Uh-oh," Daisy murmurs, watching me, understanding maybe for the first time what I really am. Bee and Jane turn toward us, their argument left hanging in the air, the two of them seeing it at the same time.

My wet mouth. Michael's limp body. That glinting, unforgivable look in my eye, the one that makes me grateful I can't see my own reflection anymore.

"Lucy," Bee whispers, her face gone gray. "What have you done?"

I want to answer her, I want to tell her it's not what it looks like, but we all know it's exactly what it looks like.

"It wasn't that much," I say, but Michael's drooping in my arms, the blood clotting on his collar, thick and dark.

The world's a blur around me, the blood settling in my veins, the decay receding. I'm starting to feel like myself again, and I hate everything about it.

We're moving now, out onto the street, Michael's body propped up between Bee and Jane, his arms slung over their shoulders. I'm behind them, not wanting to get too close. After all, I already got close enough.

"Come on." Daisy's leading us. Of course she is. She's the one who always knows the way. "There's a place we can take him."

We're back in the Haight, rushing into a dark building and up a flight of narrow wooden steps, past a circular brown sign with simple white letters. HAIGHT ASHBURY FREE MEDICAL CLINIC.

We burst into the waiting room, a motley crew, three of us dead and one on his way.

"Help us," Daisy cries out, and a nurse jolts to her feet.

"What happened?" She's clinging to a brown clipboard, her smock bright white.

"He lost a lot of blood," I say, and I wonder how much. A pint? Two pints? More than that? How much of him have I taken for my own?

The nurse hurries us through the labyrinthine hallways and into a narrow room toward the back. We have to squeeze together to fit inside, Michael slumped on the exam table, a veil of sweat on his brow, the rest of us gathered around him. He's still breathing, though, he's still alive. I tell myself that's all that matters.

A wad of gauze on his throat, red seeping through, blotching the nurse's fresh smock.

"I'll get the doctor," she says before vanishing out the door, leaving us alone with what I've done.

The room stinks of bleach and bandages and a fresh coat of paint. There's a mural on one wall, slathered in Day-Glo blue and hot pink and blaze orange, so garish it makes your eyes ache.

But it's not the bright colors, not the fluffy clouds or the too-golden suns that gets me. It's the painted faces. Dozens of them, maybe hundreds, staring out at us from the plaster. Some in profile, some turned away, a few gawking at us dead-on, all of them impassive and cold, their eyes little black splotches that never blink, that never tire. I guess the mural is supposed to make us feel welcome, but all it does is make my skin crawl.

Daisy stands back in the corner, blocking one of the faces with her body.

"This place has only been open a couple weeks," she says as though we're lucky, as though I couldn't have timed my attack better. And she's not wrong—we *are* lucky. I doubt any other emergency room in this town would admit us, and they certainly wouldn't take us in without demanding answers I can't possibly give them.

Michael murmurs on the table, and he's coming around again, his eyes still glazed but half-open now. Bee and Jane hover over him, purse-lipped like concerned mothers, and Daisy drifts forward, gingerly pressing the gauze into the wound.

"The bleeding's stopped," she says, hope blooming in her voice. "See?"

But I won't look. I won't get near him, not even when he reaches out, grasping uselessly for my hand.

"Lucy," he whispers, devoted to the last. Devoted because I made him that way.

I back against the wall. "This never happened before,"

I whisper, like that's an excuse. Like that somehow makes it all right.

Bee watches me, and for the first time, she asks me a question she knows I don't want to answer. "But haven't you ever been that hungry before?"

"Yes," I say, already knowing what will come next.

Bee hesitates before asking, "What did you do then?"

Regret hangs over me, heavy as burlap. "I drank from *him*," I say, not looking at her. "From Dracula."

It's something I've never told anyone, something I've tried for years to forget.

How I tracked him to the Carpathian Mountains, my heart already cold in my chest from what he'd done to me. What he'd still do to so many others if I didn't stop him. How when I got there, he took it as an invitation. Because once he realized I could return from dust like he did, murdering me became his courting ritual.

"For you, my darling," he'd say and turn me to ash again and again, waiting patiently for my return. Waiting for me to come back, starved and desperate.

He counted on that. He counted on me needing him. And I did. I used him because it was the only way to stop him, the only way for me to be strong enough to fight back. But it also made me a monster like him. Because it wasn't just his blood I was drinking. It was the blood of everyone he'd ever plucked from a crowd, the bodies he claimed for his own. I was drinking my own blood and Mina's blood and the blood of a thousand other girls who'd come before us. Girls whose names have been forgotten to time, forgotten even by their own families. Girls who were tally marks, aperitifs for him.

One thing those girls got, though: they were lucky enough to die. *Really* die. A stake through their hearts, and they were gone for good. They didn't come back from dust like me. Like Dracula.

"You're not the same as the others," he always whispered to me in the dark, as though it was a compliment instead of a curse.

I stand back, not saying anything else, shame boiling in me. For the way he made me just like him. For the way I went along with it, because I honestly felt I had no other choice.

"It wasn't your fault," Bee says, but I only shake my head, wishing that were true.

The eyes on the wall are still watching me when the doctor bursts into the room. He's younger than I expect—everyone's so young here—but he's got that serious look of someone who's seen enough to know enough.

A sharp snap of a plastic glove, and he inspects the bite marks on Michael before glancing up at us. "How'd he get this wound?"

None of us say a word—none of us even look at him now—and he doesn't ask again. Around here, this probably isn't the first time he's gotten a half answer or no answer at all.

The stethoscope on Michael's chest, and the doctor

listens close. "His heart rate's steady," he says, though I could have told him that. "His breathing's good too."

Daisy jumps forward a little, anxious as a colt. "He'll survive, then?"

The doctor smiles. "Looks like it."

Michael's half sitting up now, a bit of color swirling again in his cheeks. The doctor's right. He will survive— so long as I don't get hold of him again.

The urn quivers in my hands. I can't be trusted with it. After tonight, it's obvious I can't be trusted with anything. Daisy's still got her crocheted bag slung across her shoulder, and I tuck the urn inside, leaving it with her. This is the best thing I can do. The only thing I can do now. Then I'm gone, out the door.

Bee calls my name, her voice a barb in my back, but I won't turn around. I just keep going, through the impossible maze of hallways, down the steep steps, and out into the night.

The June air tastes of mist and brine, the ocean whispering between buildings, so close yet too far away to see. I wander down the block, headlights flashing across my face, jubilant voices screeching like bald tires on wet cement. I don't belong here, but then again, neither does anyone else. We're all invaders in this neighborhood, pushing into spaces where we weren't invited.

I'm lingering at a corner, a Bank of America sign overhead, when a car slows next to me, the ragged engine turning over. I jump back, startled, but when the stoplight changes, I walk on, trying to ignore it. This car won't ignore me, though. It keeps pace at my side, paying no heed to the other vehicles that honk and speed around it on the wrong side of the road.

I finally glance up, ready to tell the driver to take a hike, but my throat goes dry when I see it.

A cracked taillight, rust on the bumper, leather upholstery spewing yellow foam. The Buick. *Our* Buick.

The top's still down, so he's easy to spot there in the driver's seat. Dracula, handsome and wicked as heartbreak. In the glow of the streetlight, he looks the same as when we met, his body broad and foreboding. Dark hair, dark eyes, the weight of the night in his stare. He's everything I pretend I don't want.

And he's not alone. There's a group of long-haired girls with him, all chattering and wide-eyed in the back seat, passing a joint back and forth, so naïve that it aches bone-deep in me. He's going to eat them up alive unless someone stops him.

Unless I stop him.

Grinning, he leans across the seat, leans toward me.

"Need a ride, Lucy?" he asks, and flicks open the door.

twelve

I stare at the three girls in the back seat, all faded denim and iridescent beads strung around their necks like nooses. They're so young, even younger than Daisy. Runaways, maybe. The Haight's got plenty of those. This is a place where everyone's searching for something else, something better. And that's what Dracula's offering them. He'll break that promise, of course, the same way he'll break everything else about them.

"I know what you're thinking," he says, watching me. "That's why you should come along. Make sure I behave."

Then he flashes me that smile, the one that started all this trouble.

The streetlight flickers above us, and the girls are giggling as they blow smoke rings, their legs in a tangle in the back seat, a human rat-king.

I want to yank them out of the car, one by one, nudge them along the sidewalk like wayward toddlers, and send them on their way. But they won't listen to me, not without convincing, not without force, and I don't have time for that. Another car comes revving up behind the Buick, honking impatiently.

"Make up your mind, Lucy." Dracula still hasn't taken his eyes off me. "I don't have all night."

Except that's exactly what he has, what we both have. All night, all eternity.

The passenger door is still hanging open, like a question I don't want to answer. I shouldn't do this. I shouldn't put myself at his mercy. But then again, there's a lot of things I shouldn't do.

My heart in my throat, I slide in, and he doesn't hesitate. The car jerks into gear, and we surge forward, the sidewalk a haze around us, voices on the street fading like static into the night.

Dracula leans back, inspecting my face. "There's something different about you."

"No, there's not," I say, fidgeting, not wanting him to look any closer. Not wanting him to notice the fresh color in my cheeks, the brightness in my eyes.

But a harsh smirk blossoms on his lips, and he sees it anyhow. "So," he says, already savoring what I've done, "is that little soldier of yours still breathing? Or did you take every single drop of him?"

"Michael's fine," I say, remorse settling in my guts.

"What was he like, Lucy?"

I shiver a little, the taste of licorice, the taste of Michael still lingering on my tongue.

"I don't remember," I say.

Dracula heaves up a chuckle. "Liar."

Rage churns in me. I scan the car for a weapon, for something made of wood, but then I remember: this was *our* car, mine and Bee's. And we knew better than to keep anything handy that could kill a vampire.

My hands knot in my lap, and I need to focus. I need to figure out a way to get these kids out of the car. Only I don't really know how to do this. How do you tell a total stranger they've been dog-eared for the slaughter?

So I try something different, something to earn their trust first. "I'm Lucy," I say, turning around, smiling back at them. "Where are you from?"

A little part of me dies. Small talk. I'm making small talk.

It must be working, though, because one of the girls gives me a big toothy grin. "We're from all over," she says, and I think how their bodies will be scattered all over too, if Dracula gets his way.

We're at a stoplight now, and this is it, our perfect chance to run. I gaze back at them, at those fresh faces that believe they've figured out the world when they haven't even figured out themselves.

"Why don't we get out here?" I ask. "I know a house on Waller where we can crash."

But the kids just gape back at me. "It's way too early for that," one of them says. "Besides, he told us about this great party spot up north. That's where we want to go."

"Yeah, Lucy," Dracula says. "That's where they want to go."

We don't have much longer here. Another ten seconds, the light will change again, and the Buick will be in motion, carrying us away, carrying them to their graves.

My chest constricts, panic setting in. "You need to get out of the car," I say. "*Now*."

The girl in the middle tilts her head, one brow arching up. "Why?"

"Because," I say, my voice steadier than it has any right to be, "he's going to kill you."

This should scare them, this should do *something*, but the girl just rolls her eyes.

"Man," she says, and shoots a look at Dracula, "your old lady's a real drag."

Dracula lets out a sharp laugh. "I warned you," he says, and all the kids in the back laugh too. Laugh at me.

I sink down in the passenger seat, wondering if there's anyone left in the Haight who hasn't heard Dracula complain about me.

The light turns green, and we're off again, every road sinuous and steep. Dracula takes the curves fast, the tires threatening a blowout with every jolt of the wheel. The Buick's looking worse than before, Dracula's decay as potent as poison. The dashboard's got a crack right down the middle, the chrome on the accessories and wiper knobs peeling away, the seat belt buckles rusted around the edges. He's done more damage in an evening than I've done in a year.

Another sharp turn, and the girls in the back whoop like this is the ride of their lives. And maybe it is. Maybe they've never felt so alive. Pity that feeling won't last.

"So you're taking them back to him," I say, as the Golden Gate Bridge materializes out of the fog. "Back to your new best friend."

At this, Dracula's eyes go darker than sin. "Don't call him that."

"But that's what he is," I say. "It took you centuries, but you finally met somebody as depraved as you."

Another smirk. "You mean, when I met you?"

The Buick rockets across the bridge, as the kids chatter in the back, my prediction of their impending doom already a distant memory. Cars smear past us in the other lane, and I study the narrow concrete sidewalk next to us. It's late, and there aren't many people out strolling across the water tonight. Only a single figure up ahead that seems to be watching us. A strange bundle of a man, more shadow than human.

As we pass him, my stomach corkscrews. "Was that—" I start to ask, but Dracula rolls his eyes.

"Yes," he says, cutting me off. "He's been following me all over the city."

I stare at him, incredulous. "Of course he has," I say. "That's what you've always expected of him."

"And he's done his job now," Dracula says, waving one hand in the air, as if that's that.

Poor Renfield. He gave his life, gave his afterlife too, and now everybody wants to forget he even exists.

I watch him disappear in the rearview mirror, his body growing smaller and smaller in the dark until he's nothing at all.

"I don't know why you're so worried about him," Dracula says. "He did kill you, after all."

"Only because you told him to."

"That's true," he says with a boyish smirk, like murdering me was no more than a silly prank. "How was it over there by the way? In that waiting room from hell?"

I hesitate, peering at him in the dark. "You've been there?"

"Of course," he says. "Only for a little while, though. You and I don't get to stay."

"I know," I say, a wave of gray melancholy washing over me. I think again of Mina, who isn't like us. She's trapped in that place, and I don't know how to get her out. I don't know how to help the dead. I don't know how to help myself.

We head north, up through the Marin Headlands, along winding roads and past hills that seem to close in around us. Set back from the highway, it waits for us. Dahlia Hall, lingering in the shadows, a few stray cars pockmarking the driveway, music leaking out into the night.

The kids clamber ahead of us across the lawn, eager as schoolchildren on a field trip, but Dracula lags behind so he can walk beside me.

"Don't pretend to be a gentleman," I say, but he only grins.

"Who says I'm pretending?"

The untrimmed grass crunches beneath our feet like brittle bone, and he moves closer to me, close enough that he starts to reach out, maybe to hold my hand, maybe to break it. I want to scream, to tear at his throat, but I don't have a chance. Up ahead, the kids have stopped dead in the walkway, their eyes wide, their mouths gaping. I follow their hollow gazes until I see them.

A line of wolves standing all around the house.

There are a dozen of them, probably more, their pelts smelling of blood, their muzzles digging in the dirt. As we draw closer, they glance up, snuffing, but they don't bother to look at me. They're looking at Dracula.

"Good evening," he whispers to the wolves, a beatific smile on his face, as though he's a benevolent overlord, a merciful god. Like he even knows what mercy is.

The wolves must believe him, though, because they start to run in circles, letting out small yips at first, followed by lonesome howls, sharp and sweet and strange, their melodies ricocheting off the night sky.

The three kids still haven't moved, not unless you count the way they're shaking a little.

"What kind of dogs are those?" one of the girls asks, but the slight quiver in her voice makes it clear she already knows they're no dogs at all.

"It's all right," Dracula says, and nudges the kids on. They do as they're told, edging toward the house, carefully, quietly, the wolves sniffing at them, twining around their legs. At last, the kids reach the front step and dart inside the party.

Dracula follows behind them, waiting in the doorway, waiting for me, but I don't move. I linger out in the night, watching the wolves. They glance right past me, as if I'm a specter. I should have expected this. They helped warn me back in L.A. and even in Golden Gate Park, my own private harbingers, but I'm only the runner-up, the one they answered to when there was nobody else.

"Turncoats," I mutter, and they all look away at once, gazing off to the sky, to the stars, to anywhere that's better than here.

"Don't take it personally," Dracula says, as I shove past him into the house.

Inside it's dark, the glass walls smudged with grime. The place is nothing like it was last night. Dust soaks the floors, lightbulbs busted in their sockets, the once-pristine sofa frayed and disheveled in the corner. The house is coming apart, and I know why. It's the decay, the same kind I carry inside me, familiar as an old friend. Only, this isn't my doing. This is compliments of Dracula. He's only been back a day, and he's already leaving his mark, trailing rot and sorrow in his wake.

There are only a few people here tonight, all girls again, loitering in corners, fussing with the vinyl collection, half the records split in two. I squint through the gloom, past a shattered dome lamp, but I don't see anyone from last night. None of Rochester's followers. No Rochester, either.

A song blares over staticky speakers. It's the same band I saw earlier tonight at the Fillmore, this time the female singer crooning about wanting someone to love. Good luck with that. They might be calling this the Summer of Love, but from where I'm at, it looks like nothing but heartbreak.

I stick to the outside of the room, Dracula hovering over me, always so much taller than I remember. The three kids from the car are near the mouth of the hallway, as a couple others gather with them, listening in.

"That Lucy's a real ghoul," one of the girls says as she points at me. "She kept telling us how we're all going to die. What a weirdo, right?"

Instantly, my cheeks flush as Dracula leans in.

"Such a mouth on that one," he whispers, and his hand is suddenly on my arm. "You could fix that, you know. You could make sure she never talks like that to anyone again."

"Tempting," I say, wrenching away from him, "but no thanks."

I drift past the beige egg chair that's got a crack down the middle and the chartreuse love seat spewing out bits of its foam guts, everything fading here, everything going gray. Dracula tracks my every step, but I won't look back. I'm still searching for a weapon, for anything that can stop him.

I keep walking, one hand searching blindly across an end table, coming to rest on an antique candleholder, the kind with a spike right in the center. This might work. This might be made of silver, something I can drive straight through the middle of his miserable heart. But when I clutch it close, it's cold against my skin. If it were silver, it would feel like fire. After all, I'm a vampire too.

Dracula peers over my shoulder. "It's only chrome," he says, and he's right.

Without looking at him, I set it down and move on, gripping the edge of the end table. It's got a wood grain on the top of it. I could break it into pieces. I could use this on him.

But Dracula just snaps his tongue. "Nope," he says. "Formica."

My throat tightens, because once again, he's right. Worse than that, he knows what I'm doing. He should be afraid or at least a little angry, but of course, he's not, because this is all foreplay to him. I'm trying to kill him, and it's his idea of a perfect date.

He leans against the dividing wall, his fingers slowly tracing the seams in the paneling. "Veneer," he says. "It's got a few wood fragments in it, but probably not enough to do me in."

"How can you be sure?" I twist toward him, my teeth lengthening. "Maybe it's the ideal way to finish you. Death by tacky wood paneling."

"I'd love to see you try, Lucy," he whispers, and we waver here, our eyes on each other, the heartbeats in the house thrumming faster. My skin hums in refrain, and I think how it's only been an hour since I last ate, but I could do it again. I could draw any of these girls closer to me. He and I could do it together.

"Go on," Dracula says, and glances around the room.

"They'll give themselves to you freely. We both know they want it."

"No," I say, "they don't."

And with that, I turn away from him, sliding open the back door and slipping outside.

The patio's no better than the rest of the house. A skim of algae has bloomed in the pool overnight, cracks opening in the concrete. All the wrought iron furniture, once gleaming white, is starting to oxidize, bits of rust trimming the edges.

The moonlight shifts, refracting off the dingy pool, and I realize for the first time I'm not alone out here. Rochester's followers are everywhere, slumped over in plastic lawn chairs, their heartbeats sluggish in their chests, red welts swelling on their necks. Dracula's been greedy. There are so many here, and he's been feeding off each of them. They don't notice me in their midst—they don't notice much of anything—so I keep creeping forward.

Something moves behind me, something tall and heaving. Rochester, his dark hair mussed, crescent moons the color of bruises beneath both eyes.

I motion to the rot brimming all around us. "I love what you've done with the place."

"Not what *I've* done," he says, and sneering, he sweeps one hand across the top of a grimy table. The decay clings to his fingers. This is all so much messier than he anticipated. Rochester, a blue blood through and through. Now here he is, bringing a vampire back from the dead, and honestly expecting it to be neat and orderly.

"So," he says, "how's Jane?"

My body stiffens. "I don't know," I say. "I haven't seen her."

He gives me that ugly smirk of his. "You know, for a vampire, you're a terrible liar."

That's the nicest thing he'll ever say to me. I smile back at him. "Thank you."

I'm still looking for a weapon, anything to stop them. I wish I was stronger. I wish I was like these men. Able to use my bare hands to take whatever I want.

And Rochester can use more than just his hands. Something crawls beneath his skin, down his arms and into his fingertips. The same something that lives inside Bee and Jane.

"Why does it stay inside you like that?" I can barely form the words. "Why won't it let you die?"

Rochester examines me, one eyebrow twitching up. "Bertha never told you?"

"I never asked."

He takes a long moment. "It wants me to remember," he says finally. "Everything I did. Everything my family did."

And it forces Bee and Jane to remember too.

I stare off at a patch of algae that seems to be creeping closer to us. "Will it ever rest?"

"Maybe when I do," he says.

My eyes shift to him. "And how exactly can we make that happen?"

"Would you like to find out?" He sways closer to me, his breath like rotten milk. "There's a bed inside. We can rest all night if you want."

His hands are on my body now, sliding up along my waist, and I shove him backward. That's enough to get their attention. His followers, wilted until now, are suddenly on their feet, their eyes set on me. They're groggy as hell, their pulses weak, but they're still awake, still angry for no reason.

A knot tightens in my throat. "Aren't you going to tell them to kill me?"

He shrugs. "Why bother? You already served your purpose."

My purpose. Bringing Dracula to him.

"You can't control him," I say. "No matter how hard you try."

"Neither can you."

"We'll see."

I slink across the patio, past the ruined pool and the ruined people, and Rochester lets me go, because it proves his point, how meaningless I am. This digs into me like a ragged splinter, the way I'm a flea to him. The way Bee's a flea too. He uses people up, discarding them like shed skins when he's done.

I'm at the side door, the one that leads to the bedroom, the last place in this house that I saw something built of wood. But at the last moment, Rochester calls after me.

"That first night you came here with Bertha," he says, "you had Dracula with you then, didn't you? One of his urns in your bag?"

I seize up, not answering him. He already knows he's right.

"I should have expected it," he says. "I should have taken him from you then."

I turn back, my jaw clenched. "Who says I would have just given him to you?"

Rochester lets out a rueful chuckle. "So possessive," he says. "If I didn't know better, I'd think you were in love with him."

"It's a good thing you do know better," I say, and disappear inside the house.

The bedroom is fading, the same as the rest of the property. The violet curtains frayed on the window, the vaulted ceiling flaking off. I scan the floor, but the door they tore from the hinges yesterday is gone. I wonder if they kept the pieces. Are there wooden stakes stashed about the house, in crawl spaces and dusty drawers?

I'm ready to search for them, however useless it might be, when I hear it. Heartbeats, so faint they're no more than a whisper, even weaker than the ones on the patio.

And they're somewhere in this room.

A stirring in the oversized bed, and there they are. Bellflower, Vervain, and Rowan, twisted up together, a veil of sweat shimmering on their skin, a thin sheet halfway over them like cadavers on a gurney. Dracula must have been feeding on them since last night, gorging himself, never letting them rest, not until there was nothing left. He took too much, more than he ever used to. We come back from the dead hungry, but never this hungry. He did this just because he could. Just to prove his power. That's why the decay is taking over here, everything disintegrating in an evening. He's inviting it in.

I kneel next to the bed, and Rowan blinks up at me. "Did you come to finish us?" she asks.

My guts tighten. "No," I say.

Next to her, Bellflower shifts onto her side, shivering. "Then why are you here?"

I hesitate. "I don't know."

I told myself it was to protect those kids in the car, to stop Dracula at any cost. But maybe it's something else. Something worse. Maybe I'm here because I want to be close to him. Because after all these years, I don't know anything other than him.

"What's wrong with them?" One of the girls from the back seat is standing behind me.

Rowan reaches out, and I take her hand. "They're dying," I say.

More people drift in, and more after that, until all the girls from the party, all the ones Dracula hasn't tasted yet, are gathered around the impromptu deathbed. A few of them are whispering, and one or two have even started to cry big snotty tears.

"Call a doctor," someone's hollering. "Call anybody."

"It won't help." Dracula's in the doorway now. "Not anymore."

All their faces go gray, and these girls are finally starting to believe me. I touch Bellflower's hand, and I brush Vervain's stringy hair behind her ear, running my fingers along the scar on her jaw, as if I can heal it, as if it's not far too late for that.

I remember this. What it's like to fade away into nothing. Into an oblivion that won't last. We circle around them, silent, watching. Only for a moment, only until it's over. A final murmur from the bed, so small, so pitiful, and then no more sound at all. Not a breath, not a whisper.

"Are they—" someone asks.

"Yes," I say, and then it all breaks loose. The kids rushing back and forth in the room, panicked, hysterical. They charge through the door and down the hall, pushing past Dracula like he's a ghost, like he's not the whole cause of this. More sobs, and the front door slams, cars revving to life in the driveway, girls hollering at each other, cramming into back seats where they don't quite fit, until all at once, everything outside goes still as a tomb.

Dracula shakes his head. "I remember when you were the life of the party, Lucy. Now you're just the death of it."

The patio door crashes open, and Rochester materializes, moonlight limning his body. "What was that? Where is everyone?"

With a languid sigh, Dracula motions to me. "Dear Lucy sent them away."

A long, ugly moment. "And you let her?"

"We can always get more," Dracula says, utterly bored at this whole evening. He looks ready to retreat onto the patio and have another drink, but Rochester's suddenly across the room, looming over me.

"But she had no right," he says, and I can't even get to my feet before he closes in. "They were *mine*."

"No, they weren't," I say, and he's reaching out for me now, his hands yearning to break me in half.

Dracula stirs in the doorway. "Leave her alone, Edward."

"Why?" Rochester asks, his fury nearly choking him. "We both already know what you'd like to do to her."

"Yes, but that's me." Dracula draws closer to him. "*You* don't touch her."

How romantic. The two of them fighting over who gets to murder me.

Meanwhile, there are three dead girls in the room with us, and neither of these men can be bothered to notice. Then again, why would they be bothered? They've each had more wives than any one man needs. We're interchangeable to them, featureless as a fistful of clay, disposable as a leaky bag of garbage.

"The least you could do," I growl, "is pay your respects to them."

At once, the argument hangs limply in the air, as Dracula looks from me to the girls and back again. Then he rolls his eyes.

"Fine," he says, and with a swift hand, he tucks their wilted bodies neatly beneath the sheet, as if he's bidding them good night rather than bidding them goodbye. Their flaccid limbs slump together in a tangle, and I hate this, I hate the way death looks. So cruel. So casual.

I try to get to my feet, get to the door, but with Dracula turned away from us, Rochester takes his chance.

"I'll just have to make do with you tonight," he says, taking hold of me, my bones going soft in his hands. I slash at him, my fingernails sharper than I remember, and he cries out, a short little yelp like a wounded bird.

I've done it now. I've cut him open, a tiny gash near his wrist, but that's more than enough. The substance, thick as oil, leaks out of his body and onto the floor. It swirls before us, quick as a silverfish, and I don't stomp on it this time. I just stand back and watch as it moves toward the corner, toward a patch of cobwebs and darkness. As if it wants to merge with the decay. As if they're one and the same.

But Rochester won't let that happen. He shoves me away, bringing his foot down hard, crushing the gray tar into powder. Time twists sullenly in the room, as the three of us stare at the remnants of it, smeared across the floor.

Rochester grimaces. "Get her out of here," he says, and before I can go at him again, Dracula grabs me by the waist and lifts me up like I'm nothing, like I'm air. He drags me across the room and out onto the patio, slamming the glass door after us, shattering it.

"How lovely," Rochester mutters, and though we can't see him behind us, I can still feel him rolling his eyes.

Out front, the wolves are restless, pacing back and forth, scratching furiously in the dirt, as Dracula wrestles me into the car, pinning me down in the front seat with one hand, twisting us back onto the highway with the other. I flail against him, my body feeling so small, so useless, and by the time I finally break free, the trees are smearing past us, and we're going too fast to jump.

Dracula presses harder on the accelerator. "Now that wasn't so bad, was it?" he says, leaning back in the driver's seat. It makes my guts burn, how cool he is, how comfortable behind the wheel of a car that isn't his.

"You shouldn't even know how to drive," I seethe through clenched teeth.

He shrugs. "Why not? I've watched you do it plenty of times."

He can't help but grin, remembering how he's invaded every corner of my life, and a deep vein of rage cuts through me.

My jaw set, I reach over toward him, slowly, as if I'm about to take his hand, and he must believe that's what I'm doing, because he lets me get closer. Close enough to seize his arm and dig my fingers in, finding the soft places in his skin where he's incomplete, where the ashes are still missing. I sink deeper into him than before, my nails dragging along the bone, scraping away pieces of him from within.

His face pinched in agony, he wrenches away from me, the Buick swerving into the other lane, car horns blaring at us, pale headlights dancing across our faces. I brace for it, the twist of metal, our bodies breaking, but he straightens the wheel in time, the tail end lurching. I don't know if I'm disappointed or relieved. I sit back, expecting him to retaliate, to grab hold of me and not let go, but he just shakes his head and smiles.

"Good girl," he says, and I hate him a little more.

We drive another mile, the Golden Gate Bridge emerging in the distance, before he finally speaks it aloud. The question he's been dying to ask all night.

"Where's the last urn, Lucy?"

I gnaw my bottom lip, not looking at him. "I don't have it."

"But you know where it is."

I don't answer. I don't have to. We keep going, paying the toll, crossing the bridge, the Buick bucking beneath him.

"You're pushing her too hard," I say. "She's going to die on you."

He doesn't say anything. When we reach the other side, he eases the car off the road into a narrow alcove, and I figure this is it, he's kicking me out here. But he says something else instead, something worse.

"Walk with me awhile."

My head snaps toward him. "Why would I do that?"

There's that smile again. "Because you want to be alone with me," he says. "You want another chance to kill me, don't you?"

I always loathe it when he's right. Besides, if nothing else, I want to get that key to the Buick. I want my car back.

We climb out in the dark. From here, we could go any direction. Down to the water's edge by Fort Point or through the winding streets of the Presidio. But we don't do that. We walk back the way we came, toward the bridge. There's a narrow sidewalk that runs alongside the northbound lane, a blood-red railing to hold you in, no more than waist-high.

I inspect the traffic whizzing by, the Cadillacs and the Chevy Camaros and the Pontiac Bonnevilles. How much damage could an ordinary sedan do to his body? What about a semi, all those wheels, all that weight? It would be so quick, a hand on his shoulder, a firm shove, and there he'd be, splayed out on the white lines, his bones meeting asphalt and Goodyear tread. I bet he's thinking the same thing about me. A hundred different ways the grill of a truck could slice up my body like prosciutto.

Then I shake my head and wish it hadn't turned out like this.

"Why don't you do the decent thing and hate me?"

He tilts his head, studying me. "But why would I do that?"

"Because I murdered you, and I'm going to do it again."

"That's just it, though," he says, huddling closer to me. "Van Helsing could barely contain me for a day. You did it for seventy years."

"You didn't give me much choice."

We're together now, shoulder to shoulder, his scent so achingly familiar. Like earth and cobwebs and red roses plucked fresh in the spring. I like it more than I should. I like everything about him. That's how I got into this mess in the first place. I was a girl who liked a boy. There was nothing wrong with that, of course, but when a woman gets murdered, we never talk about why it wasn't her fault. We only talk about why it was.

Dracula stops in the middle of the bridge, his eyes on the sky, the key to the Buick glinting in his front pocket. "There's no reason to go back, Lucy. Bee and Jane have each other now." He pauses, already chewing over his next words. "You're like an annoying little sister. Always in their way."

My heart twists in my chest, and I know he's right, but I won't answer him, I won't give him the satisfaction. That just means he keeps prodding, keeps scrutinizing me, his gaze sharp as an ice pick.

"I suppose you could always run off with that tin soldier of yours."

"Leave him out of this," I say.

"Sweet Michael." Dracula gives me a harsh grin, playing it off as though he doesn't care, but I can hear it, the jealousy sizzling in his voice. "I don't understand you at all, Lucy. You leave me and a kingdom and a castle, and for what? Him and that sad little drive-in?"

"I said stop."

For once, he does what I ask, and we linger here on the bridge, the only ones on the walkway. Cars never stop passing by, but we might as well be ghosts, our bodies obscure in the fog.

Dracula puts out one hand. "Dance with me," he says. "The way we used to."

My lips part, but he doesn't wait for me to answer. I'm in his arms in an instant, not because I want to be, but because he wants me to be, everything about him as oppressive as the summer heat. He twirls me in a circle, and my hands tighten around his shoulders, trying to steady myself, trying to break away. I should expect this by now. This is the only way he's ever known how to hold me.

"I never liked dancing with you," I whisper.

At this, his eyes cloud over. "That's not true," he says, almost wounded. "You loved it that first night. Just the two of us in the dark. Away from your family, away from the world."

"That's because I didn't know you then."

He smiles. "Pretend you don't know me now."

Together, we turn faster, my head gone dizzy, my fingernails piercing his skin, disappearing inside him. The pain alone should be enough to stop him, but he doesn't even wince. He only clutches me closer. A lover's embrace he'd call it, but I've got another word for it.

His hand presses against my back. "Come away with me," he whispers, and this is it, what we've been building toward ever since he opened the passenger door. An invitation. A proposal. Something I want. Something I won't take.

"I'd rather die," I say.

Grief twists for a moment across his face. "I'm so sorry, then."

One final turn, the world a blur around me, and he dips me backward, hard and fast. I brace myself for it, the blaring of a horn, the cavalcade of headlights, my head hitting concrete. Only that's what I'd do to him—it's not what he's planning for me, not what he's ever been planning—and I don't even have time to scream before it happens.

Before my body topples over the outer railing and I plummet toward the water.

thirteen

It's a long way off the Golden Gate Bridge. A full four seconds of free fall before you're in those icy depths, an embrace almost as unforgiving as Dracula's.

As I tumble down, my muscles go weak, the wind tearing through the long tendrils of my hair. Somewhere above me, he's watching me fall, a glint in his eye, a thorn in his heart. He already knows this won't kill me. It'll just leave me battered and broken and cold as hell. But that's more than enough to satisfy him. Besides, this is probably his idea of a joke. They always say vampires can't cross flowing water. Now he won't give me a choice.

I close my eyes, as my body breaks the surface of the bay like a knife. I sink fast, my skin numbing in the chill, the brackish water filling up my lungs, choking me in darkness. I don't need to breathe, but it hurts anyhow, the pressure building inside me, the tides tossing me like garbage.

I should fight this, I should try to swim, but my body goes limp, and the ravishing current carries me away.

I slip deeper into the bay, and I'm not sure how far I make it. If it's five yards or five miles. All I know is I want to float forever, I want to dissolve into salt and sea-foam, but I won't get the chance. A small flash in the corner of my eye, and it takes a long moment for me to realize it.

There's something in the water with me.

Dread coils through my body. Nothing else should be able to survive this deep. Even sharks don't live in these parts.

But whatever it is, it's moving fast, and it's moving right toward me.

An arm hooks hastily around my waist, the figure hulking and obscure. A man, but not Dracula. This is someone else, a face I can't quite see. He fishes me out of the ocean and carries me to shore, my body thrashing against him, my thin dress soaked through.

We fall together onto the sand, and it's not until the moonlight peeks out between the heavy clouds that I see him clearly.

Renfield. His arcane silhouette leaking salt water and heartache.

"I've been waiting for you, Miss Lucy," he whispers.

"Waiting?" I wheeze, as I cough up a mouthful of dark water, seaweed in my hair. "You knew I was coming?"

He nods, half turned away, his figure a jumble of impossible shadows.

"I knew what he was planning," he says. "That's why I was on the bridge earlier."

It wasn't spur of the moment, Dracula tossing me over that railing. He must have been thinking about it all night, thinking about doing it with those three kids in the back seat as unwitting witnesses. Then he must have changed his mind and decided to wait, decided to give me a chance to stay with him. He should have known I'd never say yes.

I struggle to my feet, the echo of the ocean still pressing into my bones. "Why aren't you trying to kill me?"

"Because I don't want to," he says. "I never wanted to. That was always him."

I wring out the hem of my dress, still watching Renfield. We don't belong here. This isn't an open beach—it's private land, with a sign painted in colorful letters, faded from years in the sun.

Playland at the Beach. The nearby boardwalk's empty, but even from here, I can tell what this is. A sort of knock-off Coney Island, a nostalgic getaway with shell games and hot dog stands and ice-cream cones in every flavor. It's already closed for the night, and by the looks of it, it'll soon be closed for good, its heyday in the rearview mirror, its future foggy as the bay.

"Why are we here?" I ask.

Renfield shrugs. "This is where I'm living now," he says, darkness flickering in his eye. "Miss Lucy, there's something I need to tell you."

I squint at him, backing away. "And what's that?"

He purses his mummified lips. "I don't remember," he says. "Sometimes I get mixed up. I don't know which thoughts are mine, and which ones are his."

He turns toward me, his face still swollen from where Bee clawed him. I should claw him too, I should rip him to pieces for what he's done, but before I can say another word, before I can even move, a gruff voice cuts through the gloom.

"Who's there?" A security guard, his flashlight beam dancing across the sand. I stiffen on instinct, and Renfield puts one ancient hand on my arm to steady me, to steady us both. An aching moment before the man passes by, not seeing us in the dark.

"He'll be back soon," Renfield whispers, and looks intently at me. "Come on now. Let's hide."

In an instant, he's scurrying across the sand and onto the crumbling thoroughfare, quick as a cockroach.

I watch him go, seawater dripping off my skin. I should run the other way. I certainly shouldn't follow him. This could be a trap. Everything with Renfield and Dracula is always a trap.

But then there's another flashlight beam and another grunt of a man I can't see, and I can't help myself. I dodge across the sand, following Renfield's briny footprints into the park.

The boardwalk stinks of last week's garbage. They've got all the usual attractions here. A Ferris wheel and a wooden coaster and a merry-go-round, all the painted ponies frozen in grotesque poses, desperate to break free of their prisons. They want to be real, they want to run, but they'll never get that wish.

I quicken my steps past a place called the Mad Mine, one of those spooky rides where it's all bathed in darkness inside, where anything could be waiting around the next corner. There's a banner hanging out front. OUR MONSTERS WELCOME ALL VISITORS!

If only every monster was so accommodating.

At last, I see him up ahead. Renfield, lingering in front of a fun house, the neon marquee gone dark for the night, a giant clown head smiling above us, though I don't see what he's got to be so happy about.

Another voice coming up the boardwalk, and Renfield takes my hand, his skin withered and strange, like antique papyrus stretched taut.

"Hurry now," he whispers, as he pulls me through the door.

Inside, the fun house opens into a maze of mirrors, every angle glinting like diamonds, even in the dark. Already, I want to turn back, but Renfield holds tight to me, guiding me through. My head down, I won't glance up and see us there in the reflections, Renfield looking like a shadow, me looking like nothing at all. A blur where a girl should be.

We keep going through the maze until the narrow corridor spits us into a vast room, the ceiling vaulted, our footsteps echoing back to us. The place is filled with small wooden rides, christened with odd names. The Joy Wheel and the Barrel of Fun and the Human Laundry, each of them resembling medieval torture devices. If the power was turned on, I imagine they'd be rotating wildly, garish lights flashing, discordant music tinkling to life. But it's long into the night, long after hours, and the rides sit sullenly in the dark, waiting for patrons that one day won't return.

"We'll be safe now," Renfield says, as though he and I are ever truly safe.

I shiver, even though it isn't cold. "How long have you been hiding here?"

"Forever," he says. "Or maybe just a day."

Together, we pass by giant rocking horses, my fingers tracing the words on a faded sign, everything fading here. Of course Renfield would end up in a place like this. Somewhere that's slowly being forgotten.

"I'm nothing to him now," he says, and doesn't even speak his name. He doesn't have to.

I wish I could tell him he was wrong.

"The least he could do," Renfield says, crinkling his nose, "is snap my neck like the last time. Now *that* was a proper goodbye."

A grin cracks across his desiccated face, like he's genuinely savoring the memory. Like having Dracula break him into pieces was the closest he ever came to finding true love.

We creep along the wall, exploring the shadowy nooks behind the rides, the spaces where Renfield must hide when the park is open. I try to keep my distance from him. Everything's built of wood here, everything's a weapon he could use against me. Though he doesn't seem eager to do that. He doesn't seem eager for anything.

"There's laughter here during the day," he says, gazing up at the rafters, "but I never come out when I hear it. Because then the laughter would stop."

This makes my chest ache, the way Dracula's turned him into something to fear, his body like a curse.

We cross under another disembodied clown face, and Renfield peers at me. "Do you hate me, Miss Lucy?"

I hesitate. "No," I say finally. "I feel sorry for you."

He nods. "I'm sorry for you too."

We reach another hallway, this one darker than the others, and I seize up, not wanting to go any farther. "What is it you need to tell me, Renfield?"

He breathes deep, trying to conjure it in his mind. "That he doesn't have much time."

"Why not?"

"Because he needs the rest of him," he says. "The last urn. Until then, he's so hungry. So terribly hungry he can hardly bear it."

That's the reason he's gone through all of Rochester's followers already. It's why those three girls died in a day when it took me a week. He won't stop. He's trying to fill up the empty spaces within him.

I stand next to the bottom of a long slide. This place is painfully quaint, so silly in its nostalgia and kitsch. Everything's colorful and inviting, the soft, buttery scent of popcorn hanging in the air, and I think how I could hide here too. I could vanish in plain sight.

Renfield must read it on my face, because he's suddenly scowling at me. "You can't stay," he says flatly.

I exhale a thin laugh. "Why not? Because you've already claimed the fun house for your own?"

"No," he says, "because you've got somewhere else you should be."

My eyebrows twitch up. "And where's that?"

"With your friends," he says, and this twists in my heart.

I won't look at him now. "They're safer without me."

"Not so long as he's after them, they're not."

My head snaps toward him. "Is he?" I can barely speak. "Renfield, is he after them?"

"Of course he is." Renfield scrunches up his dust-soaked face, annoyed I haven't figured it out already. "Why do you think he tossed you off the bridge? It was to get you out of the way."

At once, my throat closes up. Dracula knew he couldn't kill me, not for good, so this was the next best thing. Skip me across the water like a stone, and I could be gone for hours, for days if the tides were in his favor. Plenty of time for him to find the last urn.

I thought I was doing the right thing by leaving Bee and the others behind. It turns out I was only making them an easy target.

I take off the way we came, past all the wooden rides and back through the maze of mirrors, still not looking at the spot where my face should be. Renfield follows behind, calling my name, warning me where the security guard likes to hide. But I don't stop. I don't have time, not if Dracula's already on his way to them.

But as I make it to the front entrance, I turn back, all my resolve withering to ash.

"I can't do this," I say. "I can't stop him."

"You're wrong, Miss Lucy." Renfield reaches through the darkness and touches my arm. "You're the only one who can stop him."

We look at each other, the last two people left in the world who understand this. Renfield pulls away from me, and for a moment I can see him there, hidden within himself, hidden in his own face. The man he used to be, all the things he would have done, the things he would have been if Dracula hadn't gotten to him first.

"Come with me," I whisper, but he only shakes his head.

"I'm sorry," he says, "but you can't trust me."

"I can't trust myself, either."

"Yes, you can," he says, and grinning, he reaches into his pocket. I brace for what he might be searching for. A stake perhaps or a piece of silver or even a bulb of garlic. But when he removes his hand, it's only a spider crawling across his gray skin. "Would you like one for the road?"

He passes the tiny creature to me, and I smile, closing my fingers around it. After all, it seems impolite not to take it.

On the street, the traffic of the Richmond District buzzing by, I get to a bustling intersection before I set the spider free on the sidewalk. It skitters away into the gutter.

The ocean whispers all around me, a spray of salt water on my cheek. Dracula could have already gotten to them by now. He could have already wrestled the urn away from Daisy and put the rest of himself back together again.

Or maybe he hasn't found them yet. Maybe I can still get there first.

My head down, I take off running.

It's almost sunrise when I get back to Daisy's house in the Haight. I burst through the front door, past the sign telling me to keep out. In the living room, the lights are off, and nobody's downstairs.

"Bee?" I edge farther inside. "Are you here?"

A creak of the ceiling above me. A distant giggle.

The whole house lurches around me as I climb the stairs, headed toward the bedroom at the end of the hall. Toward the only noise in the house.

I see his shadow before I see him. Dracula. He's turning over the yellowed mattresses, yanking out every box of useless trinkets from the dressers, searching for the last urn. Searching for himself.

His eyes fogged over with rage, he turns toward me in the doorway. "Lucy." He practically purrs. "I didn't think you'd be home so soon."

He's not alone. Those same five girls from the Fillmore are here, the ones who'd protected him, who'd been desperate to meet him. I feel so sorry that they got their wish. They're lined up against the wall now, one after another, their eyes vacant, their bodies rigid as automatons.

The thrall, poisoning them from the inside out.

"What did you expect?" A voice behind the door. "We had to replace the ones you scared off."

Rochester, stepping out of the shadows. These girls are for him. His collection, his Wunderkammer of women.

Meanwhile, Dracula doesn't care about any of them. His eyes are on me. "So," he says, "what did you do with the rest of me?"

My entire body goes rigid as I stare back at him. "What did you do with Bee?"

Rochester grunts. "She's exactly where she belongs," he says, just as a muffled voice leaks into the room.

"Lucy."

"Bee?" I search the walls, my hands pressed into the plaster, as if I'll find her there. "Where are you?"

"Here," she says, and my gaze rises to the ceiling, the realization sinking slowly into me.

She's in the attic. Rochester locked her in the attic.

"I figured we'd celebrate like old times," he says, that vile smirk on his face.

Fury blooms like cancer inside me, and I lunge at him, but there are too many of them. The girls, bewitched to their marrow, surge forward, peeling me off him. My teeth clenched, I could fight them off, I could shatter these girls into bits, but none of this is their fault. They didn't ask for any of this, not really, so I just back away from them instead, desperate to get to the door. Desperate to get to the attic.

Dracula's heavy footfalls behind me. "Wait for me, love."

The stairwell to the third floor is cramped and mildewed. I rush to the top, shadows dancing in the gap beneath the door.

"Lucy, is that you?" Bee on the other side.

"I'm here," I say, but there's a lock on the outside, and I struggle to open it, my fingers shaking. Dracula's behind me now, his arm looped around my waist. I whirl around to face him, and we're so close again, everything about this as intimate as a nightmare.

He reaches out, slowly, carefully, twirling a strand of my still-wet hair around his finger. "You know you belong with me," he whispers, his breath hot on my cheek. "Flesh of my flesh, blood of my blood."

"Stop saying that." I grit my teeth. "I hate it when you say that."

It's the same line he gives every girl, the one he used on me all those years ago. The one he tried to use on Mina, too.

My hand fumbles behind me, and at last, the lock gives way, and I force open the door.

Inside, it's a single room, the wooden ceiling pitched, the place stinking of mothballs. Bee's pressed against the wall, her face pallid, Jane trying and failing to comfort her. This is their worst fear incarnate, the past repeating into the present like mirrors reflecting back on themselves to infinity. I kneel beside them, and Bee curls into me.

"It happened so quick," she whispers. "The way they chased us up here."

"It's all right now," I say.

Nearby, Michael's still half-delirious from what I did, and Daisy sits at his side, doing her best to calm him. She's still clutching her bag, but Dracula doesn't notice her. He's watching me, the way Michael reaches out for my hand.

"I've defended kingdoms," Dracula says, sneering. "Fought off whole armies. And that's who you choose over me? A soldier who didn't even want to go into battle?"

I glare back, wishing my gaze could turn him to ash. "Not everyone's a born killer."

"But you are." Dracula takes a step closer. "We're the same, you and me. That's why you won't stay dead."

"I'm nothing like you," I say, only half believing it.

A sharp creak in the stairwell, and Rochester's climbing the steps now, along with his corps of mesmerized girls. Jane sees them, sees herself in them, and she twists toward the farthest corner, her hands over her eyes. She won't watch what comes next, this thing she helped to create.

"I'll ask you once more, Lucy." Dracula edges toward me. "Where's the last urn?"

"I already told you. I don't have it."

"That's strange. Because I've looked everywhere for it," he says, before turning to Daisy. "Maybe you know where it is."

He rips the crocheted bag away from her and rifles through it, his face twisted, his hands gnarled. But it's all for nothing. The bag's empty.

Daisy stands back, grinning at him. She's clever, always one step ahead of the rest of us. She must have known they'd come for it. That's why she's hidden the urn somewhere else.

"You," Dracula says, eyeing her up. "Come here."

Daisy backs away. "Forget it."

He smiles. "It wasn't a request."

I always forget how fast he can move. I don't even have time to scream before he's across the attic, his mouth already on her throat. The sounds that follow are so terribly familiar.

The soft tearing of flesh. Her breath catching. His lips sticky against her skin.

Daisy lolls back in his arms, her eyes filmed over but still watching me, silently begging me to help her. I rush forward, my hands on Dracula, nails digging deep into his skin, into his jacket, too, ripping off the collar, the pocket, half the lapel, anything to yank him away from her.

He withdraws from Daisy long enough to grin at me. "I always love it when you tear off my clothes," he says, before going back for more of her.

Another hand is suddenly on my body. Rochester. His fingers splayed around my throat, his muscles twitching, everything about him so much stronger than I expected.

He closes his hand around my neck, my body lifting off the ground, my feet barely grazing the floor.

"Enough," Dracula says, his mouth smeared red. "Leave her alone, Edward."

"Then give me that one." Rochester nods at Daisy.

A shrug. "Fine." Dracula passes her limp body over to him, an obscene barter between men. Without hesitating, Rochester shoves me toward the wall, and takes the one he really wants. A new bride, too bloodied and glazed over to fight back.

For a moment, I remember what Daisy said in the car, about what Rochester had done to her before. She never fell under his spell like the others. She was the girl who got away. The girl he wouldn't let escape for long.

His arms tightening around her body, Rochester smirks again before carrying her off, the other girls on the steps parting like the Red Sea to let them pass. I start toward them, my teeth sharpened, but the stairwell's too narrow, and the crowd closes behind Rochester like pus filling a wound. They force me back, and I topple to the attic floor next to Michael. By the time I scramble to my feet, Dracula's vanishing through the door behind them.

He turns back once, gazing at me, with that same injured look from before. As if the only thing I'm good at is disappointing him.

"Goodbye, my Lucy," he says, and the lock slams shut behind him.

fourteen

I rush to the door, clawing and pounding at it, until I'm sure it'll break loose. Only it doesn't break, it barely moves at all, the latch on the other side holding fast. I shove my whole body against it, but it doesn't matter.

We're locked inside, and there's no way out.

It's nearly sunrise now, and noise from the street seeps through the windowless walls. Someone's outside on the sidewalk below. Two someones, and they're arguing, their voices sharp and urgent. Rochester and Dracula. I crouch on the far side of the attic, my ear pressed into the plaster. Another moment of quarreling, something about the Buick, and then their voices go silent, replaced with the whir of an engine. From the rasp of the muffler, it's that same Volkswagen bus from before.

They must have come into the city separately, Dracula meeting Rochester after he was finished with me. This must have been their plan all along. Dracula wanted the urn, and Rochester wanted the girls.

But they're leaving our car behind now, and I know why. The fragment of his jacket I tore off in a frenzy. In the ripped pocket, something glints up at us.

The key for the Buick.

This is why they were arguing on the street, why they left together. Dracula lost this and couldn't risk coming back for it.

I pluck the key from the floor and hold it in the palm of my hand. It's worth more than a gold mine to me. For all the good it'll do here, locked away in the attic.

It doesn't seem fair. Bee and Jane and I are immortal, but we're so vulnerable too. A turn of a lock, a flick of a match, a fragment of wood. That's all it takes, and we're undone.

Dracula and Rochester must know this won't kill us. This is just a cruel prank, the best these men can do to hurt us. Force Jane and Bee to relive that attic in Thornfield. Force me to linger next to Michael where the only thing I can hear is the gentle murmur of his heart.

In the corner, Bee's fingernails drag along the wall, plaster flaking off like dry flesh, her shoulders caving in like she wants to fold up and vanish.

"It looked just like this," she whispers, glancing up at the rafters. "Only it was darker. So dark I could never see that thing coming."

That thing, that gray tar that lives inside them. I can spot it crawling beneath her skin even now. Crawling beneath Jane's, too. The two of them sit on the dusty floor, not looking at each other, shame hanging over them like an invisible veil.

Bee's hands knot into fists. "I remember that last night in the attic," she says, and looks up at Jane. "After it had gotten you. After he'd taken you away. I remember finding that match. It seemed like the only way out."

"I tried to get back to you." Jane shivers a little. "I tried to get you out before it was too late."

"I know." Bee hunches over, her head in her hands. "But it wasn't all bad at Thornfield. Remember when he caught us together?"

Jane exhales a small laugh, a shadow of delight across her face. "He didn't know what to do about that."

"No, he didn't." A thin smile. The first time I've seen Bee really smile in days. "He'd been so afraid of so many things. But he'd never worried about losing his wives to each other."

This is the final piece of their story, one I'd never known until now. How he'd locked them up together, abandoning them in that attic. How they'd found each other in the dark. They couldn't keep that terrible thing away from them, from burrowing beneath their skin, but that couldn't keep them apart, either.

An aching silence as Jane edges closer, resting her forehead against Bee's. For a moment, they look so content together, like nothing in the world could ever come between them. Then it's as if the past settles over them again, and Bee remembers everything at once.

Swallowing a sob, she pulls away, and Jane doesn't argue. She just crawls across the floor to the far corner, her knees tucked into her chest.

Jane Eyre. She was so steel-willed once, so uncompromising. But years at Rochester's mercy have left her like this. It's the one thing he's good at, forcing her and Bee to carry the weight of his sins. And he did it just because he didn't want to be alone. It's the same reason he's got a houseful of girls up north. The same reason he took Daisy. His loneliness has become a burden the whole world has to bear.

The street outside bustles to life, and I call out through the wall, but no one hears me, the revelry of the day already brimming at full volume. No one will come for us. Not with that sign on the front door, not after the girls sent everyone away.

Bee rocks back and forth. "What are we going to do?"

Michael struggles to sit up. "We could last a few days up here," he murmurs, but we all know we can't wait that long. We need to be ready by sundown. Otherwise Daisy won't stand a chance. Trapped in this room with me, Michael won't stand a chance either.

I pace across the attic and back again, only a few steps, these claustrophobic walls closing in on us. It should be dawn by now, but we can't see anything in this room. Nothing except a pale yellow light leaking through the gap beneath the door. I stare at it, a realization settling like a stone in my chest. That gap isn't much, no more than an inch, but it could be enough. It could be a way out.

For me, anyhow.

I cross to a water-stained patch of the ceiling, and with a steady hand, break off a piece of the wooden rafter. Just a small one, its jagged edges digging into my palm.

"Bee," I say, leaning down next to her, "there's something I need you to do."

I place the piece of splintered wood in her lap, and it takes her a long moment to understand what it is I want.

"No," she says, and tosses the stake to the floor, as if it's made of fire. "Lucy, that isn't the way."

"But it'll work." I sit next to her, motioning to the opening beneath the door. "It's the *only* thing that will work."

Michael glances between us, barely able to fathom what I'm suggesting.

"You can't do this," he says, and he's almost right. Michael can't do this. The thrall would make it impossible for me to ask him, to put this stake in his hands, and Jane's so shaky, her whole body quivering with grief, that she's liable to miss my heart altogether.

It has to be Bee. She's the only one I trust.

"There has to be another way," she says, but I shake my head.

"We can't wait," I whisper. "Daisy won't make it. And if Dracula finds that last urn before we do—"

I don't finish that sentence. I won't push Bee into this. If she doesn't want to do it, I won't ask again. I won't be another person in her life expecting impossible things from her.

The makeshift stake waits sullenly on the floor between us. She stares down at it, and without a word, she remembers everything. How we've spent years protecting those urns, giving up everything to hide them away. How we've spent years running from Rochester too, keeping him at bay. Now it's nearly lost, slipped right through our fingers. More girls will die. Girls just like us.

Something shifts in her, her face still as stone, her gaze the color of iron.

"You'll come back, right?"

I force a smile. "I always have before, haven't I?"

"And what if you don't this time?"

I don't answer her. I just march to the door and stand against it. When it's done, the ash of me will slip through that gap and out into the stairwell.

His head still heavy, Michael's desperately trying to get to his feet, trying to argue with us, but he doesn't get a say in this. This is between Bee and me. After everything, this has got to be between us.

She edges toward me, the tears already starting to come. "Are you sure?"

"Yes," I say, and close my eyes.

A bottomless moment, and I'm sure she won't do it, that she'll back out after all. Then the floor creaks before me, and with an agonizing cry, she buries the stake in my heart.

It hurts more than I expect.

For an instant, I open what's left of my eyes, and see them there. Bee, weeping, covering her face with both hands. Jane wrapping her arms around her, neither of them looking, neither of them wanting to see what's become of me. Michael, on the other hand, can't stop staring. He crawls across the floor to me, reaching out, even though there's nothing left of me to hold.

"It's okay," I try to say, but the words dissolve on my lips, as I dissolve too, the whole world melting away like a thousand cigarette burns on a movie screen.

The last thing I hear is Bee calling my name.

AND NOW HERE I am again, in the afterlife. In this drab waiting room, like I'm some would-be ingenue on a casting call, wide-eyed and eager, my heart full of the very hope I learned long ago never makes a damn bit of difference.

My vision returns to me, slowly at first, until at last, I see this place clearly. It isn't the same as I left it. The room is darker than before, the ceiling sagging, the plaster chipping away. Everything's decaying, the same way it decays in the spots Dracula and I touch.

But one thing hasn't changed. Mina's still here, looking the way I remember her. The girl I grew up with all those years ago.

Smiling, she steps toward me, but I shake my head.

"I can't stay this time," I whisper.

She nods. "I know."

Mina must have heard us making our meager plan, our voices seeping through from the attic.

Other voices seep through as well, more urgent than before. A thousand voices, murmuring just beyond the twisting plaster. I gaze at the crawling walls, and I swear they're gazing back at me.

"Are you all right here?" I ask.

She swallows hard, as a hand emerges, grasping for her. "I'm not sure."

A chill settles over me. "Are they getting worse?"

"Maybe not worse," she says. "Just more restless."

That's one way of putting it. All around us, the walls are liquid, the ghosts hungrier than before, the whole room looking ready to collapse, as if it's no more than a cheap set. Something not built to last.

I huddle next to her, the two of us watching every flicker of movement. It doesn't feel like I've gotten very far. From the attic to here, from one confined space to another. But at least I'm with Mina. At least this feels familiar.

Mina. The friend who never forgot me, the one who ended up trapped in this purgatory. Ever since she died, she must have been stuck in between. A girl who was bitten, who was earmarked as Dracula's property. A girl who didn't die from it. That's why she's inside the room and not beyond it. She doesn't belong with the living, but she doesn't belong with the dead, either.

At my feet, the makeshift stake that brought me here rolls back and forth, making a hollow sound across the floor.

"Why am I not here with you? Why don't I stay

dead?" I seize up, half choking on my next question. "Is it because I'm like him?"

Mina hesitates. "That's not how I'd describe it."

But it's true. Dracula was right. He and I are the same.

The hands reach out all around us, fingers writhing, arms coiling like snakes.

I drift forward. "Are they all from him? From what he's done?"

Mina shakes her head. "There are others, too. Voices calling out different names."

Dread churns in me. "Rochester?"

"Sometimes," she says. "But there are so many of them. From Dracula. From Rochester. From men we've never met."

A knot of melancholy twists inside me. This place where the forgotten are left behind.

I don't want to leave Mina here, I don't want her to be forgotten too, but I have no other choice. Already my body's dissolving like a sugar cube in boiling water.

And there's something else. I told Bee I'd come back. Even if I want to stay with Mina—even if I want to stay dead—it can't be this time.

Mina knows that. She can see the resolve on my face. "It's all right," she says, and flashes me that small smile of hers, the one that could crack a heart in two.

I reach out and try to take her hand, but my fingers slip right through her. The other hands, though, are stronger than mine. They jut out of the walls, farther than before, and they latch on to her, wrenching her toward them. She rasps out a scream before pulling away and cowering in the center of the room. The only place they can't touch her.

The shadows grow a little longer, the room contracting and expanding like a beating heart. I want to stop all of this, but my skin goes translucent, and it's almost time.

"I'll come back for you," I whisper.

Mina brightens for a moment. "Promise?"

"I promise," I say, and reach out again for her, but it's too late. My body folds into itself, soft as porridge, and all at once I'm gone, torn back into the world.

fifteen

When I open my eyes, I'm huddled at the top of the stairwell, my knees pulled into my chest, my body stripped bare. Fresh skin tightens on my bones, my sinews snapping into place, but I barely feel it, everything in me numb.

Or almost everything. The same as always, I've come back famished, my head dizzy, my guts grinding together.

But what matters—the *only* thing that matters—is it worked. I'm on the other side of the door now.

My hands shaking, I struggle to my feet and wrench open the lock. It's such a simple motion. A clang of metal, a flick of the wrist. I never should have had to die for this. Then again, I never should have had to die at all, at least not the way that Dracula did it.

The door lurches open, and inside, Bee's collapsed in the far corner, her face red, her cheeks stained with tears. She blinks up at me, as if she doesn't believe I'm real.

"Are you all right?" she asks.

"I'm fine," I say, shivering.

Jane crouches nearby, that strange gulf opened between her and Bee again. I wonder if they've spent the whole day fighting.

The floor creaks beneath me as I step into the attic. It's late in the day, almost night now. I can feel it. We don't have much time. Dracula's been resting all afternoon, but he'll awaken soon. And he'll be even hungrier than before.

"Come on," I whisper, and reach for Bee. Wiping away the last of her tears, she squeezes my hand before drifting down the narrow stairwell, her steps soft as an apparition's. Jane follows behind her, keeping a safe distance, not wanting to get too close, not if Bee doesn't want her to.

Michael lingers in the attic with me, averting his eyes, my naked silhouette backlit by the bare bulb overhead. For a moment, I forgot I was naked. Without looking up, he takes off his jacket and passes it to me. Shivering again, I slip into it, the sheepskin lining soft and comforting, the numbness in me fading away.

He glances at me now, his cheeks flushed. "Are you really all right?"

"I'm really here," I say. "Isn't that enough?"

Together, we start toward the steps, but before we close the door behind us, I pluck the Buick key from the floor. It feels heavier than I remember. It also feels like mine. Something that Dracula stole from us. Something we've now reclaimed.

At the bottom of the stairs, I hesitate, the second-floor hallway unfurling before us.

"You go on ahead," I say to Michael, his heartbeat bleating in my ears. It isn't safe for us to be alone like this.

"I'll meet you downstairs," he says.

When I'm sure he's out of reach, I stumble into the nearest bedroom, searching through tangled piles of dirty laundry strewn across the floor, desperate for something that will fit me. Something more than just a jacket.

I find it turned inside out, pushed to the back of a mildewed dresser. A pale muslin dress with tiny red flowers stitched along the neck. Another of Daisy's secondhand treasures, no doubt. Hopefully, she won't care that I'm borrowing it. Hopefully, she's still alive to care about things at all.

My body quivering, I pull the dress over my head and step into a pair of woven sandals in the corner. Now here I am, looking like a girl who belongs in the Haight. Like someone other than me.

Unless this *is* me now, what I've become. After all, I was a socialite once. Maybe that's what I could be again. A girl who's part of the world rather than just standing outside it.

From the street below, voices float up like ghosts, too far away to see. I gaze out the window, daylight fading away, as a voice rises within this room too. A whisper, as familiar as my own.

Dracula.

He's long gone, but in spite of himself, he left something behind. It's in the back of the closet, tucked away like a dirty secret. Another spot in the wall where a furnace grate used to be. On my tiptoes, I reach inside and wrench it out. The last urn, right where Daisy must have hidden it.

Dracula should have heard it, but this has always been the quiet urn. The one that caused me the least grief. Now it's the only thing standing between him and everything he wants.

Downstairs, Bee, Jane, and Michael are gathered together in the empty living room.

Leaning against an open window, Bee looks at me. "We have to get Daisy."

"I know," I say, and hold the last urn tighter.

Another thing I know: whatever happens next, I can't let Dracula find this. I can't lose the rest of him.

I also can't let anyone else get hurt.

"I need you to head home," I say to Michael. "Back to the drive-in."

"And what about you?" he asks.

"We'll follow you in the Buick," I say. "After we get Daisy."

"And me?" Jane's watching Bee. "Where am I going?"

Bee won't answer her. She won't even look her way.

"You go back to L.A. too," I say. "It'll be safer for both of you."

The evening air hangs heavy with humidity as we head outside, lingering for a moment on the sidewalk. This is it, the last time we'll be here. In this strange, heady neighborhood in this strange, heady city.

Beneath a flickering streetlight, Jane tries to say good-bye to Bee, to say anything at all, but she doesn't get the chance. Bee spots the Buick and rushes on ahead, leaving the rest of us behind.

Jane's face goes pink with shame. "She'll never forgive me, will she?"

"I don't know," I say.

Jane peers at me. "Do you forgive me?"

"Forgiveness doesn't matter much," I say. "It's about doing the best we can now."

"And how can I help with that?"

"Take this." I pass the urn to Jane, and her eyes go wide.

"Why me?" she asks.

"Because if something happens to me and Bee—" I start to say, but instantly Jane blanches, already antici-pating what I'll say next.

So I don't say it. Instead, I close her hands tighter around the urn. "You just keep him from finding it. All right?"

At this, Jane nods, a steely resolve in her eyes. "I can do that," she says, and there she is, the girl she used to be, the one who could stand up to anyone.

I cross the street, and Bee's already in the passenger seat, her shoulders hunched. She's too tired to drive, so I slide behind the wheel. From the sidewalk, Michael and Jane bid us goodbye, but I turn away, refusing to look back, part of me afraid of what comes next. Afraid we'll never see them again.

Only, I won't think of that now. The Buick grumbles to life, the engine rattling worse than before, and we start down the road. Heading north one more time, back to the Marin Headlands. Back to Dracula and Rochester.

It's Friday night, and the Haight's coming alive. Kids on every block, flowers in their hair, hope brimming in their eyes. I remember what that's like. This place made me remember. I'd wanted to forget who I was, how naïve I'd been the night Dracula found me. But that's one thing this place has got in abundance: the belief in something better. Sometimes, that doesn't seem like much. Sometimes, it seems like everything.

We're almost to the highway when Bee turns to me.

"You shouldn't have trusted Jane with the urn." She gnaws her bottom lip. "All of this is her fault, Lucy."

"I prefer to think it's Rochester's fault," I say. "He's the one who lied to her. Or only told her half the truth."

When she came to Los Angeles, Jane genuinely believed I was holding someone against their will. And she wasn't wrong. She just didn't know why. Rochester never told her that part. He made her believe she was doing the right thing.

Maybe that's not a good enough excuse. Maybe it would be easier to put this all on Jane. That's certainly what Rochester wants. But it's something I finally learned, though it took me years to figure it out: how a girl should never be the one to blame for the lies of men.

The Buick charges across the Golden Gate Bridge, traffic flanking us. I try to pick out the spot where Dracula tossed me into the water, but it's dark, and everything's blurring together.

"You shouldn't have left us last night at the free clinic," Bee whispers.

"I thought it was the best thing to do."

"You don't get to decide what's best for everyone else, Lucy."

"I know," I say. "I'm sorry."

Bee leans back in the passenger seat, her gaze set on the clouded stars. "What are we going to do when we get there tonight?"

"Whatever we can," I say, but a heavy silence hangs between us, because we both know that won't be enough. We can't just leave Dracula and Rochester in San Francisco. But it's the same question we've been asking ourselves for years: How do you stop someone who won't die?

Something flickers inside me suddenly. "Bee?"

"Yeah?" She doesn't look at me.

"After the fire," I say, swallowing hard, "where did you go? I mean, what did it look like when you died?"

She hesitates, her lips pursed, her shoulders gone rigid. I've never asked her this before.

"It's hard to describe," she says.

We drive a little ways, off the 101, the shadowy hillsides devouring us, and I figure that's all Bee's going to say about it, until she shakes her head.

"One thing's for sure," she says, and looks at me now. "I could do without all those hands in the walls."

I heave up a small laugh. "Me too."

Of course Bee goes to the same place I do. She and I are more alike than we ever believed. And we never should have kept all these things from each other.

"Even after everything," I say, "even after all the times I died, Dracula always thought I should be grateful."

"So did Rochester," Bee says, her jaw set. "He acted like he did me a favor when he married me. A Creole girl from Spanish Town."

The trees creep closer, the highway narrowing, as Bee lets out a long sigh.

"He always expected me to be ashamed. To be afraid." Her eyes glint in the moonlight, a determination settling in her face. "Never again."

When we come around the last corner, the tires squealing against concrete, I ease the car off the road, our figures bathed in shadows beneath the laurel trees. Then, together, Bee and I gaze up at Dahlia Hall.

Or what's left of it.

Gone are the gleaming lights and the sweet music lilting up into the evening sky, an endless party, an endless good time. There's nothing good about it now. The whole property is sullen and quiet as a grave. The sagging roof, the windows grimier than before, decay hanging from every shingle, thick as kudzu vines.

Bee climbs slowly out of the Buick. "What happened to this place?"

"Dracula," I say.

This was Rochester's new Thornfield, his pride and joy, his eager future. Now it's on the verge of ruin. It took him years to find a place like this, and it only took Dracula overnight to spoil it.

But one thing hasn't changed. The wolves are still standing guard around the house, a thick perimeter of glistening fangs and mangy pelts and ancient grudges I can't even fathom. They lower their heads as we inch closer, up the driveway and across the lawn. Bee takes hold of my arm, maybe to steady herself or maybe to pull me back.

"It's all right," I whisper, and put one hand out to them. Their red eyes glare back through the gloom, and for an instant, they're all I can see.

Then with a quiet snuff, they let us pass. For now, anyhow. They probably figure if they change their minds, our throats will be just as good for shredding when we're on our way out.

Bee and I sneak around the side of the house, along the narrow stone walkway, dodging drooping tobacco brush and bitter cherry, all their leaves gone ragged and gray.

Around back, the decay is everywhere, shimmering in the dark, the pool veiled thick with algae. Something floats past in the water, but I won't look close enough to find out what it is.

There are other things I won't look at. Like the figures slumped over in lawn chairs. They haven't budged since last night, and as we pass them, I realize why. There are no heartbeats on the patio anymore. No sluggish breath, no movement at all. Dracula's taken what he wanted, leaving their bodies behind like empty cicada shells.

But there's still one heartbeat nearby, its gentle rhythm calling out to me. I follow the sound through the shattered glass door. That's where we find her.

Daisy, curled up in the same bed where the other girls went to die.

Her skin's pale as clotted cream, her breath rasping from what he's done to her. But she's alive. That's what matters.

As Bee and I kneel next to the bed, Daisy's eyes flutter open. "He's coming back soon," she whispers. "Coming back to finish."

We help her up, her arm hooked around Bee's shoulders. A muffled voice down the hall, and a shadow moving closer.

"Go on," I whisper. "Get her out of here."

Bee's eyes flash in the dark. "And what about you?"

I squeeze Bee's hand. "I'll be right behind you."

They disappear through the patio door, just as the shadow devours the whole room.

Dracula. He regards me, nothing about him looking the least bit surprised to see me.

"Good evening." He strolls nearer, a crust of red in the corner of his mouth. "Did you have a nice rest in the attic?"

"Of course," I say, and give him a smile as if I don't hate every last inch of him. "Aren't you disappointed it's only me here?"

"Disappointed to see you?" He snaps his tongue. "Never, my Lucy."

He's standing right before me now, his scent like roses and earth as overwhelming as ever. I try to edge toward the patio door, toward freedom, but he cuts me off first.

"You're looking a little peaked tonight," he says, already sensing my hunger.

"I'm fine," I say, but he knows I'm lying. My bloodlust is like a beacon to him.

"I can help you with that," he says, flicking open the buttons on his shirt, one by one. I watch him, enjoying it more than I should.

His bare skin glistening in the moonlight, he presses a long fingernail across his chest, and in an instant, the blood's flowing from him like the sweetest merlot. Like a cure I never asked for. I drift toward him. That's the problem—he knows me well enough to know I can't help myself. He made me this way, and now he gets to enjoy it.

I'm close enough to drink now, but I start to pull away, grimacing.

"It's all right," he whispers, and threads his fingers through my hair, pressing softly on the back of my neck, forcing me toward him. Toward what he knows I want. My eyes sting with tears, but I part my lips, ready to get this over with.

Then all at once, a scream seeps through the broken door.

"Lucy?" Bee calls out, and the sound of her voice jolts me back.

I shove Dracula away, my hand slick with his blood.

He crashes into the flimsy paneling, the wall bowing against his weight. Then he exhales a braying laugh.

"You could have just told me no, Lucy."

Outside, they've already surrounded Daisy and Bee. Rochester, along with the girls from Daisy's house, their expressions blank as fresh paper. Still under Dracula's thrall, they don't know what they're doing. They never asked for this. None of us ever do.

The girls keep watching us, their faces blending together, anonymous as Jane Does. I don't know their names or where they're from or why they hitched up the interstate to the Haight, why they came to California at all. They'll lose their lives at the hands of the same monster who murdered me, but that doesn't make us intimates. We each die alone in the end. Men like them make sure of that.

Dracula drifts out onto the patio, his shirt still hanging open. My cheeks flush with shame at the sight of him, and I turn away. There's movement again in the pool, and this time, I can't stop myself. I gaze into the murky water and see them. Bellflower, Vervain, and Rowan, their limp bodies floating to the top like chum.

Rochester watches them, the rotting remains of the girls he recruited. Then he just shakes his head. "Look what's become of this place."

Dracula glances around, seemingly pleased with himself. "I'd call it an improvement."

"I'd call it a blight on property values." Rochester sneers, his shoulders broadening. "It wasn't supposed to be like this. You were supposed to make things better."

A small grin blooms on Dracula's lips. "Why in the world would you expect a vampire to do that?"

Rochester's face goes dark, and time stretches thin, nobody moving, nobody speaking.

"My mistake," he says finally. "How about I fix that? How about we find that last urn and put you back in the dark where you belong?"

Dracula's grin grows wider. "How delightful it would be to watch you try."

The two of them edge nearer, their hands twitching into fists, and I think how much I'd like to witness them pummel each other into infinity. But this is our chance. With no one watching us, Bee and Daisy start to stumble forward, and I try to move with them, but at the mouth of the walkway, I hesitate, looking back at the other girls. I don't want to leave them behind.

Maybe they don't want us to leave either, because they're beaming at us like they know something. That's when I see it. In the pool, Bellflower's eyes flick open, and she looks right at me.

And she's not the only one. They're all awakening now, macabre Sleeping Beauties, monsters these men have created. Along the crumbling border of the pool, a dead girl rises from her plastic lawn chair, her legs unsteady, her gaze set on us. Once she's up, another one resurrects, and another after that, all their necks cracking as they lurch forward, their mouths gaping open like beached carp. They haven't broken in their new bodies yet, and I cringe because I know what that feels like.

Nearby, Vervain's stirring in the water, and so is Rowan. There's movement all around us, like the skittering of roaches. The wolves are closing in too. Everyone here, everyone watching.

"About time," Rochester says, as they force us back across the patio, closer to the house, past the moldering pool where the girls climb out on hands and knees, their limbs strange and angular as spiders.

With Daisy wilting between us, Bee and I dash back inside, trying for the front door, stumbling past all the things that can't be used as weapons. The Formica table, the chrome candleholder, the wood paneling that isn't really wood at all.

Of course, we could have brought a stake or a piece of silver or even a small cross, but that seemed too dangerous. Anything we can use on Dracula, someone else could use on me.

And maybe I don't need a weapon at all. Maybe I'm more than enough on my own, my hunger tightening like a screw in my belly, the decay rising inside me, crackling in my fingertips like a dark spell ready to unfurl.

We're at the front door now, and Bee wrenches it open, but I turn back. Dracula's right behind us, tracking us into the house, and he must sense it within me, the resolve budding inside my cold heart.

"Don't even try it, Lucy," he warns, his eyes darker than sin, and I can't help but smile.

"It's only fair, though," I say. "You did the same thing to our house, didn't you?"

I close my eyes, and it doesn't take much. Only a little coaxing, my hunger heavier now, before the decay bursts forth from me. It puddles beneath my fingertips and drips out, bit by sticky bit, leaking onto the floor, cracking it in two. The decay that's already here, all the deterioration Dracula's wrought on this place, must be jealous, because it ripples through the walls and floors, greeting my own decay, the rot mingling together until the entire foundation is starting to shake beneath us.

"Stop," Rochester says, tripping over himself, nearly toppling into the chasm I've cut clean through the center of the house.

Bee's eyes go bright as fire. "Stop?" She gazes at Rochester. "You want us to stop?"

He doesn't answer her. He doesn't even move. That quiet look on her face must be one he recognizes. The same look before she turned his last house to cinders.

"Bertha," he says, his hands extending slowly, his palms turned upward. "Bee. Please."

But it's too late. It's been too late for years. Her face like stone, Bee pierces the tip of her ring finger. It isn't much, but it's more than enough, the gray tar leaking toward the walls, toward every shadowy crevice. The last bit of rot this place can take.

For a long moment, the whole house trembles around us, the egg chair quivering in the corner, the chrome candleholder tumbling to the stone floor.

And then everything gives way.

Shrieking, the girls on the patio leap back, escaping

the worst of it, but Rochester stays inside, pressed against the wall, trying to hold up the whole house, as if his sheer willpower can keep this place from disintegrating.

But the house keeps buckling around us, and Bee lets out a whooping cry of joy. This is like Thornfield all over again—only this time, she didn't have to burn to see it crumble.

Dracula yanks a yelping Rochester onto the patio, the roof sloughing off around them. Our arms looped tighter around Daisy, Bee and I take off through the front door and across the lawn. At our backs, the wolves charge after us, baring their teeth, bearing down faster, but we tumble into the car, and Bee cranks the engine, twisting the Buick back toward the highway.

Chaos echoes into the night air, girls fleeing the wreckage in all directions, the men's voices calling after them, their ire rising like smoke rings. But as the dark trees rush past, they feel a thousand miles away. With Daisy tucked in the back seat, Bee and I look to the road ahead, as the rest of Dahlia Hall turns to dust behind us.

sixteen

We're already south of San Jose when I spot the first wolf.

He's no more than a blot along the shoulder, something barely there, more phantom than fur, and I hardly see him in the dark. He shouldn't be here at all. The Buick's cruising at an even fifty down the 101, but somehow, the wolf's still keeping pace with the car.

"They're tracking us," I whisper. "They'll probably follow us all the way home."

Bee scoffs. "Let's see them try," she says, and presses the gas pedal harder.

The eucalyptus trees smear past, but it's another full mile before the wolf finally vanishes in the rearview mirror. Even then, I swear I still hear him howling.

The wolves aren't the only ones following. Rochester and Dracula are on their way too, that cream Volkswagen somewhere on the highway behind us, the color so nondescript, so bland that it's practically invisible. They could be right next to us before we'd even notice.

Shivering, I recline in the passenger seat as Bee fiddles with the radio, twisting the dial, anything to occupy her nervous hands.

"Do you think the urn's still safe?" she asks, and I nod, my feet on the cracked dashboard.

"I'm sure Jane's doing her best."

Bee exhales a grunt. "That'd be a first."

I don't say anything, but my heavy silence is more than enough.

Bee's eyes dart from the road to me and back again. "You think I should forgive her, don't you?"

"No," I say. "I think that's for you to decide."

"That's the problem, though." Bee gnaws her bottom lip. "I don't even know who she is anymore. Maybe I never knew."

Another mile, the highway stretching long and lonesome in front of us, before she adds, "Maybe it's all too late."

My chest constricts, her words aching inside me, but I won't argue, because I'm wondering the same thing myself. That maybe everything's too far gone to set right again.

I ask Bee if she wants me to drive, but she just shakes her head.

"I need something to steady me," she says, her hands trembling on the wheel.

We stop off for gas, using a twenty Michael let me borrow back in the Haight. The whole time the attendant is filling the rusted-out tank, Bee and I keep watching the hills, waiting for the wolves to catch up with us. But for now, we're safe. Or as safe as we can be in a car that's disintegrating around us, the seats sinking, the ignition nearly too tired to turn over. All thanks to what Dracula's done.

With the breeze in our hair, the top still down on the Buick, we head south along the 101, the road winding before us. An hour north of Hollywood, Daisy stirs in the back seat, her limbs in a tangle against the torn upholstery. I peer at her, like a concerned mother.

"How are you?" I say, and it seems like the silliest question in the world to ask a girl who was just a midnight snack for a vampire.

Daisy's a good sport, though. She smiles and plays along. "Been better," she whispers.

She falls back asleep, and I gaze up at the sky, the indigo clouds melting around us. It'll be sunrise soon, only a couple hours left. Part of me is afraid we won't make it back to L.A. before morning does. Then all at once, the hills snake away, and there it is.

The steel skyline. The rickety Hollywood sign peeling in the distance. Bee and I have never come home from the north before, and seeing the city this way feels inside out, like the whole world's been turned backward.

"Are we heading to the drive-in now?" Bee asks.

I shake my head. "Let's make a detour first," I say, and Bee doesn't even have to ask where. She takes the exit back to Wilshire.

Back to the pile of rubble we once called home.

Bright yellow police tape surrounds the debris, construction sawhorses blocking off the driveway. We pull around them, parking in the desiccated yard, the engine cutting out, as we stare at what's left of the house.

Our former life, no more than a petty crime scene now.

It's nearly morning, sprinklers awakening in nearby lawns, rolled-up copies of the *Los Angeles Times* thudding sullenly against doorsteps.

I climb out of the car and pace the ragged outline of the rubble, carefully reconstructing the house in my mind. The front door we won't ever unlock again. The foyer with the statue of Venus always standing guard over us. Our bedrooms and the stairwell and the cellar where the worst of Dracula used to live.

And the parlor, our favorite room in the whole house. If I close my eyes, I can almost still hear the Victrola, lilting in the morning air. It used to be right here. That means what we need should be right here too.

I cross into the wreckage, my borrowed sandals slipping between chunks of horsehair plaster and crown molding cracked in two. Among the uneven terrain, I find it, toppled on its side. The rolltop desk that once sat in the corner.

It's charred from the fire, the single drawer splintered and sticking, but with both hands clenched, I manage to pry it open. Inside, there's the last of my dowry. A ruby necklace, the ash caked half an inch thick. My wedding jewels for a wedding that never came.

There's something else in the drawer too, glinting up at me. The letter opener Mina gifted me all those years ago. I reach inside, and it sears into my skin, the silver more potent than fire against me. Wincing, I wrap it up in the hem of my dress before starting out of our house for the last time.

Bee waits at the edge of what used to be the foundation, and when I'm close enough, she reaches out and guides me from the wreckage.

"Do you think that'll help us?" she asks, nodding at what I'm holding, the necklace and the letter opener in a jumble in my hand.

"We'll find out," I start to say, but a shadow, jagged and heavy, passes over us. Together, we twist toward it, my lips parting, ready to scream, convinced it's them, caught up with us already. Then I see that familiar sour-grape face glaring back at us.

"Tyrone," I say, almost disappointed.

He's still wearing those same striped flannel pajamas from the other night, and I wonder for a moment if he's been standing on his front porch the whole week, just waiting for us to return. Waiting for someone to admonish.

"I should call the police on you two." He crosses his arms, snuffing at us like an angry Pekingese. "The way you ran, after that fire? That's against the law."

I roll my eyes and start back toward the car, but he catches my arm first.

"Not so fast," he says, and I thrash against him, my

teeth sharpened. I want to finish him, to devour him in what will soon be broad daylight, but I don't get a chance. That's because we're suddenly not alone.

A low growl, a flash of gray, and the wolves are in a ring around us, emerging as if from nothing.

Tyrone's face goes pale as sea-foam, and I choke up a laugh.

"You want to call the police on them too?" I ask, as he lets go of my arm and tries to back away. Not that it does him any good. They're everywhere now, circling faster, their bodies a haze of fur and claws around us.

Bee huddles closer to me. "What should we do?"

I look to the wolves, and they look back at me, their teeth glistening, their gazes bright as holly.

"Go on." I advance a single unsteady step. "Get out of here."

The promise of morning hangs in the air, and I'm convinced this won't work. That they'll charge us in an instant and tear out our throats. And let's face it: we just don't have time for that today.

But that's not what they do at all. Their tails tucked, the wolves slink away, one by one. Tyrone should be happy now, but instead of being grateful, he just glares at me.

"What *are* you?" he asks, and he looks liable to take hold of me again.

"Don't," I say, rage searing through me, and there's a sudden jolt of movement beneath us. At first, I'm sure it's another earthquake, as familiar as an old friend in these parts. But it's not the ground that's shifting. It's the rubble. And it's moving because of me, because I'm coaxing it to life. All the decay that I thought had burned into nothing is shimmering at our feet. It rises, bit by bit, fragments of cobwebs and ash and dust. The rot I trained in my bedroom is here with us, and it's ready to do my bidding.

"There he is," I whisper. Then I stand back and smile as it slithers toward Tyrone.

He edges away, one careless step after another, his eyes wide. "What is that?"

"It's me," I say, and for the first time, I'm a little bit proud of it.

Tyrone's halfway across the street now, his gaze darting over his shoulder, looking for the rot. Looking at me too. "Get out of here," he wheezes, "and don't come back."

I can't help but laugh, as the decay settles down again, returning to the wreckage. "Don't worry," I say. "We won't."

Back in the Buick, I tuck the letter opener and the necklace in the glove box, and Tyrone watches us leave from his own doorstep, that ugly glower still on his face. I wave goodbye, not to him but to the house.

Bee glances back in the rearview, the wreckage shrinking smaller and smaller in the distance. "It wasn't all bad here," she whispers.

"No," I say, my heart twisted in my chest, "it wasn't."

The sun's spilling over the horizon when we pull into the drive-in. Bee's barely put the Buick in park before Michael comes bounding down the front steps, smiling like the fool he is.

"I was worried you wouldn't make it back before dawn." He turns to Bee. "Jane's inside waiting for you."

The engine croaks out, but Bee doesn't move. "And the urn?" she asks, accusation sizzling in her voice.

Michael shrugs. "It's inside too."

Bee starts in, as if to confirm for herself, as if she can't possibly believe Jane did what she said. I linger in the Buick, the sun creeping closer, as I stare down at Daisy in the back seat. Her heartbeat's quieter than before, a meek little rhythm in her chest.

"Maybe we should get her to a hospital," I say.

At this, her eyes snap open. "Please," she murmurs. "Don't send me away."

Daisy, afraid of being discarded, of being left behind.

Maybe they couldn't help her anyhow—it's not like a blood transfusion did a damn bit of good for me—and besides, we'd be in the same predicament as we were with Michael. We couldn't explain this to anyone.

Though I don't ask him to, Michael lifts Daisy from the back seat, and she clings to him, her arms around his neck, her face nuzzled into his shoulder. Jealousy stirs in me again, but I fall back a step, so they can go on ahead, Walter flicking open the screen door to let them pass.

In a room at the end of the hall, a twin-sized bed with faded sheets is already made up and waiting for her. Michael tucks her in, and I kneel next to the mattress.

She gazes up at me, her eyes bleary. "Will I become like you?"

I brush a thin strand of hair out of her eyes. "Let's hope not."

Her hand unsteady, she reaches out for me and traces what's left of my meager lifeline. "It's almost gone now," she whispers.

I pull away. "Get some rest, all right?" I say, and I'm almost to the door when I hear her again.

"Lucy?" Her voice is frail as ancient bone.

I turn to her. "Yeah?"

"Thanks for coming back for me."

I smile. "That's what we do here," I say. "We help each other."

Michael's waiting in the hallway, and I gaze back at him, my hunger churning in me. He looks ready to say something, when fervent voices break through the wall. Bee and Jane in the next bedroom.

"How do we know we can trust you? That you're not still on his side?"

"He locked me in that attic too, remember?"

"Maybe that's all part of your plan."

"I'm so sorry, Bee. I'm trying to fix it."

"Please just stop." Her words sharp as a bayonet. "I can't listen to this anymore."

Heavy footsteps across the floor, and Bee comes bursting into the hallway, holding the urn away from her like a grenade.

"Take this," she says, and shoves it into my arms. "I don't trust her with it."

And with that, she's gone, vanished out the front door.

I want to go after her, but the sun's too strong now. I want to check on Jane, too, but she's already closed the door.

Michael and I stand together, neither of us speaking a word, before he finally sighs.

"Come to bed," he says, and disappears inside his room at the end of the hallway.

I hesitate, remembering the last time we were here. How fast I ran from him in the dark. How it was the only reason he survived the night.

"I trust you, Lucy," he says, his voice floating out into the hall, and I want to trust myself too.

His bedroom is cramped, the ceiling low, the walls arrayed in yellowed tape, posters tacked up that must be a decade old. Pictures of old B-52 fighter planes picked out when he was no more than a child, back when war was only theoretical to him.

The bed was built for one, but I climb in next to him, Michael curling close to me. I hold him with one arm and the urn in the other. His body's warm, his skin soft and tan and unblemished, everything about him electric and alive. He's the inverse of Dracula. The inverse of me, too.

I stare up at the ceiling. We're safe from the others for now. They'll wait until it's dark. That's when Dracula will be at his peak. We can rest for a little while.

"Sleep," I whisper, but Michael doesn't close his eyes. He just keeps watching me.

"Is there anything you need from me first?"

I shake my head, even though it's not true. I could use

what he has very badly, only I won't hurt him again. I'm holding it back, holding it in. This hunger blooming inside me is mine, and so is the decay. I won't let one drop of it go to waste.

His heart beating faster, Michael's hands move slowly beneath the sheet. "I love you," he murmurs, and I wish I could say it back. But you can't really love something you've trapped, a butterfly beneath a bell jar, a bird in a gilded cage.

He's asleep in a minute, his chest rising and falling like the tides. I watch him, already knowing I should stay awake. I should get ready for this evening, for what's to come. But last night's still heavy in my bones, and before I can stop myself, I close my eyes too.

IT'S ALMOST SUNDOWN WHEN I jolt awake, Dracula's voice stirring inside me. They're close, somewhere inside the city limits.

I sit up, the urn still in my arms. Beside me, the bed's empty, the sheets crumpled and cold. Michael's long gone. I shrink from the mattress, my eyes bleary.

In the next room, Jane's with Daisy, sitting in an antique rocking chair next to her bed.

"How is she?" I ask.

Jane forces a smile. "Better, I think," she says, and holds a compress to Daisy's forehead.

The light through the window is fading fast, and I grip

the urn tighter. "You stay with her, okay? No matter what happens tonight, you two just stay locked in here."

Jane shrinks away from me, defeated. "You don't trust me around him, do you?"

"I don't see any reason to chance it."

"Bee doesn't trust me either." A long moment passes. "I don't blame her."

I ask Jane if she needs anything—for her, for Daisy— but she only shakes her head.

"Close the door behind you," she says, and I slip back into the hallway, my heart heavy inside me.

In the kitchen, Walter's hunched over a flimsy card table, his coffee cup gone cold next to him. When he sees me looming in the doorway, he gives me a big, toothy smile.

"So," he says, leaning back in his chair, "Michael tells me you're a vampire."

I sigh. Small talk. Walter wants to make small talk about me being a monster.

"I guess that's true," I say.

He wipes the sweat from his brow. "I saw that love bite you left on him."

My body goes rigid, and I brace for it. Retaliation. That fistful of buckshot I've been fearing since the first night I brought Michael back here, my black heart oozing bad intentions.

But Walter just shakes his head. "Kids these days," he says.

The night sneaking closer to us, I start toward the screen door, but at the last moment, I look back.

"You'll be in here, right? Holding down the fort with Jane and Daisy?"

"Sure," he says, his eyebrow arching. "They're coming, aren't they? The men Michael warned me about?"

My stomach clenches. "I think so."

"So I'm going to meet Dracula himself," Walter marvels, sucking air through his teeth. He glances down at his smudged overalls. "I wish I had something nicer to wear for the occasion."

With a small laugh, I lock the door behind me and disappear out into the dusty lot.

Michael's perched in the projection booth, unloading film from bulky spools. He looks up, brightening when he sees me.

"I figured I'd let you sleep," he says, and it's such a simple thing, a courtesy really, but one that shouldn't have been possible. He shouldn't have been able to decide that. He shouldn't have woken up before me at all, not when I coaxed him to sleep in the first place.

I know what that means. The thrall's fraying between us. That's what happens when you don't keep tightening it like a noose, the way Dracula has with Renfield. Soon, Michael will drift away from me. This is how it should be. Exactly what I want, and exactly what I don't want, too.

A radio crackles, and a monotone reporter gives the news report on the hour. Yesterday, there was a protest right here in Los Angeles over in Rancho Park. Against the war and everything that goes with it.

I run my hands across a pile of moldering film posters, rolled up and stacked in the corner like firewood ready for burning. "If you weren't with us," I say, "would you be there with them? Protesting what's happening in Vietnam?"

Something glints across Michael's face. "I doubt they'd want me. I fought there, remember? I'm the enemy now."

I seize up, watching him. "But none of that was your choice."

A sharp laugh, harsh as sandpaper. "There you go with that word again," he says. "It doesn't matter whether or not it was my choice, Lucy."

"It *does* matter." I tighten my hand around one of the posters, and the thin paper crumbles between my clenched fingers. "It's the only thing that matters."

This hangs in the air between us, an impasse. I turn away, searching through the metal tins in the corner. It's a tall stack, dozens of films, maybe a hundred, and though it takes me a moment, I finally find what I'm looking for.

"Could you put on these two?" I nudge a pair of film reels toward Michael. "You know, for old times' sake?"

I flash him a smile, sweeter than marzipan, and we both know he won't say no.

His hands steady, he starts feeding the projector. "I'll be in here if you need me," he says, and despite everything, he still hopes I'll stay with him. That I won't ever leave.

I flick off the radio. "Lock the door behind me," I say, and disappear into the night.

The urn tucked under my arm, I wander across the lot and back to the Buick, gazing between the big screens, a pair of blank canvases. Michael will start the films soon. The last two pictures ever to be projected at this drive-in.

Of course, I shouldn't be loitering out here, waiting for the show to start. I know what I'm supposed to be doing right now, all the elaborate preparations I should be making. After all, I've seen the movies enough times. If I were Van Helsing or Jonathan Harker or even Peter Cushing, I'd be melting down silver in some arcane apparatus, forming one perfect bullet with Dracula's name on it, a third-act promise the audience knows I'll keep.

Or I'd be whittling oak and elm into the sharpest stakes you've ever seen, practicing how to hit the heart on the very first try. (A little to the right and straight on till morning.)

Or at the very least, I'd be stringing up bulbs of garlic like garish Christmas lights all around the house until the place is foul with it and even we don't want to stick around.

But I'm not those men, and I won't do any of that. Instead, I settle down behind the wheel of the Buick, holding the urn in my lap as I rifle through the glove box, pulling out the necklace and the letter opener. The last souvenirs of the life I tried and failed to build.

The sun's vanished on the horizon, and they'll be here soon, their arrival as inexorable as the tides.

I don't know what comes next. Even if I can get him

back into this urn, then what? Another seventy years of standing sentry over his ashes? Is this all I'll ever be, the girl who guards Dracula?

"I figured you'd be awake by now." Bee's standing next to the Buick. The night air's getting colder, and she's wearing a used khaki jacket, borrowed from Walter, no doubt. She slides into the passenger seat, and we sit together quietly. The silver letter opener burns a mark into the palm of my hand, but I hardly notice.

"We could still run," she says. "We could hock that necklace at some pawnshop and leave tonight."

I glance at her. "Would we take Jane?"

She looks back at me. "Would we take Michael?"

There's a howl in the distance, echoing up through the canyons, and neither of us says anything for a long time.

"Do you really want to run?" I ask at last.

"No," she says, her face hard as granite. "Do you?"

I shake my head. "We've been hiding for years. I'm tired now."

"Me too."

Another howl, closer this time, and with their claret eyes flashing in the dark, the wolves are here. So is that pale Volkswagen, lumbering across the gravel lot past all the abandoned speakers, the muffler rattling like a warning shot.

We could race back inside. We could shriek to the sky, alerting the others. We could do a lot of things. But we just sit right here, the radio crackling. No more than ten yards away, the Volkswagen's engine cuts out, and the rusted door slides open, a dozen faces materializing in the dark like apparitions.

The girls creep out first, the ones without heartbeats, their limbs long and loose as insects. Then the girls with heartbeats, weak as they are, their throats blotched red. Dracula must have been busy in that back seat.

Bee watches them for a moment before turning back to me. "He's lying, you know."

A choir of hideous giggles lilts through the air like a rancid lullaby, but I won't listen to them. I just look at Bee, only seeing her. Only seeing my best friend. "Lying about what?"

"You're nothing like him, Lucy," she says, and her words ache inside me. She doesn't know what Mina told me, about why I keep coming back.

I exhale a ragged sigh, as the last two figures emerge from the bus. Rochester and Dracula, side by side, towering as tall as nightmares.

"And what if you're wrong?" I say to Bee. "What if I am like him?"

A sea of shadows dances across our faces, but Bee smiles, not missing a beat. "Then use it against them," she says, and with a final laugh, they surround us.

seventeen

The girls without heartbeats are blocking our headlights now, their bodies like a noonday eclipse. Bellflower and Vervain are at the front, smiles on their faces,
barbed wire in their veins.

They've each got a small wooden stake tucked up their
sleeve. I wonder if they know yet what an occupational
hazard those things can be. Right now, all they care about
is getting close enough to me to use them.

The Buick's already on, the engine rattling softly beneath us. The necklace and the letter opener slide on the
seat next to me, and I've got one hand on the wheel, the
other never letting go of the urn.

"Ready?" I whisper, and Bee nods back at me.

"Ready," she says, and I throw the Buick into gear, the
tires spinning for a moment before we lurch forward, dirt
and stone kicking up around us.

We rocket across the lot, away from the little shotgun house and straight toward one of the movie screens. Rochester and Dracula step aside, because they know they don't need to follow us. The girls do it for them, leaping at the car, clinging to the sides, their arms flailing wildly, the wooden stakes aimed at my heart.

"Lucy," they hiss, and their voices are like asphalt against my skin.

I shift gears, the Buick bucking beneath me, but I can't shake them. I can't shake the wolves, either. They're tracking us now, a whole line of them, yipping at the rust on the bumper, slobbering on the faded paint job.

The drive-in blurs around us, and the only thing that matters is drawing them away from the house, away from Jane and Daisy. Away from Michael and Walter, too.

The girls are crawling closer now, but they still can't quite reach us, so they do the next best thing. They start pulling the Buick apart, piece by rotting piece. It's been falling apart for ages, helped along by my decay and then by Dracula's, so it makes their work easy. They tear off the bumper and the canvas top and thick handfuls of upholstery.

"That's not fair," I seethe, as the car jolts, and the girls lose their tenuous grip on the back seat, their bodies flung to the dirt like flotsam. I jerk the wheel, but the Buick fishtails across gravel, lurching to a stop right next to our favorite speaker. The best one in the place, never once been broken.

The world goes still around us, Bee and me heaving in

the dark. We're stuck now. These men are determined to steal our ride, one way or another.

But we've got something else on our side. On the dueling screens, the films flicker to life, and the floodlights cut out, the whole lot plunged into darkness. Michael, in the projection booth. Doing exactly what I asked him.

The girls are shaking themselves off, ready for round two, and the wolves are closing in, their howls almost deafening. I hold the urn tight with both hands, and Bee reaches across the seat, grabbing the letter opener and the necklace, tucking them in the pocket of her jacket, these last souvenirs from the house.

"Come on," she says, and we race down the empty rows, cranking up every speaker as we go, loud enough to drown out the whispering urn. Loud enough to drown out our own footsteps, too.

We dodge behind a storage building. They don't see us here.

"Keep looking," Rochester calls, and they're scattering like wedding rice. This is what I'd hoped for. To spread them out across the sprawling drive-in.

Besides, there's something else to distract them now. I didn't choose just any movies from the dusty stack in the projection booth. I found a pair I wish I could forget. *Jane Eyre* and *Nosferatu*. These films like ghosts, haunting us, spinning their lies into gold, into a story that's turned Bee and me into afterthoughts.

Only this time, it's different. This time, we're using the

films for us, for a distraction, and it's working. Rochester and Dracula can't take their eyes off the screens. Like Narcissus gazing at his own reflection, they see themselves, the way the world fancies them.

Rochester, so brooding, so Byronic, a villain in hero's clothing.

Nosferatu, so brooding too, but not quite so dashing, not with those pointed ears and that bald head pale as the moon.

A sly grin on his face, Rochester glances back and forth between the screens, sizing up the actors, realizing he got the better deal. He turns to Dracula, elbowing him like an old chum.

"Better luck next time," he says, and for an instant, I'm sure Dracula's going to break him into pieces and save us the trouble. He searches the lot for me instead, glaring into the dark, as if to say this is my fault. That I'm to blame for him meeting Rochester.

"Nobody made you come back from the dead," I mutter, as Bee and I dash to the edge of the lot and behind the crumbling ticket booth.

The overgrown weeds biting at our ankles, Bee searches the desolate landscape. Out on the road, there isn't a single car in sight.

"Should we try for the highway?" she asks. "Should we lead them farther away from here?"

I look back at the house. "What if they go after them instead?"

That's the one thing neither of us wants. We need to keep them safe.

A rustling outside the ticket booth, and a blot of a man emerges among the shadows. I'm ready to scream, until his twisted face stares back at us in the moonlight.

Renfield. He's followed us, all the way down the coast, all the way to Dracula. Maybe to help him. Maybe to help us.

Bee snarls at him. "What are you doing here?" she asks, her hands curling into claws, ready to scratch out his other eye.

"Wait," I say. "Give him a chance. Back in San Francisco, he rescued me."

Bee gapes at me. "Was that before or after he killed you?"

"After," Renfield and I say at the same time.

The girls are calling out all around us, their voices ricocheting like bird shot. They're getting closer.

I put one hand on Renfield's ancient arm, his skin crackling at my touch. "You could help us now," I whisper. "Can you do that?"

He purses his lips, his head down, resolve settling over him. "What do you need, Miss Lucy?"

"You can hear him, right? The things in his head?" I lean in close, and I taste Renfield's breath, pungent as garlic, heavy as heartache. "What's he thinking right now?"

A long moment dissolves between us as he stares off, seeing everything and nothing. "About you," he says finally. "About how much he wants to crack you open and find out what you look like inside."

In spite of myself, I tremble a little, but we can use this. Because of the thrall, because Renfield can scry into his mind, we can track Dracula. Together, the three of us sneak across the lot and duck behind a blocky building. The lobby.

A wolf is sniffing at the edge of the building, only a few yards away. He'll spot us soon. He'll tell the others we're here.

I turn back to Renfield. "What else is Dracula thinking?"

"He's saying I was never as loyal as I claimed to be." A pained look twists across his face. "But that's not true. I *was* loyal. For years, I waited for him."

"I know," I say, and put a careful hand on his back. "Come on now."

Inside the darkened lobby, we latch the front door and snake quietly through the red velvet rope, so bleak and matted now.

Bee and I help Renfield over the counter, the three of us crouching on the stone floor among husks of stale popcorn and crushed gumdrops gone hairy and gray.

"He's still looking," Renfield says, his milky eye vacant, peering into places I'll never go. "He's worried, too. He didn't think you'd survive this long. He's a little impressed."

I scoff. "I doubt that."

His gaze shifts, and Renfield looks at me now. "You're wrong," he says. "He keeps thinking how you're the one he sees in the sunlight, when the past comes for him. You're the only thing that frightens him, Miss Lucy."

This instantly chills me. "Where is he now?" I ask.

A long, unforgiving moment. "He's right outside the door."

I start to crawl toward the back, toward the only safe way out, motioning them to follow, but then I see it in him. Renfield's not just in Dracula's head now. Dracula's returning the favor.

"No," I cry, but Renfield's vanishing right before our eyes, the thrall yanking him away.

"I told you not to trust me, Miss Lucy," he says, sorrow twitching across his face, and I'm sure I see Dracula behind his gaze, laughing at me.

With a single heave, Renfield puts his hands on the urn and tears it from my arms. I topple back against Bee, the two of us splayed across the sticky floor.

I struggle to my feet again, charging after him, but Renfield's already to the door. So is Dracula. In the gloom outside, he's nearly invisible. All I can see is his hand, emerging from the shadows, pressing against the window.

"I've got the rest of you, Master," Renfield says, and matches his own hand through the glass, as though the two of them are touching.

"Open the door," Dracula whispers, and even in the dark, I can hear him smile. He knows he's about to get everything he wants.

Renfield moves toward the lock, but I get to him first. Fear rising inside me, I could reach out and break him into nothing. I could slash at his skin, delicate as vellum, and unravel him into ribbons. But I do something else instead.

I knit my hand with his, carefully entwining our fingers, and without hesitating, he holds on tight to me. Tighter than I've ever been held. As though nobody's ever embraced Renfield once in his whole life.

"Thank you," he says, and with a heavy hand, he passes me the urn.

Renfield, making his choice at last.

Dracula shoves hard against the other side of the door, rage flickering across his face, quiet but unmistakable. He's not used to being denied. He's certainly not used to Renfield denying him. The shadows dance around him, and he leans closer, his lips nearly pressed against the smudged glass.

"Are you sure this is what you want?" he asks.

"Yes," Renfield whispers, and that's all it takes.

With his eyes burning, his silhouette growing longer, Dracula says something else. Something I never expect.

"I release you."

It's such a simple phrase. So quick, so irrevocable.

Instantly, Renfield feels it, stirring inside him, the way the thrall snaps like a taut rubber band. Seventy years ago, this would have been a mercy. This would have freed Renfield for good. This would have given him a second chance. But his body's too far gone now, the decades far too unkind to him.

His arms outstretched, he staggers into me, a single

agonizing step, before collapsing to his knees. I kneel beside him, desperate to help him up, but there's no way to stop this now.

His body breaks apart like chunks of plaster, desiccated and bloodless.

My hands are frantic, trying to hold him together, like he's a puzzle to reassemble, but Renfield doesn't fight this. Maybe it's what he's been yearning for all these years. With a final wheezing breath, his head lolls back, and he smiles up at me.

"Goodbye, Miss Lucy," Renfield whispers, and he crumbles to nothing in my arms.

I clutch the bits of him to my heart, but I don't have time to hold him. The glass door shatters around me, like a spray of diamonds.

I fall back, but Bee's right beside me, pulling me to my feet.

"This way," she says, his shadow devouring us as we shove between the dingy velvet ropes and behind the counter, desperate to reach the other door. We're almost outside, almost to the closest thing to freedom we've got, when the necklace slips from Bee's pocket. She turns back for it, but I shake my head.

"Leave it," I say. Our last chance at another life, discarded in the dark.

Back out in the night, the air is sticky with summer, and we clamber across the lot, the smooth gravel slipping beneath our shoes.

The shotgun house is less than fifty paces away, and

on the front porch, Daisy's breezing down the steps. The screen door bursts open behind her, and Jane and Walter are charging after her, trying to pull her back, but she keeps wandering, her eyes fogged over, her body not her own.

"Get back inside," I call to her, but Daisy can't help herself. Dracula's whispering on the wind to her. He's taken her blood into him, put her under his thrall. So far as he's concerned, she belongs to him now.

There are others who belong to him too, and scattered across the drive-in, they see us now. Bee grabs my hand and pulls me one way toward the projection booth, only for Bellflower and Vervain to block our way. I wrench Bee toward the nearest movie screen, but the outlines of other girls are blotting the view.

They're everywhere, as unrelenting as the July sun. One by one, they surround us, their faces gaunt and ravenous, and we've got nowhere to run this time. No Buick to carry us off. They close in, quicker than before, and I try to count them in the dark. A dozen perhaps, or it could be more than that. The thing is, it doesn't matter. All it takes is a single hand to drive a stake through a heart or strike a match that won't be quelled. There are so many ways they could destroy us and so few ways we can escape.

But they haven't all joined the throng. Across the lot, Rowan's huddling against the cinder block walls of the projection booth, her dirty knees pulled into her chest.

"I'm so hungry," she keeps saying, and I wish I could

tell her that feeling will pass, but it won't. It'll only get worse.

Rochester glances back at her, rolling his eyes. "Looks like I picked the wrong one again."

At this, his gaze flits to Bee, and he expects her to shrink beneath the weight of his insults. But she doesn't even flinch. For years, he could unravel her with a word, but no more.

So he decides to unravel her in an entirely different way. He motions to Jane, still standing on the front porch of the house.

"There you are," he says, and puts out a steady hand to her. "Come on now. Show's over."

She stares at him. "What are you talking about?"

"We've finally got them." Rochester smirks at her, and the greasy look on his face turns my stomach. "You don't have to pretend anymore. You can come on back to me now."

His hand is still extended to her, but Jane's not looking at him. She's gaping at Bee, something frantic in her face.

"He's lying," she whispers. "Bee, I promise you he's lying."

But Bee won't listen. She's already backing away from Jane, that wounded look in her eyes, as if she knew it all along.

From the lobby, Dracula's coming up behind us, less than twenty yards away, but Vervain and Bellflower won't wait for him. They shove Bee out of the way, and then they shove me down, just so they can loom over me, their shadows long, the stakes quivering between their delicate fingers. I crawl backward in the dirt, but they keep in step with me.

They can't do this, not tonight. By the time I return, it'll be hours from now, and there might not be anything to come back to. No Daisy or Michael. No Bee or Jane, either.

That's if I return at all. I might not have any more afterlives left in me.

A lonesome howl behind us, and Dracula's in our midst, joining us at last. All around, the wolves are more restless now, braying at the moon, braying at these men. Their eyes burning brighter, they look to me, as if waiting on a cue. I stare back at them, wishing I knew what they wanted.

Dracula seizes up next to Rochester, still watching me. "Go on," he says to Bellflower and Vervain, his latest protégés, his cold-blooded killers-in-training. The ones who will be better versions of me.

Grinning, the girls gaze down at me. They're ready to turn me to ash, but all I can do is rasp out a ragged sigh, regret seeping into me.

"I'm so sorry for what they've done to you," I whisper, and I expect this to be it, a final insult, their reason for dispatching me. But that's not what happens at all. Instead, something passes between us, something small. A memory, a moment. That last night on their deathbed when I was there. When the men were nowhere to be found.

Bellflower suddenly isn't looking at me anymore.

"Where were you?" Her eyes shift to Rochester. "When we were dying, where were you?"

Rochester steps back as if he's been punched. "I . . . thought I'd leave the three of you to rest."

"You mean, you thought you'd leave us to die alone?" Bellflower doesn't move. She doesn't go for me. She doesn't do anything at all. Neither does Vervain—or any of the other girls. They just keep waiting, expecting a better explanation that never comes.

"It's not like that," Rochester keeps murmuring, and I shake my head.

"It's exactly like that," I say, as I start to crawl away, desperate to clamber to my feet, to get back to Bee.

Next to me, Vervain watches him, her gaze gone inky black. "It didn't bother you at all, did it?" she asks. "You really never cared what became of us."

Rochester searches the faces around him, clearly convinced someone will be on his side. But nobody is. His Wunderkammer of women, suddenly on an impromptu labor strike. Even from here, I can tell he senses it in the air. It's all starting to fray, starting to slip away. His dubious plan, not built to last.

I'm waiting for him to scream or to argue with them, but he just grins instead.

"You're right," he says. "I never did care what became of you."

Five steps. That's all it takes. Then he's standing with us, his jaw set, a thick sinew quivering in his neck. He wrestles the stake out of Bellflower's hand and gives it right back to her. One quick thrust, and Bellflower's heart is shattered to pieces. A whimper from a wolf, and she's gone, vanished into the night.

Vervain lets out an agonizing cry before she drops to her knees, desperately searching the dust. "Bellflower," she keeps whispering, and the tears are coming now, running thick as honey down her face. These strange girls, these unlikely sisters. Rochester never counted on that. He never counted on anything except himself.

But the others see him now, what he really is, what he's always been. His collection of would-be wives, not so eager to belong to a man who will discard them like last week's leftovers. Vervain's on her feet again, her venomous gaze set on him, and the others look to her, taking her lead.

And together, they're coming right at him.

"Do something," Rochester practically spits in Dracula's face, but Dracula barely notices. All he cares about is what I'm holding in my arms. If Bellflower and Vervain won't bring it to him, he'll have to get it himself.

"I'm not waiting any longer, Lucy," he says, and he's at my side, always moving faster than I remember.

I don't even have time to lunge at him before he plucks the urn from my arms and lifts it above his head, bringing it down hard. The clay, shattering in the gravel like porcelain.

The ash swirls in the air, shimmering in the glow of the movie screens, and this is it. He's becoming whole again. Becoming everything he once was.

I should weep or scream or cower in the dark of the drive-in. I should be afraid like before. But rage boils up in me instead, raw as heartbreak, and all the wolves are looking right at me. Right into my cold and silent heart, and they finally understand. Who I am and what I want. Their heads down, their jaws gaping, they turn to Dracula, and they surround him.

The wolves. At my command instead of his.

The last dust settling on his body, Dracula edges away from them, and I can't help but smile.

"You told me I'm like you," I say. "Then maybe it's time for you to run now."

And with the wolves at my side, we're upon him in an instant.

eighteen

Dracula and I fall together into the dirt, our bodies tangled, sliding across gravel toward the projection booth. I've got my hands around his neck, and he's got his hands around mine, and with my hunger and decay unraveling, it feels like we might be evenly matched for the very first time.

"I love it when you touch me like this," he wheezes, and I tighten my hands a little more.

The wolves are with us too, tearing at his clothes, ripping them off, piece by piece. Grimacing, he lets go of me long enough to strike them openhanded in their slathering muzzles. They fall back a step, and he stumbles to his feet, wilting against the outside of the projection booth, right next to Rowan, still cowering on the ground.

"I want to go home," she sobs, and Dracula glowers at her, looking ready to break her in two, simply for being a gnat in his way.

But these girls are more than that. They're powerful, and that's what Rochester and Dracula never understood. You can only silence someone for so long before they learn how to scream. Before those screams become deafening. The girls are closing in around Rochester, backing him against the projection booth.

"Help me," he rasps at Dracula, as though there's a playbook for this.

Bee's trying to rush at them, so are Jane and Walter, but the throng of girls is stronger than the rest of us, a united front not wavering, not breaking.

Daisy's gathered among them, still looking dazed. She's so new to all of this, the thrall barely settled over her, everything about her in a disarray. Rochester senses this, her vulnerability, and with a calloused hand, he yanks her from the horde, gripping her by one arm like a rag doll.

"Leave her alone," I cry out, my voice ricocheting off the night sky. It must be louder than I think, because Michael emerges suddenly from the projection booth, his eyes wide, his back ramrod straight, all his battlefield instincts kicking in.

But I don't need him out here, another potential casualty.

"Don't," I say, but it's too late. Dracula's already spotted him.

"Hello again," he says, and seizes Michael by the throat. Dracula glances back at me, grinning, before he drags him into the booth. Rochester wrenches Daisy after them.

The girls close in around the door, but as much as I'd love to watch them tear these men to shreds, we don't have time for their grudges.

"Get them out of our way," I whisper, and the wolves nip at the girls' heels, dispersing them for a moment, just long enough for Bee and me to cut through the crowd like a knife and slip into the projection booth.

It's dark inside, the space no more than a shack. Out in the lot, the films are still flickering on the screens, and a bit of pale light bounces back in, illuminating figures against the wall. Daisy and Michael have backed into a dusty corner, their hands wrapped tight together, desperate to hold on to something. A stack of metal film cans has toppled over behind them, the reels unspooling at their feet like a tangle of satin ribbons.

Right next to me, something moves. Dracula, only inches away in the shadows, leaning back against the cold wall. "So which one of them should we start with, Lucy?" he asks. "The one I've already had, or the one you've had?"

"Leave them out of this," I say.

Growling, the wolves are going wild now, looming in the doorway.

"Such traitors." Dracula shakes his head. "But it proves my point, doesn't it? You're just like me, Lucy."

Bee takes a long step forward. "She's nothing like you," she says, and Dracula only laughs.

"That's because she hasn't told you everything, Bee."

His gaze flits to me. "Remember what you were like before? So charming, so persuasive. How many men proposed to you in one day? Was it four?"

I grit my teeth. "It was three."

"And that was before you ever even met me," he says. "You're not the nice girl you pretend to be, are you, Lucy?"

I smile. "Who wants to be a nice girl anyhow?" I ask, and with the snap of my fingers, the wolves charge in.

Shadows dance sharply on the ceiling, and Rochester and Dracula dodge out of the way, their hands over their faces, but this isn't about them. In a flash, all the wolves shepherd Michael and Daisy outside, the night air sticky and unrelenting. I watch from the doorway, as Jane and Walter rush to them, their arms outstretched. Daisy curls into Jane, half-dazed, but Michael turns back.

"Lucy," he says.

My heart aching, I take one last look at him. "I'm sorry," I say, and slam the door in his face, locking him out. Locking all of them out. This is what Bee and I want, what we've been waiting for. To have everyone out of the way. To have Dracula and Rochester all to ourselves.

We're in this together or not at all.

She waits inside the door for me. Even this claustrophobic booth can't stop her now.

Rochester and Dracula are hovering next to the projector, their eyes black as cinders.

"You were always trouble." Rochester gnashes his teeth at Bee. "Trouble to be married to, and trouble even after. You're all I've heard about for the last hundred years."

Bee gapes at him. "From who?"

"From Jane, of course," he says with a sneer. "The way she kept talking about you, it's like I never got rid of you at all."

A wave of relief washes over Bee. What Jane said was true. She's always loved Bee. She's always regretted not going with her.

"Thank you," Bee says to him.

The men stand across from us, and they're the ones frozen now. They can't leave this booth, and they know it. Between the wolves and the girls, there's nowhere left for them to run.

But maybe they don't need to go anywhere. In a way, this is right where they belong. In this city that helped to make them legends. Hollywood. The movies. This is their native soil now, and there's no better place for them than in the heart of this drive-in, in this projection booth, cold and dark, like one giant urn.

A tomb where they can be laid to rest together.

In her pocket, Bee's still got the letter opener. Her hands steady, she takes it out and drags it up one arm and down the other. Everything he's ever done to her comes leaking out.

And we're not done yet. My hunger, burning bright inside me, is a weapon too. I close my eyes, and it unfurls from my fingertips, climbing up the walls like ivy, blighting everything, turning it all to dust.

What Rochester and Dracula did to Bee and me was different, but in the end, men like them are always the same. That means they can die the same too.

The gray tar climbs over everything, and Rochester falls to his knees, trying to pound it to dust, but there's just too much now. Too much of the decay from me and Bee, the things they put inside us.

The rot climbs up and over the projectors, leeching into the film spool. Outside, on the screens, the movies burn away to nothing, the pictures of Rochester and Nosferatu dissolving like cigarette burns, the blots on the celluloid reminding me for a moment of the liquid light shows in the Haight, everything splotchy and wild.

The decay seeps down the walls and into the electrical outlets, and heavy sparks explode in every direction. On the desiccated rafters. On the cache of crumbling film posters. On the unspooled nitrate film spilled across the floor.

We've always loved it here, but let's face it, this dated drive-in is a tinderbox, and it only takes a moment, barely long enough to blink, before the whole projection booth is alight.

Another fire, the same as Thornfield all those years ago, the same as our beloved house. This should be Bee's worst nightmare. But she doesn't look afraid this time.

She looks ready.

"Hurry," she says to me, and we push past the men,

their clothes already starting to smolder, the two of them still trying to put out the fire, to chase off the decay.

The door is dripping thick with cobwebs and sludge, sealed tight at the edges, sealing us in. But there are still the windows, two of them, one for each projector. One for each of us, Bee and me.

The gray tar is fogging up the glass, caking in the corners, closing in around us. We don't have much time, so we start climbing, folding our shoulders in, making ourselves as small as we can to fit through the opening, escaping through the same spot where all the films we've ever seen here have escaped too.

Jane and Michael are on the other side, flanked by girls and wolves, and they're reaching for us, desperate to pull us free.

"Bee," Jane says, sobbing, and their fingers entwine as we crawl through to freedom.

But these men won't give up. Rochester's fiery hand reaches out and grasps Bee's thigh.

"We stay together," he seethes, and though she kicks him square in the chest, he manages to grip her tight around the waist. Through the window, Bee stretches one last time and kisses Jane. It's so quick, so sweet. It's goodbye.

Then Rochester wrenches her back into the projection booth.

Outside, the wolves are whimpering, begging me to come to them. I could still make it through, I could still escape, but I won't leave Bee. She would never leave me.

Michael screams something, so does Jane, but in the

rush of flames, I can't hear them as I drop back into the projection booth. Rochester's got Bee pinned against the wall, and though she's flailing against him, more than holding her own, the fire is outmatching them both. It's rising faster now, and it's greedy, even greedier than these men. It's consuming everything.

I call out Bee's name, but I can't get to her, Dracula blocking my way, the flames licking his body like an eager lover. Only his skin isn't burning to cinders. Instead, he's turning gray, as if all the colors have been leeched out of him.

"You know I'll only come back from this," he whispers, smoke pouring from his lips. "And so will you."

I back against the wall. It's true. We'll never stop this cycle. We'll just keep going around and around until we're both dizzy with infinity.

Unless there's another way.

The silver letter opener glints up from the floor. This keepsake, this gift, this glorious weapon.

I lunge for it in the dark, but Dracula sees it too, and with a quick leap, he grabs it first.

"For you," he says, and with his skin puddling at my feet like pancake batter, he thrusts the letter opener through my heart.

A strangled sob, and my skin goes soft and useless. Across the booth, Bee stares back at me, her body burning, my body dissolving, the two of us dying in plain sight. The men are dying too, the smoke and the blaze too much for them.

With the last fragments of his strength, Dracula leans in close, his lips pressed against my ear. "See you there," he whispers, as the world fades to gray.

I GET TO THE other side first.

The room—if you can even call it that anymore—is almost too dark to see. It takes a moment for my eyes to adjust before I spot her there.

Mina, crumpled up on the floor, her legs tucked into her chest, the hands groping all around her.

"Lucy," she whispers, and I fall to my knees next to her.

"I told you I'd come back," I say, and shivering, we sit together on the floor, the walls crawling and eager.

These hands, these restless hands. I envision them just beyond, waiting in the dark. They're the same as the girls back in the drive-in. They're so enraged at what's become of them, and even from here they can feel it, what those men have been up to. How more girls will soon join their ranks.

But these hands can't stop them, they can't break through. It's all they want in the world, and the one thing they're denied.

Another arm juts out, and Mina and I dodge the other way, sliding past something on the floor.

The silver letter opener.

"You kept it," Mina whispers, and with a delicate hand, she scoops it up, passing it to me.

"Of course I did," I say, holding it tight.

It's all I can bring through with me. The very thing that killed me.

The air shifts in the room, and there's suddenly some-one else with us. She's no more than a shadow at first, her spectral figure soft and unformed. Then she emerges, bit by bit. Her dark hair, her nervous hands, that face I know so well.

Bee. She curls into herself, her whole body shaking. This is unfamiliar to her, only the second time she's died. She's not an old pro at it like me.

A long sigh, and she opens her eyes. "Hello, Lucy," she says, and her gaze shifts. "Hello, Mina."

At this, Mina brightens. "Hello, Bee."

They've never met, but they know each other anyhow. They know the stories, all our secrets laid bare in this place.

An echo beyond this room, and the men are getting closer, the flames devouring them. We can feel them coming, and so can the others, the walls rattling, hard and fast.

"What are we going to do?" Mina asks, and Bee and I each take her hand as we wait for this.

The men materialize among us, obscure at first, be-fore becoming stronger, more solid. More dangerous. They gather themselves to their feet, their shadows so much darker, so much longer than before. The arms are reaching out for them, but both Rochester and Dracula sidestep every one, grinning to themselves, remembering how they put them here. This purgatory of souls they handpicked. Souls they condemned to this.

Dracula turns toward us. "Sweet Mina," he says. "So lovely to meet you again after all these years."

Mina whimpers as we slide back across the floor, but there's nowhere to go, nowhere that isn't reaching out for us, reaching out for them. This is it. What Bee and I have been running from for decades.

Bee looks at me, the darkness edging closer. "Now," she whispers, and I clutch the letter opener tighter.

Dracula sees it in my hand. "That won't do you any good here," he says. "I'm already dead."

"It isn't for you." Smiling, I turn toward the wall. "It's for them."

I wait until an arm pulls back, far enough out of my way. Then I plunge the letter opener into the wall and cut straight through the plaster, gone soft and liquid. It opens up like flesh, like an infected wound, and a hundred fingers emerge, slithering like Medusa's crown. But one gash isn't enough. I slash again and again, dozens of times, trying to make room for all of them to crawl right through.

Rochester exhales a shriek and tumbles toward me, his hands aimed for my throat, but I toss the letter opener to Bee, and, howling with delight, she finishes the job. When she's done, the whole room is ragged and gaping open, and they're coming now, even faster than I expected.

Dracula twists toward me, agony in his eyes, because this is what he never planned for: how well I know him. How I knew if given the chance, he'd use this letter opener to murder me. That's why I brought it, why I plucked it from the wreckage of my life. So I could get it into this room, get it into the afterlife, and have a weapon waiting for me.

"Well done," Dracula says finally, as he and Rochester come face-to-face with all the girls they'd forgotten. It never occurred to these men that the girls never forgot them.

But as the figures pour out of the wall, it isn't just girls. There are so many of them—faces I recognize and faces I don't. The maidens that Dracula dispatched centuries ago, and others too, the families the Rochesters evicted. The fathers who worked their hands to the bone before becoming bones themselves, the mothers who watched their only progeny wither away to dust, the children whose names have been blotted from the ledgers, tally marks and nothing more.

Except they've always been more than nothing, and they are going to remind Dracula and Rochester of that now.

They take Rochester first, and he doesn't even have time to scream before their hands are cupped over his mouth and shoved straight through what's left of his heart. It's a blur of faces, all these countless families, and Bellflower too, right at the forefront, flowers in her hair, a smirk on her lips.

"So good to see you again so soon," she says, and

they drag him through the torn wall and into the gloom on the other side. As they vanish together, a macabre family all their own, the only thing we can hear is something like old leather tearing in two. It's the rending of flesh. And this is eternity, after all. That rending could go on a long time.

Another moment before the hands materialize again. Dracula should look afraid. He should try to scream too. But when he turns back to me, he can't help but smile.

"You know you can't stop me forever," he says, and he's probably right. Even the darkest depths aren't bottomless, and if anyone can find their way out again, it would be him.

"That's okay," I say. "I'll settle with stopping you for now."

A final hand emerges from the darkness, and I recognize it at once, even though it's healed and smooth and strong again.

Renfield grins out at me. "Thank you, Miss Lucy," he says, before pulling Dracula down into the gloom.

At last, the stale air is silent, the walls go still, and there are two fewer of us standing in the room.

Rochester and Dracula aren't the only ones who have vanished. The whispering voices are gone too. No more hands reaching through. No more restless ghosts.

Bee stares into the empty sockets in the wall. "Where are they?"

"Somewhere they can rest," Mina says, and it's somewhere we can rest too. The shadows shift beyond the walls, and I can feel it in my bones, the afterlife calling to us.

Mina can feel it too. She holds out her hand. "Are you ready, my Lucy?"

I hesitate. "I think so," I say finally. Mina's been waiting a long time for this, for the beyond to unfurl to her. I've been waiting a long time too.

My throat tightening, I look at Bee, and her face has gone frantic.

"Lucy, don't," she says, pleading with me, grabbing my hand, but I pull away. She doesn't understand. There's a reason for her to return, a life she can stitch together, a lost love she can repair. I don't have that. It's like Dracula said. I'm the annoying little sister, the one who's always in the way. The one who belongs here.

My chin tipped up, I put both hands on the wall, the gloom hungry and eager for me. And I'm eager for it, ready for this to be over.

But then I hear something else, echoing from a thousand miles away.

Rowan and the other girls back at the drive-in, nursing their newfound hunger, their fear bone-deep. They're lost, exactly the way Dracula and Rochester wanted them to be.

I know what that's like, to be abandoned with nothing. I know all too well. Only it isn't hopeless. I could show them how you can survive it, how you can control it, how it doesn't have to control you. What those men did to us isn't destiny. We deserve more than that. We deserve our own story. I could help those girls. They could help me, too.

It's something I should have realized by now: that Dracula was wrong about a lot of things. Maybe I've never been in the way. Maybe I have a reason to go back.

I look to Mina, and she sees it in me, a vague hope swirling behind my eyes, a chance for a future that was stolen from me. A future she once had. She got to grow old, got to build a life, free of fear, free of Dracula. Now I get to have mine.

My heart twists in my chest, and I squeeze her hand, the hand of my friend, my very first friend, the one who never forgot me.

"Next time," I whisper. "I'll stay next time."

"Promise?" she asks.

"I promise."

I wish we could linger here a little longer. I wish we could sit in what's left of this room, the three of us laughing at those men, laughing together, me with Mina and Bee, my two best friends united at last. But that will have to wait for another day. Voices break through from the other side, Jane and Michael and Daisy and all the girls we left behind, and it's time. It's time for Mina, too, the darkness beyond the walls filling with a golden light, more blinding than the California sun.

I give Mina one last smile, and she smiles back, as our bodies dissolve, slowly at first until there's nothing left, Bee and me disappearing back into the world.

This time, it doesn't hurt a bit.

nineteen

It's past sundown in Los Angeles, and we're sitting cross-legged beneath the Hollywood sign.

Bee and Jane and me, the dust settled around us, the wind whipping at the NO TRESPASSING signs.

I shiver. "I always forget how cold it gets up here at night."

It's already October, the months creeping away from us quicker than we can hold on.

Bee and Jane are nestled beneath the rickety letter *H*, the two of them giggling, bantering back and forth. There are no more secrets between them. Between any of us. We used to think keeping quiet would keep us safe, but it turns out there's nothing more dangerous than that.

Jane's brought a portable radio with her, and we listen to the day's news. Somebody's performing nuclear tests over in Europe. And closer to home, all the kids in the

Haight held a mock funeral this afternoon. "The death of the hippie," they called it.

"People need to move on," one of the organizers tells the reporter, the static of the city crackling behind them. "Summer's over. Go home. We're done here."

Jane shakes her head. "We couldn't go back even if we wanted to," she says, and I smile, because that's the way it should be.

I lean back beneath the sign, my long hair whispering in the wind. It isn't so bad up here, especially without any urns to bury. And there won't ever be another urn again. We've combed through the slog of the projection booth, every charred rafter, every half-melted film cannister, but there are no ashes from those men, no remains at all. They're gone, and this time, they're not coming back. All the hands in that room have made sure of it.

The ghosts are no longer restless. They're no longer bound by these men either. Neither are we.

"Look," Bee whispers, and something slight, something almost too small to see, twitches beneath her skin. We all watch, our voices hushed, until it settles again, quiet and calm inside her.

"That's the first time we've seen it in a month," Jane says, and squeezes Bee's hand.

The two of them are different now. That gray tar inside them is drying up. There's no reason for it to stay. No Rochesters left to keep the grudges growing.

There are other changes too. We've noticed it in the small things, the kind nobody else would ever see. A single strand of silver in Jane's hair. A laugh line around Bee's eyes. A tiny liver spot on my hand.

We're aging now. Slowly, in real time, like we always should have. It's something those men thought they'd stolen from us forever, but forever wasn't up to them.

The decay that used to unfurl from me is still here, but it's within me now. It's twining its way through my body, my constant companion, carefully turning my viscera to gray, and one day, many years from now, it will be my undoing. And when that day comes, I'll welcome it.

But in the meantime, we've still got many evenings ahead of us. With a sharp howl, the wolves have arrived, skulking out at sunset, and Jane squeals as they run circles around us. Back at Dahlia Hall, they were ready to rip out our throats. Now they're just content to do parlor tricks. Children of the night, indeed.

And someone else has arrived too, sneaking up the dusty hill. I don't spot him at first, but Bee does, her face brightening.

"Hello, Michael," she says. Then she regards Jane, a conspiratorial glance passing between them. "I think we're going to take a walk."

The two of them scurry off, leaving Michael and me alone. He watches me, his eyes clearer than before. The thrall is faded now, nearly vanished altogether, but the echo of what I did to him is still strong enough that he can find me here. Strong enough that I still want him to find me.

"You're leaving tonight, right?" I ask.

Michael nods. "We've got the truck all packed up," he says, and then says no more about it. He doesn't have to. I already know. They're headed up the coast, six hundred miles away, to where Walter got a job managing a quaint indoor theater in downtown Eureka.

"There will be a lot fewer bloodsuckers in that projection booth," Walter told us, and when I gave him a sideways look, he only chuckled. "I meant mosquitos, Lucy."

I fold my hands in my lap. "And Daisy's going with you?"

At this, Michael blushes. "I guess so. My grandfather invited her along. She wants to be an usherette or something."

"I'm glad," I say. "You two are cute together."

He squints at me. "Don't try to play matchmaker, Lucy," he says, but I don't have to do anything. This is practically etched in the stars. Some couples have identical wedding bands. The two of them have identical scars, a mark on their throats that won't ever quite heal.

The moon shifts in the sky, and without a word, we both know it's time.

"See you around, Lucy," he says finally.

"Goodbye, Michael."

He heads back down, but only makes it a few steps before glancing at me again. "Is what Dracula said true? Did four men really propose to you in one day?"

I exhale a thin laugh. "It was three."

He nods again, his lips pursed. "Lucky guys," he says, and starts to walk away.

But I can't let him leave like this. Not with that ache inside him, the curse I planted in his heart.

I know how to fix it now. What Dracula did to Renfield at the drive-in, how he severed the thrall in an instant— I never realized it could be so easy. Or maybe I did, and I never admitted it to myself.

It was too late for Renfield, he was too far gone. But it's not too late for Michael.

The wind whips around me again, the wolves edging closer, and it takes a long moment before I can bring myself to speak those three little words.

"I release you," I whisper at last, and I feel it happen. A dull twinge in my chest, as the thrall snaps in two.

Michael feels it too. A hitch in his step, his back straightening, everything holding perfectly still for a moment.

He turns to me, one last time, and I'm expecting a blankness in his eyes, as if he's gazing at a stranger. But he only smiles. "You could still come with us, you know."

I shake my head. "Maybe I'll catch up later."

And with that, he disappears into the Santa Monica Mountains, headed back to Walter's Ford pickup. Back to civilization, to the future. I close my eyes and listen for his heartbeat, so clear, so familiar. I keep listening until he's too far away, and the melody inside his chest joins a thousand other hearts, all of them bleeding together in the autumn night.

Bee wanders back up the hillside, a sad look in her eyes. "You let him go?"

A lonesome ache settles inside me. "Of course I did."

There are no Hollywood endings, not even in Hollywood, and that's the way it should be.

The rest of the story's unwritten. *Our* story's unwritten, the one they tried so hard to steal from us.

A giggle from far off, and the other girls are coming, Rowan and Vervain leading them. All the ones without heartbeats. Every night they meet us in this spot where I once buried the urn, buried my fear. They meet us, and I share every secret I've ever held in my heart.

"I'll tell you everything about what we are," I say to them, and they listen. They listen, even though there are no guarantees.

We'll never stop hungering. Nothing can change that. And what they become isn't up to me. It's their move, it's their choice. I can't make them promise to behave, to banish their bloodlust like it's no more than a bad habit. I can't trust them because I can't even always trust myself. Together, we might rip this town apart.

Or maybe we'll do something else. Maybe we'll prove that just because you come from a monster, it doesn't make you one.

Their soft voices lilt up from the canyon, and the wolves lope in eager circles, ready for the evening to begin.

With the moonlight slicing through the clouds, I unknit my hands in my lap and glance down at my palms.

My lifeline's gone now. So are my second chances. This is it, my last go-around. My last time to prove Dracula wrong. To prove I'm more than just the girl who withers in his shadow.

And with the gloom of California brimming in my heart, I'm going to make it count.

acknowledgments

First and foremost, thank you to my husband, Bill, who is a force of nature when it comes to supporting my writing. Personally, I wouldn't want to be married to a moody author, but he seems to manage just fine, and I appreciate it more than I can ever express.

So many thanks to Christa Carmen and Sara Tantlinger for listening to me talk about every single aspect of this book to the point that they probably wanted to mute my messages on Facebook. I'm certainly grateful they didn't mute me, and I seriously encourage everyone to read their books, because they're not only amazing friends, but also two of the most incredible horror authors writing today.

It's impossible to write these acknowledgments without also giving a respectful nod to some people I don't even know—namely, all the varied versions of Lucy Westenra who came before. There are so many Lucys that I adore, from Frances Dade in *Dracula* and Carol Marsh in *Horror of Dracula* to Soledad Miranda in *Count Dracula* and Isabelle Adjani in *Nosferatu the Vampyre* to Sadie Frost in *Bram Stoker's Dracula*, and of course, Bram Stoker's incandescent creation in the original novel: the lovely Lucy that started them all. Every iteration has brought something new to the character (including a lot of new last names), but above and beyond all else, I hope I've honored each one in some small way in writing *Reluctant Immortals*. So thank you to the Lucys, both in literature and in cinema, for inspiring me.

While they've rarely gotten the page or screen time of the Lucys, I also want to thank all the Bertha Antoinetta Masons of books and film, in particular the uncredited actress from the 1943 version of *Jane Eyre*, which was my very first exposure to the story back when I was a kid. (Also, a shout-out to my dad who enthusiastically recommended we watch the film one Saturday afternoon. Because if nothing else, we loved all things strange and gothic in our household.)

Back in the real world, thank you to everyone at Saga Press who helped bring this book to life. It was such an astounding experience to have so many people working at once to conjure my tale of Bee and Lucy into the world. In particular, thank you to my editor Joe Monti for helping me to hone this story into the very best version it could be. There's nothing as important to a writer as a truly skilled editor, and I'm so grateful that this book had such a great one.

And last but not least, all my heartfelt thanks in the world to Charlotte Brontë and Bram Stoker for creating these characters. I've cherished both *Jane Eyre* and *Dracula* for almost my entire life, and the opportunity to craft this psychedelic sequel/retelling is possibly the most fun I've ever had writing a book. So thank you to Charlotte and Bram's gothic spirits, wherever they may roam.

about the author

GWENDOLYN KISTE is the Bram Stoker Award–winning author of *The Rust Maidens*, *And Her Smile Will Untether the Universe*, *Pretty Marys All in a Row*, *The Invention of Ghosts*, and *Boneset & Feathers*. Originally from Ohio, she now resides on an abandoned horse farm outside of Pittsburgh with her husband, two cats, and not nearly enough ghosts. You can also find her online on Facebook and Twitter @GwendolynKiste.